Sign up for our newsletter to hear
about new and upcoming releases.

www.ylva-publishing.com

Other Books by Rachael Sommers

In Too Deep
Chemistry
Fool for Love
Never Say Never

Love NEXT DOOR

Rachael Sommers

Acknowledgments

My thanks, as always, go to Astrid and the rest of Ylva team for making this book a possibility. Some days, I still can't believe I get to live my dream of being an author, and none of that would be possible without you. Thank you for continuing to believe in me.

My incredible beta readers, Yan and Sarah, made this story so much better than the initial draft. I am so grateful for the time you spend helping me make tweaks and improvements, and I appreciate it more than I can say.

Thanks also must go to my brilliant editors, Lenir and Michelle, who have been wonderful at helping my writing improve. This story is better for all of the work you have both put into it, and I am very thankful for your guidance. I must thank my sensitivity reader, Mey, too, for ensuring that Bea was written in a respectful way.

I wrote this book during a very difficult time in my life, and I don't know if I could have finished it without the support of my wonderful girlfriend, Laura. Thank you for everything you do for me.

Chapter 1

"CAN WE WATCH THE NEW *Matilda* before I have to go to Dad's?" Tyler hoisted his skateboard higher on his shoulder as he and Kim waited for the elevator. "It's on Netflix now."

Kim would love nothing more. They'd never gotten around to watching it in the cinema, and the original had been one of her favorites as a kid—she hoped sharing the new one with her son would be as meaningful. But…

"It depends. Have you finished your homework?"

Tyler's heavy sigh as they stepped into the elevator was all the answer Kim needed. Sometimes it sucked having to be a responsible parent to a nine-year-old.

"That's a no, then?"

"I can do it after."

"No chance. We can watch the movie after." Hopefully, they had time before John came to get him—otherwise, they'd have to wait another week.

The elevator doors opened on the fourth floor, where a sea of boxes and furniture greeted them. The apartment next to their own had been empty for a few months since Mrs. Wood had moved into a retirement home closer to her family, and Kim hoped the new tenant would be as nice.

The boxes were marked with generic labels like *kitchen* and *bedroom*. But she did spot a giant box of records among the piles, which piqued her interest. Her own collection was gathering dust at the bottom of her closet; maybe it was time she dug them out.

A bark echoed from inside 4C as she stepped over a box and rooted around in her pocket for her keys.

Oh no.

Tyler's head whipped around, his eyes widening, and Kim smothered a groan. He'd been pestering her for a dog ever since his best friend had gotten a puppy a few months ago. How much worse would he be if he met the one living next door?

"Mom, can we go and say hello?" He turned to her with pleading eyes.

"You have homework." Kim pushed their front door open.

"But—"

Whatever Tyler had been about to say was forgotten as a brown and white dog bounded out of 4C and made a beeline for Tyler, nearly knocking him off-balance. The dog was half his size, and Kim tensed, hoping it was friendly.

She needn't have worried—the dog's tail wagged furiously, and Tyler giggled as it licked his hand.

"Cari!" A voice shouted from inside 4C, followed by hurried footsteps. "Get back here you little—oh." A white woman rushed through the door and skidded to a stop in front of Kim and Tyler. "I'm so sorry. She slipped out." Bending to grab the dog's collar, the woman pulled the animal back from Tyler.

Kim got her first look at her new neighbor. *Wow.*

A red beanie half covered her short, blonde hair. The hat's color matched the flush on her cheeks. She was probably in her mid-twenties, a couple years younger than Kim, and pretty, with gorgeous blue eyes. The woman's tentative smile lingered as she readjusted her grip on the dog's collar.

Her gray tank top revealed toned arms covered in tattoos, and Kim could see more of them on her legs through the wide gaps in her ripped jeans.

"It's okay," Tyler said, looking disappointed that the dog had been hauled away. "Can I keep petting her?"

Kim shrugged when the woman glanced toward her. In Kim's eyes, the damage was already done, and she was resigned to hearing about puppies for the rest of the day.

"Sure. Though I'll try and make her behave herself this time. Sit, Cari."

The dog complied, her tail swishing along the wooden floor, and the woman let the collar go. The intensity of her wagging increased as Tyler approached.

"That's a nice name." Tyler dropped his skateboard so he could pet the dog with both hands—a high honor. The board might as well be surgically attached to his hip most days. "What breed is she?"

"She's a mutt," the woman said. "I rescued her off the streets, so I have no idea. Part lab, part terrier, and part spaniel, if I had to guess. I've thought about doing one of those doggy DNA tests to find out for sure, but I've never gotten around to it."

"Well, whatever she is, she's cute," Tyler said, falling to his knees so he didn't have to keep bending over.

"And she knows it." The woman smiled. "I'm Riley," she said to Kim, extending a hand toward her. "As you've probably guessed, I'm your new neighbor."

"Really? You're moving in?" Kim raised an eyebrow as she shook the woman's hand. "I hadn't noticed."

Riley grinned. "Observation not one of your special skills?"

"I've been told it could use some work. I'm Kim. And seeing as he's too busy playing with the dog to introduce himself, this is Tyler. Welcome to the building."

"Thanks." Riley glanced at Cari, who was lying on her back with all four legs in the air as Tyler scratched her stomach. "I think she feels at home already."

"It certainly looks like it."

As Riley's fond gaze settled on Cari, Kim appraised her new neighbor and wondered what she'd be like. Kim had to admit the tattoos were cool. She'd always admired them but was too much of a wimp to get any herself. She knew some people would find so much ink intimidating, but Riley's face was kind, her expression a little shy, and Kim had a feeling they were going to become fast friends.

Not least because Tyler would be asking to pet her dog whenever they crossed paths.

Did Riley live alone? There was no ring on her finger, but that didn't necessarily mean anything.

Riley's mouth opened. "I—"

"Hey!" Another person stepped out of 4C behind Riley. "When we offered to help you move in, it wasn't so we could do all the work while you chat up pretty women in the hall."

Kim's cheeks warmed. Well, she supposed that answered the question about whether Riley was single.

Riley seemed unperturbed. "It wasn't? Isn't that what little sisters are for?"

Kim could've guessed they were sisters. While Riley's sister had a mop of red curls, they had the same lanky frame, pale white skin, and bright blue eyes.

Riley's sister stuck out her tongue and rolled her eyes at Riley before disappearing back into the apartment.

"I'd better go"—Riley turned back toward Kim— "start clearing away the tripping hazard." She waved toward the things strewn all over the floor.

"Mm. I'd get to it before Ms. Watkins sees."

A puzzled look crossed Riley's face. "Ms. Watkins?"

"4A." Tyler pointed to the door across the hall. "She's scary," he whispered.

"How scary are we talking, kid?"

"Oh, you'll find out for yourself soon enough." Kim laughed when Riley's face turned alarmed. "Don't worry, she's harmless. Just has a tendency to get involved in other people's business."

"Ah. I had one of those at my last place. He used to steal people's parcels."

"She's not too bad. She'll just tell you off for stepping too loudly."

Riley snorted.

"Riley," another white woman poked her head out of 4C's door, her dark hair buzzed short and a vine of tattooed flowers snaking across her wrist, "if you don't come back soon, Bea's going to start unpacking for you. And you know she's going to put things in the most random places to annoy you."

"Yeah, yeah. I'm coming, Ash." Riley lifted the box of records onto her hip and whistled.

Cari scrambled to her feet.

"Say goodbye to Tyler, Cari."

"Bye," Tyler said, already looking glum as he gave the dog one last pat.

"I'll see you both around. Come on, Cari."

Cari followed Riley back into her apartment.

As Kim stepped into her own, Tyler's gaze bored into her back. She dropped her purse onto the couch, steeling herself for what she knew was coming.

"Mom, can we get a dog?"

Kicking off her shoes, Kim sighed. It was going to take her ages to get Tyler to start his homework. "No."

"Why not?"

"Because we live in an apartment—"

"So does Riley," Tyler said, "and she has one."

"And no one would be home with it all day, which wouldn't be fair to the poor thing."

Tyler looked crestfallen, but he'd get over it. It wasn't the first time they'd had this argument. Now, thanks to Riley and Cari's close proximity, Kim suspected it wouldn't be the last.

"What about a cat?" Tyler tried, following Kim into the kitchen.

"How about a goldfish?"

"Goldfish are boring."

"Mm, but they're much less work, and we both know I'd be the one doing the bulk of it." Kim kissed him atop his head.

"I bet Dad would let me have a dog."

"Well, why don't you ask him when he picks you up later?" Kim glanced at her watch. "Speaking of…if you want to squeeze in *Matilda* before you go, you'd better get started on your homework."

With another huge sigh—Kim already wasn't looking forward to his teenage years—he trudged off to his room.

Riley hauled the last of her boxes in from the hall and set them beside the rest inside her new apartment.

"Please tell me we're done," Bea said from her spot on the floor, flopped onto her back with her head in Ash's lap. "I can't take anymore."

"You're so dramatic." Riley poked her sister's thigh with a socked foot. "There weren't that many boxes."

Bea lifted her head to glare. "Are you kidding? Look around, Riley. You have way too much shit."

"And you don't?" Riley knew full well Bea had as much stuff as Riley did—she'd seen the inside of her closet.

"No."

"Please. Besides, this is all your fault for kicking me out of our apartment."

Bea's jaw dropped. "I did not kick you out! You wanted to leave!"

"'Cause I was sick of you two lovebirds." Riley couldn't pretend to be upset about it. She was glad Bea was happy—and that they both finally had a space to call their own, though it would take some getting used to. Riley had never lived on her own before.

"Please," Ash retorted, a grin on her face. "You love us."

"I do," Riley said. "But you don't have to stay. You should go. Enjoy having the place to yourselves."

Bea and Ash shared a glance.

"You don't want us to stay?" Ash said. "Grab a pizza or something?"

Riley shook her head. "Seriously, go. I need to start unpacking anyway." The floor was more cardboard than wood. It was only a matter of time before Cari would start to barrel into boxes instead of going around them.

"We can help you," Bea said.

"Nah. I'd rather do it myself—at least I'll know where everything is."

Still, Bea and Ash were reluctant to leave.

"We don't want you to be lonely," Bea said, a small frown between her eyebrows.

"I'll be fine, okay? I'm a big girl. And I've got Cari."

Not that Cari was currently being much company. She was curled up, taking a nap on her favorite armchair, snoring.

"Okay." Bea climbed to her feet. "But we're meeting for lunch tomorrow, right?"

"I wouldn't miss it." Riley hugged them both goodbye.

Once they were gone, she tried not to think about how quiet everything was.

Taking a deep breath, Riley reminded herself this was something she'd been working toward for years. She looked around the apartment, barely believing it was all hers. She'd fallen in love with it on her first viewing, with its open-plan kitchen and living room and the large bay windows that looked out over the city. She was on the fourth floor, but it was still a beautiful view, with the rays of the weak winter sun filtering through the glass.

It had two bedrooms, one of which she'd be using for storage. The only thing in her own bedroom was the bed she'd lugged over from Bea and Ash's that they'd spent half an hour rebuilding.

At least if she didn't get much else done, she'd have somewhere to sleep.

Her first priority was setting up her record player in the corner of the living room. Her favorite thrift store find, Riley was looking forward to utilizing it more than she'd been able to when living with Bea and Ash. It was safe to say they didn't share the same taste in music, as much as Riley had tried over the years.

Once it was set up, Riley carefully loaded one of her favorites—*Nevermind*—and cranked up the volume—though not too loud. She didn't want to annoy her new neighbors too much. Having Cari escape her apartment to bother them had been bad enough, though at least Tyler hadn't minded.

She stood with her hands on her hips in the middle of the room with no clue where to start. How had she managed to accumulate so much stuff over the years? And where was she going to put it all?

———◦✕◦———

Riley had barely gotten through three boxes before Cari woke from her nap full of energy, bounding to a stop in front of Riley and staring at her with big brown eyes.

With a sigh, Riley abandoned unpacking. She grabbed her jacket and Cari's leash, clipping it onto the dog's collar and letting herself be pulled into the hall.

The early-evening Seattle air was chilly. It was the second week of January—winter was well and truly underway—and her Doc Martens splashed through puddles as she took Cari to the park around the corner from their new home. The air smelled of rain, and the stormy gray clouds in the sky suggested more was on the way.

"I hope you like it here," she said as Cari sniffed the base of a tree, probably trying to find the trail of a squirrel.

The new apartment was a big change for Cari, too; she had never lived anywhere else, and Riley hoped Cari wouldn't miss Bea and Ash too much.

At least their old place was close enough to visit. Riley had still wanted to be able to walk with Cari to work, so she had only moved a few blocks over.

It meant they were still close to her favorite pizza place, and once Cari had done her business, Riley swung by on their way home to pick up a pie.

In the elevator heading back up to the fourth floor, Riley's stomach rumbled at the smell of pepperoni wafting from the pizza box. From the hopeful look in her eyes when she glanced at Riley, Cari was clearly hungry, too.

"There's no way in hell you're getting a slice of this," Riley told her. "You know Bea was always your best bet for table scraps."

Despite knowing dogs couldn't pout, Riley swore she could see the beginning of one on Cari's face.

When the doors opened, Kim was standing in her open doorway talking to a tall white man with dark hair. An overnight bag was tucked under his arm.

Tyler leaned against the wall next to the man, his green eyes lighting up when he saw them enter. "Cari!"

Cari hurried toward him, yanking Riley down the hall with her, and Tyler dropped to his knees to fuss over her, his curly brown hair falling into his eyes.

The man looked at Tyler in disapproval. "Tyler, don't bother this nice lady and her dog."

"Oh, it's fine," Riley said. "I think he might be her new favorite person."

Usually, Cari hated strangers fussing over her, but Tyler was an exception. And the boy appeared to be smitten, too.

"She's my favorite dog."

"Be that as it may, we'd better get going, Tyler," the man said.

Tyler sighed, slowly getting to his feet.

"Don't forget about his soccer practice on Wednesday," Kim said.

"You mean the same after-school soccer practice he's been going to for the last three weeks?" His voice was tinged with equal parts exasperation and amusement. "Honestly, Kim, sometimes I'm sure you think I'm an imbecile."

"I won't make the obvious comment," Kim said. "You be good for your dad, Tyler."

"I always am."

"Can I have a hug goodbye?"

"I guess so," Tyler said, his grin cheeky. "Bye, Mom. I'll see you next weekend." He turned back to give Cari one last pat before following his dad to the elevators. "Bye, Cari! And Riley."

"See ya, kiddo." Riley dug her left hand into her back pocket for her keys—they proved elusive—while her right balanced the pizza box.

"Need some help there?"

Riley turned to find Kim watching her, an amused look on her face.

"No, I got this." Hooking her thumb around her key ring, Riley crowed in victory. "See? Not a problem."

"No, it looked easy. Very smooth." Kim's voice was dry, a twinkle in her green eyes.

Riley grinned.

Her new neighbor was gorgeous—a couple of inches shorter than Riley and with curves to die for. Her brown hair fell past her shoulders in soft curls, and her white skin glowed even under the hallway's fluorescent lighting. Riley had to look away before she was caught staring.

The last thing she wanted was to make Kim think she was rude.

Or have her notice Riley checking her out.

Which was inappropriate. They'd just met, and as much as Bea had teased Riley about flirting in the hall, Riley wasn't about to make a habit of it.

"What can I say? Smooth's my middle name." As if the universe were out to get her, the pizza nearly toppled to the floor as Riley attempted to unlock her door.

Kim stepped forward to grab the box's other side, stopping Cari from having an all-she-could-eat buffet drop on top of her head. "Smooth, huh?"

"Usually more than that." With the door unlocked, Riley nudged it open with her foot and unclipped Cari's leash to let her bound inside. "Thanks for saving this," Riley said, waving the pizza box. "Want to come in for a thank-you slice?"

"I've already eaten."

Riley tried not to be disappointed. "Maybe next time."

"Maybe." Kim stepped back toward her door. "Have a good night, Riley."

"You, too."

Riley glanced back at Kim one last time before she shut the door to her apartment. She was going to like it here.

Chapter 2

THE NEXT DAY, RILEY WAS back at work. She wielded the tattoo gun with practiced ease, its noise a comforting buzz ringing in her ears.

Her client's face was screwed tight in pain.

Riley patted their thigh with her free hand. "Not much longer now," Riley said. "Do you need a break?"

Sam shook their head. "No, thank you. I think I'd rather get it over with."

"I'll be as quick as I can."

Riley poked her tongue between her teeth as she finished coloring the butterfly on Sam's forearm. Yellow, white, purple, and black—it was meant to represent the nonbinary flag. As Riley leaned back in her seat to admire the ink, she couldn't help but smile.

"All done." Riley set the tattoo gun aside and leaned back in her chair. "I'll clean it up for you, and you can take a look." Gently, Riley swiped Sam's arm with her trusty soap solution, wiping away any excess ink and leaving the butterfly shining brightly beneath her tattoo studio's lighting. "There you go," Riley said, tossing the wipe into the trash and snapping off a pair of black disposable gloves.

Sam's eyes widened as they took in the tattoo, lightly touching their fingertips to the newly inked skin.

This was the moment Riley loved—and feared—the most in her job. Because as much as she could pore over designs with her clients before marking their skin, it would never look exactly like it did on paper. But seeing Sam's expression, Riley knew she'd done a good job.

Sam's bottom lip wobbled. "It's amazing. Thank you so much."

"Worth the pain?"

"Yep. Though I don't think I'll be coming back in a hurry—no offense."

Riley chuckled. "None taken. Do you mind if I take a picture of it for my portfolio? And then I'll wrap it for you, and we'll go over the aftercare instructions again."

"Sure. Could you take one on my phone, too? Based on these"—Sam waved a hand at the photographs lining the walls of Riley's room in the studio—"you'll take a much better one than I will."

Riley obliged, and, once she'd bandaged Sam and sent them on their way, she headed to the break room for a much-needed drink before her next client. Caffeine was in order. Her Monday-morning exhaustion was worse than usual, thanks to spending the whole weekend settling into her new place.

Her boss, Stephen, was already sitting at the table, and he waved when she stepped inside. "Hello, trouble. Another satisfied customer?"

"Uh-huh." The air smelled of coffee, but Riley grabbed a Coke from the refrigerator, feeling like something fizzy. She dropped into the seat beside him. "How about you? You finish your sleeve?"

Stephen'd been working on the same client for weeks, doing a full sleeve that had been months in the making.

"I did! Wanna see?"

"Obviously."

He took out his phone and showed her the finished artwork, and Riley admired the smooth lines and the bright color. Stephen might have taught Riley everything he knew, but that didn't mean she was anywhere near as good as him. He did have an extra fifteen years of experience on her, though.

He'd been the one she'd trusted to do most of her own ink, after they'd spent hours agonizing over the designs together.

"It's gorgeous."

"Just like me," Stephen said.

Riley snorted, rolling her eyes.

Stephen wasn't short on confidence—but as a six-foot-four Black man who spent a healthy amount of time lifting weights, Riley supposed he shouldn't be. Much to his husband's despair, Stephen definitely had more than his fair share of admirers.

"I employ you, you know," he said. "You should be nicer to me."

"Like you'd ever get rid of me. You like having me around too much."

The door opened, and one of the other tattoo artists, Tess, stepped inside and waved at them both. Her bright blue hair stood out starkly against her white skin, drawing the eye.

"Do I?" Stephen continued. "Or do I tolerate you?"

"I think I'm the one who does the tolerating around here," Tess said with a grin.

Riley looked at Tess in disbelief. "Are you kidding me? You are so the most annoying."

"How rude. You love me." Tess leaned over the back of Riley's chair to pull her into a hug.

"Sure," Riley said, heavy on the sarcasm, but she didn't shrug off the embrace. Tess was like another sister to Riley—one that, unlike Bea, enjoyed playing the same sports as her. Bea liked watching soccer more than playing it, and Riley had never been able to get into softball, no matter how many times Bea had tried to lure her into enjoying it. "How's your knee?" Riley said when Tess pulled away to make a drink. "It looked like you fell on it awkwardly last night."

"Don't tell me you two were tackling one another again," Stephen said. "I thought players on the same team were supposed to be nice to each other."

"I was nowhere near Tess at the time, thank you."

"It's true. For once, it wasn't her fault."

"I caught you one time. One!" Riley exclaimed.

"Need I remind you I had to wear an ankle brace for three weeks afterward?"

"And you've never let me forget it since," Riley said.

Stephen grinned. "There's never a dull day with the two of you, is there?"

Beginning her workday over forty minutes late wasn't the start to the week Kim had hoped for. Nor was the downpour.

Bursting through the doors of Cake My Day, she shook off her umbrella and breathed in two of her favorite aromas—coffee and pastries.

Thankfully, the bakery was quiet—though from the tired look on Tina's face, Kim had missed the worst of the morning rush. Flour was smudged across her cheek, standing out against her Black skin.

"I'm sorry I'm late," Kim said. "You've got a little flour…" she motioned to her cheek.

"When don't we?" Tina smiled as she wiped it away. "Is everything okay? You're not usually late when you don't have Tyler."

"No, but it is his fault. John called to tell me Tyler had forgotten his history homework—I swear that boy would forget his own head if it weren't attached to his body—and I got cornered by a few members of the PTA when I dropped it off for him."

Tina shuddered. "I do not miss those days. One of the few perks of having teenagers is no longer having to deal with that. My two would die if I ever dared involve myself in their high school. Although maybe I could use that threat as leverage the next time they refuse to clean their rooms."

Chuckling, Kim shoved her bag and coat into the back room and grabbed her usual apron. "Is the use of threats a good parenting technique?"

"Oh, just you wait until Tyler hits puberty, Kim. Just you wait. Though maybe boys are easier than girls. And at least you only have one."

"I don't think I could've coped with another one. Especially not a year apart; I don't know how you and Nathan did it."

"Honestly? Neither do I. Though sometimes—after a particularly big argument—I wish I could go back to when they were babies and they couldn't talk back." Tina let out a wistful sigh. "Did I tell you Sophia has a boyfriend now?"

Kim could remember when Sophia was a wide-eyed six-year-old standing on a footstool and "helping" Tina and Kim bake. "They grow so fast."

"Tyler will be next."

"I don't think so. He still thinks girls have cooties."

Tina snorted. "Yeah, hold on to that for as long as you can."

Kim intended to. "How busy was it this morning?"

"So-so. Nothing I couldn't handle. By the way, I'll have to leave early on Thursday—Sophia has a game."

The system she and Tina had come up with when they'd opened Cake My Day two years ago had been arranged with both their families in mind: Tina opened so that on Kim's weeks with Tyler she could take him to school, and Kim closed so that Tina could ferry Sophia and Brianna to their various after-school activities.

"That's fine. Soccer or hockey?" How Tina and Nathan kept on top of their girls' schedules, Kim would never know.

"Soccer. Silly me, thinking having two girls would mean I wouldn't have to suffer through things like that."

"Like you don't love watching them."

"I do, but ninety minutes of soccer on a Thursday? You come and sit through a few of those and tell me you wouldn't complain."

"I think that might be in my future."

"Tyler's enjoying soccer practice at school?"

"Oh yeah. I don't think it'll be long before he'll want to join a team."

"And then it's game over for you," Tina said. "Hey, if you want to get a head start, you're more than welcome to come to Sophia's game with me tonight."

"What a shame, but someone has to stay here and close…"

"How convenient." Tina whipped a towel toward Kim, who leaped out of the way.

Kim's phone buzzed four times in quick succession.

Tina raised her eyebrows. "Someone's popular this morning."

"It's the dating app." Kim glanced at her screen. "This guy is the type to send four messages at once."

Tina held out her hand. "Ooh, let me see."

Kim hadn't had the best of luck in the dating department, so she handed it over—a second opinion from her best friend wouldn't be unwelcome.

Getting back into the dating scene had been a struggle. Kim and John had met in college, so she had never needed to use dating apps. It was only recently that Kim had felt ready to dip her toe back into the water—five years after the divorce.

"He's cute. When are you going out?"

"We haven't arranged anything yet; we've only been speaking for a couple of days."

"Looks like he has a lot to say," Tina said, scrolling back through the messages.

Kim snatched her phone back before Tina started criticizing her conversation technique. "We'll see how it goes."

"He can't be any worse than the last one."

"Don't jinx it!" Her luck was bad enough without Tina saying things like that.

Tina held out her hands in surrender. "Okay, okay. I'm going to go and start the next set of bakes before our first interviewee gets here—are you okay manning the counter?"

"No problem."

As the clock struck nine fifteen, only a few customers sat quietly with their books and laptops. Kim leaned against the counter and listened to the clanging of bowls from the kitchen, observing the bakery she and Tina had poured so much blood, sweat, and tears into over the last two years.

It was small—with eight wooden tables dotted around in front of the large glass counters showcasing their cakes and bakes—but since most of their business was takeout, the size had never been a problem.

And it was much more manageable that way. Kim didn't know how they'd cope if the place were much bigger.

She'd never expected to have a job she loved. The bakery had been a dream for so long—most of her life—that sometimes, even when Kim was standing inside it, she felt as if she had to pinch herself to believe it was real.

That it was really hers.

That they'd done it.

The bell above the door jingled, and Kim climbed off her stool, greeting the customer with a smile, ready to take on the rest of the day.

Chapter 3

Pausing outside the lobby doors of her apartment building after work the next Thursday, Kim raised an eyebrow at the sight of a person halfway down the street, staggering beneath the weight of a wooden desk, perilously close to knocking over everyone else on the sidewalk.

Wait a minute…

Kim recognized those tattooed arms.

What the hell was Riley doing?

Deciding it would be cruel to let the woman continue to struggle, Kim hurried toward her; Riley smiled when Kim reached her.

"Let me give you a hand," Kim said.

To her amazement, Riley shook her head. "No, thanks. I'm all good."

"Are you serious?"

Breathing heavily, sweat beaded at Riley's brow, and her arms were visibly shaking. "Uh-huh. I've made it this far. What's half a block?" She took another few teetering steps.

When she nearly took out an elderly lady with a Zimmer frame, Kim had to intervene. "Okay, you clearly aren't all good."

Kim grabbed the other side of the desk before Riley could argue, and together they managed to wrangle it into the building's lobby. "You don't like accepting help, do you?" Kim accused. She pressed the button for the elevator.

Riley looked sheepish as the doors opened and they lifted the desk inside. "It's not in my nature."

"How far have you carried this thing?" Kim rapped her knuckles on the desk's solid surface.

"Ten blocks."

"Ten blocks? On your own?!"

No wonder Riley looked exhausted. The thing was *heavy*.

"The guy I bought it off did offer to carry it," Riley said, "but he implied it would be impossible for me to do it myself, and I couldn't let that slide."

"So you're stubborn, too?"

"When it comes to proving I don't need a man for anything? Hell, yeah."

"Is it worth putting your back out for?"

"Ask me again in the morning."

When they reached the fourth floor, Kim ignored Riley's protests and helped her carry the desk out of the elevator.

"I can handle it from here," Riley said when they reached her front door.

"I may as well help you finish the job."

Riley unlocked the door, and Cari nearly leaped into her arms, tail wagging with such enthusiasm, it was a wonder she didn't take off. "Oh, I know," Riley said, giving the dog a fond pat. "I had the audacity to leave you here all on your own. The nerve."

Cari whined, and Kim reached out a hand for her to sniff when the dog approached, tickling Cari under the chin. Her fur was soft beneath Kim's fingertips.

"Huh." Riley looked at Kim thoughtfully. "She's usually wary of strangers."

"Didn't seem like it when she met Tyler."

"No. That surprised me, too."

"I wish she'd been wary of him—he hasn't shut up about getting a dog since he met her."

Riley gently moved Cari out of the way with her foot and grabbed the edge of the desk once more. "It's not my fault she's so damn cute."

Kim followed Riley's lead as to where she wanted the desk. The two of them set it beside the window that looked out onto the street.

"Thanks for your help," Riley said. "You didn't have to."

"I know, but I couldn't have lived with myself if I'd seen you barely able to walk tomorrow morning."

Riley grinned, her eyes bright in the afternoon sunlight.

Not wanting to be caught staring, Kim blinked and seized the opportunity to take in the apartment around her. It was a mirror image of her own, but that was where the similarities ended: Riley's place was sparse compared to Kim's—which reflected the presence of a messy nine-year-old— and Riley's decor was a mishmash of different styles.

Noticing Kim eyeing the mismatched three-piece suite, Riley folded her arms across her chest. "It's a little eccentric, but it's all mine."

She sounded defensive, and Kim was quick to reassure her. "Hey, I'm not judging. I kind of like it—it works, in an odd way. Is this your first place?"

"First of my own." Riley leaned against the arm of a blue leather armchair, scratching behind Cari's ears when she jumped to put her front paws on Riley's thighs, begging for attention. "I used to live with my little sister."

Kim remembered the redhead she'd seen in the hall. "She was one of the people helping you move in, right?"

"Uh-huh. Bea." A fond look crossed Riley's face. "The only time we didn't live together was when I went to college. It feels weird without her. Too quiet."

"I can empathize with that," Kim said. "Tyler's at his father's this week—and every other week. It took some time to get used to not having him around."

"Oh. I'm sorry."

"Don't be. We divorced years ago. And it's the best thing for all three of us."

"Would you like to stay for a beer?" There was a note of hesitancy in Riley's voice. "Or a glass of wine? As a thank-you for your help."

The hopeful look on Riley's face reminded Kim of the silence of those awful nights when Tyler had stayed somewhere else for the first time.

The lemon-orange cupcake frosting she needed to make could wait.

"That sounds lovely," she said.

Riley made her way toward her refrigerator, ignoring the burn in her arm muscles. She was going to be sore tomorrow, but at least her new desk looked nice, nestled into the corner of her living room. And it had led to her spending some more time getting to know her cute new neighbor.

"Wine or beer?"

"Beer, please. I can't stand the taste of wine."

"A woman after my own heart." Riley grabbed two bottles from the top shelf. The only reason she had any wine at all was in case Bea and Ash dropped by and forgot to bring their own. "Here you go." Riley passed Kim one of the ice-cold bottles, and they settled onto either end of Riley's gray couch.

Cari took the opportunity to launch herself into the space between them.

"Sorry," Riley said. "I can get her down—"

"It's fine." Kim settled a hand on Cari's back, her fingers combing through the short fur. "I don't mind. Besides—it's her home."

"And, boy, does she know it," Riley muttered because Cari had settled in immediately.

"How long have you had her? You said you rescued her off the streets?"

"Nearly three years." The anniversary was approaching—Riley would have to get her a new toy as a present. "I was working late one night when I heard a commotion in the alley out behind the shop.

When I went to investigate—usually nothing good happens out there after eleven p.m.—I found a scrawny puppy digging through the trash. Persuaded her to come inside with a few pieces of ham, and I've been stuck with her ever since."

"I don't know how people can abandon their animals."

"Me either." Riley had been furious when she'd taken Cari to the vet and found out how bad her condition was. "She was so skinny, she wouldn't have survived much longer if I hadn't found her."

"What kind of shop do you work in that's open so late?"

Stretching one inked arm along the back of the couch, Riley grinned. "I'll give you one guess."

Kim's expression turned puzzled before a spark of realization flashed across her face. "Tattoo artist?"

"Yup."

"That's cool." Kim nodded toward Riley's arm. "Did you do those yourself?"

"Nah. Tattooing yourself isn't the easiest thing in the world. I did design them all, though."

"I've always thought about getting one, but I don't think I have the nerve."

Riley had heard that one before. "A lot of people say that to me. But if you ever change your mind, hit me up. I'll give you a good deal."

"How many do you have?"

"It'd be quicker to list the places I don't have them," Riley said. "I don't have much skin to spare."

"Masochist."

Riley laughed. "Yeah, probably. My ribs were the worst." She pressed her fingers to where the phoenix rising from the ashes was inked on her skin, wincing even now as she remembered the hours spent in the chair. "But I think that one is my favorite."

"Can I see?"

"If you want to." Riley lifted her shirt, grateful she'd put on one of her nicer sports bras that morning. She was under no illusions—

Kim was most likely straight, and Riley shouldn't be flirting with her neighbor anyway—but still. It would be a shame for Kim to see one of the ratty, holey ones kicking around the bottom of her drawers for when she hadn't done laundry in a while.

"Wow, that's beautiful. Does it have any special meaning?"

"It's for my sister." Riley dropped her shirt and took a sip of her beer. "She went through a shitty situation, but she came out the other side stronger than ever."

"You really care about her."

It didn't sound like a question, but Riley nodded anyway. "She's my everything. And we're the only family we've got."

"I'm sorry."

"Don't be," Riley said, her voice more venomous than she intended.

Kim's eyes widened in alarm.

"Sorry, it's just…" Riley sighed. "It's a touchy subject."

"I get it. You don't have to talk about it."

"No, I don't mind. My parents kicked Bea out when she came out at fourteen." Riley kept the details deliberately vague—Kim didn't need to know Bea was trans, and it wasn't Riley's secret to share. "She always was braver than me. I never had the guts to come out to my parents, but I guess that's a good thing. Anyway, Bea didn't have anywhere to go, so I dropped out of college, found a crappy apartment for us to rent, and moved her out here with me. No one in my family was interested in helping us—or cared we were struggling—so I cut them all off and haven't spoken to any of them since."

"Jesus, Riley. I'm so sorry. How old were you?"

"Eighteen. Five months into my freshman year."

Kim drew in a sharp breath.

It was a reaction Riley was used to, and she shrugged. "It's okay. We got through it, and now Bea's happier than ever."

"And you? Are you happy?" Kim met Riley's gaze.

Kim's irises had specks of gray in the green, and Riley tried not to drown in them. "Yeah," she said, meaning it more than she had in a long time. She was proud of how far she'd come in the last few years. "I am."

"Good. Are you—"

Whatever Kim had been about to say was cut off by the sound of the lock clicking. Riley glanced at her watch. She hadn't realized the time.

"Yo!" Bea's voice called out.

Cari scrambled off the couch to go and greet her.

"I brought food and beer ready for the gam—oh." Bea's eyes widened when she saw Kim sitting beside Riley on the couch.

"You're supposed to knock now that I have my own place," Riley said, watching Kim gulp the last of her beer before setting the bottle carefully on a coaster on Riley's coffee table.

"Then why'd you give me a key?" Bea said. "But sorry. Didn't realize I'd be interrupting anything."

"You're not."

Bea glanced between Riley and Kim, eyebrows twitching, and Riley rolled her eyes.

"I'll leave you to it," Kim said, climbing to her feet.

"You don't have to go." Riley was enjoying getting to know Kim—she didn't want the time to be cut short. "You can stay and watch the game with us if you like. As long as you're a Sounders fan, anyway."

"Sorry, I don't watch baseball."

Riley grinned. "That's all right, seeing as it's soccer."

"They're all the same to me," Kim said with a wave of her hand.

"Okay. Well, then, thanks for your help."

"Thanks for the beer."

Kim let herself out, and Bea whistled as soon as she was gone, throwing herself onto the seat Kim had vacated. Cari, not wanting to be left out, leapt onto Riley's knee, and Riley winced when a sharp elbow dug into her ribs as Cari made herself comfortable.

"I was kidding when I accused you of flirting with her the other day, but now I see you're already making moves," Bea said.

"I am not making moves."

"Then what was that?"

"She helped me drag that desk in here," Riley gestured to the item of furniture in question, "so I offered her a drink as a thank-you."

"A likely story." Bea reached for the TV remote and turned on the pregame commentary. "She's cute."

"Yeah, cute and probably straight. Not that I'd go there anyway."

"Why not?"

"Because she lives next door? It's bad enough when I run into an ex at a random bar somewhere. Can you imagine in the elevator each morning?" Riley shuddered at the thought. "Plus, she's got a kid."

"And? You love kids," Bea said.

"Yeah, but I've never dated a woman who has them."

"Fair enough." Bea shrugged. "So, speaking of dating"—the segue was smoother than Bea normally managed—"when are you going to get back out there? It's been months since you and Lizzy broke up."

"I don't know."

Truthfully, Riley hadn't thought about it. She was fine being single—had needed to be, considering her disastrous dating history—and she had more important things to focus on. Like work. And Cari. And saving enough to buy matching furniture.

"I'm not in a rush. And I don't want to talk about it anymore," she said as Bea opened her mouth to argue further.

"Fine, fine."

Riley shook her head as Bea shoved six chips into her mouth at once. "You eat like an animal."

Bea shot Riley a pointed look. "Where do you think I learned it from?"

Riley stole the bag of chips before Bea could grab another handful. "I thought Ash was coming too?"

"She was supposed to be, but she ended up having to do some last-minute prep for her lessons this week. She's being evaluated."

Unable to think of anything worse than being observed—and judged—while at work, Riley felt a stab of sympathy. "I don't envy her."

"Me either. She sends her love, though."

As much as Riley adored Ash, it was nice to spend some one-on-one time with her sister. They'd bonded over soccer when they were little, and watching the Sounders had become tradition—even during those brief months when they'd been apart, they'd watched matches together over Skype every week.

"How are you settling in?" Bea said.

"Okay. The peace and quiet is nice." Riley ducked when Bea threw a pillow in her direction. "Just kidding. I'd be lying if I didn't say that it's taking a bit of getting used to. "

"Yeah. I feel the same way. Like, it's nice for me and Ash to have our own place, but…sometimes I miss having my big sister around."

When Bea leaned closer into her side, Riley wrapped an arm around her shoulder. "I know what you mean."

"You know, I never…I've never really thanked you for everything you've done for me."

Riley tensed. "You don't have to thank me, Bea. I did what any decent person would have done."

Bea leaned back and captured Riley's gaze. "No, they wouldn't. You basically gave up your life for me. And I know you wouldn't have it any other way, but, still, you didn't have to quit college. You didn't have to work two jobs. You didn't have to put your own dreams on hold until I was in college. And I just…I want you to know that I appreciate it so fucking much, Riley. And I'm so proud that you've managed to achieve everything you wanted in spite of it all."

"Stop it," Riley said, her throat tight with tears. They'd never been a particularly emotional family. "You're going to make me cry, and I haven't done that since Lizzy and I broke up."

Bea chuckled. "Okay, okay. I'll stop. As long as you know it."

"I do." Riley rested her head on top of Bea's. "Thank you." Reaching for another handful of chips, Riley turned back to the TV screen where the teams' lineups were shown on the screen and groaned. "Why are we going with that defense again? We're screwed."

Chapter 4

The bell above Cake My Day's door jingled as Kim was carefully removing a tray of brownies from the oven, and she was glad Tina was out front to greet the customer. After the morning flurry passed, Kim liked to use the precious two quiet hours before lunch to bake as many sweet treats as she could to fill the display cases.

"Morning!" Tina's bright voice carried through the open door of the bakery's kitchen. "What can I get for you?"

"A black coffee to go, please."

Kim nearly dropped the tray when she recognized the voice. Thinking she might be mistaken, Kim set the brownies down, turned off the oven, and stepped out of the kitchen to look. Sure enough, Riley stood behind the counter, hands buried in the pockets of a brown leather jacket.

"Kim?" Riley gave Kim's apron a once-over. "You work here?"

"I own the place," Kim said, unable to stop the slight puff of her chest—she was proud of what she and Tina had managed to cobble together after years of hard work.

"No way." Riley cast her gaze around, taking in the bakery and its handful of tables. "I guess that's my bad for spending too much time talking about myself and never asking you what you did for a living."

"It's not like we've spent much time together," Kim said, resting her arms on top of the counter.

Behind her, making Riley's coffee, Tina cleared her throat, and Kim knew she was waiting for an introduction.

"Riley, this is my co-owner—and annoying best friend—Tina. And, Tina, this is Riley. She moved in next door a couple of weeks ago."

"Welcome to the neighborhood," Tina said, eyeing Riley curiously. "Your dog is adorable."

Kim glanced out of the window to see Cari tied to a streetlight outside. "You could've brought her in."

"I couldn't see a sign saying dogs were welcome, so I thought I'd better not. And she loves being outside."

Cari did look happy enough sitting patiently on the sidewalk.

"So, what brings you here?" Kim said. "Morning dog walk?"

"I walk past here now on my way to work, and I thought it was cute. This morning my coffee machine gave up on life, and I know I won't get through my first appointment today without caffeine, so I thought it was about time I checked it out."

"What's so bad about your first appointment?"

"I've tattooed her before, and the woman does not know how to shut up. Trust me when I say I do not need to know every detail of her personal life." Riley's nose wrinkled in distaste.

Kim laughed. "Maybe that's how she distracts herself from the pain."

"She could at least have the decency to make an afternoon appointment."

"One black coffee," Tina said, setting a to-go cup on the counter in front of Riley.

"You're a lifesaver, thank you." Riley took a sip and hummed in obvious satisfaction. Her gaze fell to the display cases—empty aside from a small collection of leftover breakfast pastries. "I'm starting to think it's a travesty I've never been to this place before. Salted caramel brownies?" Riley read out one of the signs in a section waiting to be filled. "Oreo cupcakes? I've been missing out."

"I'd offer you one, but they're not ready yet."

"Maybe I'll come back at lunch."

"I'll save one for you."

Riley grinned as she reached for her wallet. "How much for the coffee?"

"Two fifty," Kim said when she realized Tina had wandered off into the kitchen.

Riley handed over three dollar bills. "Keep it," she said waving a hand when Kim went to hand Riley her change. "I'd be paying double if I went to Starbucks."

Kim couldn't argue with that.

Riley glanced at her watch. "Shit. I'd better get going or I'm going to be late—see ya around!" Riley spun on her heel and hurried out the door onto the busy street beyond, grabbing Cari and jogging out of view.

Kim returned to the kitchen, where Tina was starting to whip up the batter for red velvet cupcakes.

"Your new neighbor seems nice."

"She is." Kim began gathering the ingredients for the topping of her salted caramel brownies, keeping an ear out for the bell in case they had any other customers. "And she has Tyler smitten."

"It's the dog, isn't it? How many times has he asked you for one?"

"So freaking many." Her phone buzzed, and Kim smiled at the notification on her screen.

"That the guy from the dating app again?"

"Darren, yeah."

"Things still going well, then?"

"We're going for dinner next time Tyler is at John's."

"Ooh, how exciting. I hope he's the one."

Kim would settle for a second date. Her track record wasn't great, but there must be someone out there for her.

She just had to find him.

Practices where they played 5-a-side games were always everyone's favorites—and no one on Riley's team wanted to be on the losing side.

It meant the pace was faster and the competition was fierce, and Riley was jostled by her teammates as she vied to be the first one to head the ball sailing through the air toward the goal. But instead of connecting with the ball, Riley caught an elbow to the face and went down—hard. The impact knocked the wind out of her.

"Ow."

"Shit, Riley, I'm sorry." Jodie dropped to her knees beside Riley as their coach blew her whistle. "Are you okay?"

"I'm good." Riley accepted Jodie's hand and winced as she was hauled to her feet. "I'll walk it off."

It wasn't the first hit Riley had taken, and it wouldn't be the last, either. She blamed it on her exhaustion—her morning tattoo appointment had taken longer than expected, and she'd spent the rest of the day scrambling to catch up.

All she'd wanted to do after finishing her shift was go home and collapse on the couch, but instead she was running around a field in the February rain in mud-splattered shorts.

Riley couldn't remember, but she was pretty sure she'd landed in a puddle; her underwear was unpleasantly damp.

When Tess spun neatly to tap the ball past Riley and into Jodie's path, Riley knew it was only going to end one way: with the ball in the back of the net.

Sure enough, Jodie scored, leaving Riley's team down nil-one. Riley groaned at their coach's whistle that came a few minutes after the restart, signaling the end of the game.

"Losers buy the first round of drinks tonight?" Tess proposed, knocking Riley's shoulder with her own as they trudged back to the changing room for a well-deserved shower.

"I don't think I'm up for drinks tonight," Riley said, sure she'd fall asleep at the table. When her reply was met with groans, Riley held up her hands. "I'll buy two rounds next time to make up for it."

"We'll hold you to that," Tess said.

Jodie approached Riley with a sheepish look. "Is your cheek okay? Oh, gosh, it's already bruising."

Riley glanced in the mirror. Jodie was right—the skin was red and puffy, and she couldn't deny it was stinging. But Riley wasn't about to admit that. Jodie would already feel bad enough.

"Hey, don't worry about it. It happens. And I've had worse."

If nothing else, it would be a story to tell her clients tomorrow.

Riley showered and headed home, leaving the rest of her teammates to their regular after-practice hangout at the lesbian bar across the street.

As she stepped through her front door twenty minutes later, Cari leapt up, her paws on Riley's ribcage, and Riley scratched her.

With a yawn, she dropped her kit bag to the floor and padded into her kitchen. She was relieved the previous night's leftovers were still in the refrigerator. The art of cooking for one wasn't a thing Riley had managed to master yet.

A knock sounded as Riley was about to put her bowl of spaghetti bolognese in the microwave. Cari barked, and Riley shushed her as she dragged herself over to answer the door. She had no idea who it was—Bea would never knock, no matter how many times she was told. She smiled when she opened it a crack and standing on the other side were Kim and Tyler.

Kim gasped when her eyes met Riley's. "Oh my God, what happened to your face?"

"You should see the other guy," Riley said, regretting the joke as Kim's eyes widened. "Kidding. I got elbowed in the face at soccer practice. But I'm fine. It looks worse than it feels."

Mostly.

"You play soccer?" Tyler's face lit up with interest. "Me too!"

"Oh yeah?" Considering Kim hadn't known who the Sounders were, Riley was surprised. "What position?"

"I don't have one yet—I don't play on a team. I started playing a few weeks ago at school."

"That's okay. You can try different ones and find where you like best."

"Where do you play?"

"Striker, usually. But I can play wherever they need me to."

Tyler's questions came quick and fast. "Do you play games?"

"Uh-huh, every couple weeks."

"Can I come watch?"

"If you want to." Riley glanced at Kim, who was still looking at her cheek in concern. "Though we don't have one for a while."

"Oh." Tyler looked crestfallen.

"But, uh, maybe you could come to one of my practices? The team would love to have you there. Maybe we can teach you a few things, too."

"Can I, Mom?" Tyler's pleading gaze turned to Kim. "Please?"

"We'll see. It depends on whether you finish all your homework."

"So"—Riley wanted to distract Tyler before he started arguing his case further—"what brings you two over here?"

Kim produced a box from behind her back. "I wanted to give you these because you never came back to the bakery today."

"And I wanted to see Cari." Tyler peered hopefully around Riley.

"You can come in and say hi." Opening the door wider, Riley ushered Tyler and Kim inside.

Cari launched herself at Tyler, her tail wagging frantically and her favorite stuffed toy in her mouth. As Tyler played with her, Riley took the box from Kim and opened it to find two brownies and a cupcake, the chocolatey smell making her mouth water.

"Thank you. You might be the best neighbor in the history of the world."

Kim smiled, a light flush on her cheeks. "I doubt that."

"No, seriously. These look incredible." Brownie for dinner sounded much more appealing than bolognese—Riley was touched Kim had thought of her. "Definitely the highlight of my day."

"I'm glad it beats an elbow to the face."

"I guess when you put it like that, it doesn't sound like a high bar."

"So, soccer, huh? I don't know. First, you make my kid obsessed with wanting a dog, and now you're going to have him drag me to a soccer game? I'm starting to think you might be trouble."

"Guessing you're not a fan?"

Kim's nose wrinkled. "I can think of better ways to spend my time. Unless your games fall on John's weeks with him—then he can watch as many of them as he likes."

Riley chuckled, though she'd much rather see Kim waving from the sidelines than the ex-husband she hadn't been properly introduced to. "I'll see what I can do. And I'm sorry I never came back earlier—it ended up being a busier day than I thought."

"I thought your customer might have talked you to death."

"It was close. How much for them?" Riley waved toward the box.

Kim shook her head. "Nothing. They were left over at the end of the day."

"Doesn't mean I can't give you something."

"It's fine. They'd be going to waste anyway."

"Do you have leftovers often?"

"Depends on how busy we've been."

"Why do I get the feeling living next to you is going to be danger-ous for my waistline?"

Kim laughed. "I guess you'll have to start taking take Cari for more walks."

"How do you manage not to eat everything you make?"

"It's less tempting when you're the one who makes them."

"I dunno." Riley glanced at her sleeve. "I spend my whole day around tattoos and I'm covered in them."

"Clearly, you have no self-control."

"Burn," Tyler said from his spot on the floor—he sat cross-legged with Cari's head in his lap.

Riley lifted a hand to her chest. "Ouch. True—but ouch."

When Kim grinned, Riley tried not to think about how pretty she was when she smiled.

"Come on, Tyler." Kim turned toward him. "Let's leave Riley in peace."

Tyler pouted. "Do we have to?"

Riley was half-tempted to tell them both to stay, but she was exhausted.

"Yes," Kim said, folding her arms across her chest. "But perhaps if you ask nicely, Riley might let you come back to see Cari later this week."

"Tomorrow?" Tyler looked at Riley with hopeful eyes. "Can we take her for a walk?"

"Uh, sure. We can do that. I usually take her after I finish work—which is four tomorrow."

"Why don't you meet us at the bakery?" Kim said. "Tyler hangs out with me there after school. Though he will have to finish his homework before he can go with you."

"*Mooooom*," Tyler groaned as he climbed to his feet. "That is not cool."

"Tough," Kim said, poking him on the nose. "Perhaps this will make you more inclined to finish it quicker."

Riley grinned at the look on Tyler's face. "Okay, sounds good. I guess I'll see you both tomorrow."

"Enjoy the brownies." Kim edged toward the door.

"Thank you. Maybe I'll pay you back with a tattoo sometime."

"Don't count on it."

Riley grinned. "See ya, Tyler."

"Bye!" He gave Cari one last hug before scampering next door with Kim.

———✦———

Kim was serving a customer when Riley strode through the door of the bakery with Cari in tow. She waved, and Kim nodded toward Tyler, who sat at the table in the corner with a pencil between his lips—he'd yet to get out of the habit of chewing on them, no matter how many times Kim nagged him. He'd also yet to finish his homework, despite Kim's insistence he wouldn't be going for a walk with Cari until it was done.

By the time Kim had served the customer, Riley was sitting on the chair opposite Tyler. Cari sat beneath the table with her head on Tyler's lap, and he stroked her with the hand not holding the pencil.

"Okay, so if this equals three," Riley said as Kim approached, "what would the answer be?"

"Tyler," Kim said, setting her hands on her hips as she came to a stop by Tyler's shoulder. "I'm not sure Riley signed up to help you with your homework."

Riley smiled. "Oh, I don't mind. It's making me feel smart."

"So long as you don't tell him the answers."

"Hey, I'm no amateur when it comes to tutoring math. I used to help Bea with her homework all the time."

Riley eyed the display cases while Tyler carefully wrote his answer.

"What can I get you?" Kim said.

"Am I that obvious?"

"There is some drooling."

Riley narrowed her eyes.

"Kidding." Kim smiled. "But seriously—what do you want?"

"Surprise me."

Kim chose her newest and currently most popular creation, a combination of a brownie and a cookie—in her favorite flavor, chocolate orange.

"Wow, that looks amazing," Riley said when Kim set it beside her. "Thank you."

"No problem."

The bell jingled, and Kim returned to her spot behind the counter, leaving Riley and Tyler to it. They seemed happy enough. Riley was good with him, probably because she'd had to look out for her sister from such a young age. She had a protective instinct most people didn't, and it meant Kim felt Tyler was safe with her.

And Tyler liked Riley, not to mention Cari. Kim didn't think a day went by without him mentioning one or both of them.

"Mom!" Tyler's voice carried across the bakery. "I'm finished! Can we go now?"

If only he was that enthusiastic to do anything with her. "Go on, then."

Tyler bounded to his feet and began shoving his things into his backpack.

Riley approached Kim at the counter with an uncertain expression. "You're not coming with us?"

"I have to stay here and close up. But you two go, have fun. Let him talk your ear off about soccer."

"You trust me with your kid?"

"I don't see any reason why I shouldn't. He's nine, not four. And I do know where you live. I'll give you my phone number, though, in case you need anything."

"Sure."

Riley handed Kim her iPhone, and Kim added herself as a new contact.

"I'll send you a text so you have mine, too," Riley said, and Kim's phone buzzed a few seconds later. "Should we meet you back here?"

"Back at home is fine. Tyler has a key if you get there before I do. Though he might try and persuade his way into your apartment to spend some more time with Cari."

"Okay. I'll see you later." Riley went back to the table, where Tyler was waiting, backpack slung over his arm, and handed him Cari's leash.

"Have fun," Kim said. "And be good, Tyler."

"I always am, Mom."

The air smelled of wet grass, and the sound of screaming children and barking dogs filled their ears as they wound deeper into the park.

It felt odd, walking through Volunteer Park with Tyler by her side. Riley had only met him a handful of times, and never alone, but Tyler wasn't a shy kid, and his constant stream of questions made him easy to talk to.

They paused to let Cari sniff a particularly interesting tree.

"How many walks does Cari need a day?" Tyler said.

"I usually take her out three times. Once first thing in the morning, once after work, and once at night before she goes to bed. And she walks to and from work with me, too."

"You get to take her to work? That's so cool!"

"It is."

Not that Cari interacted much with Riley when she was there. She curled up on her bed and snored the day away. It only served to make Riley jealous when she was on her fourth appointment of the day and wishing she could nap so freely.

"I want a job where I can take my dog to work."

"Well, what do you want to be?"

"I dunno yet." Tyler glanced at Riley as Cari finished her sniffing and moved onto the next tree. "What do you do?"

"I'm a tattoo artist."

"Is that why you have so many? Did you design them all?"

"I did."

"That's awesome. I like the Spider-Man one." He pointed to the symbol on her bicep, mixed into the sleeve of other comic book characters. "He's my favorite superhero."

"He's mine, too. I used to read a lot of his comics when I was your age."

As they approached the skate park, Tyler became distracted, paying more attention to the people doing tricks than to Cari.

Riley remembered seeing him with a board the day they'd first met. "You like to skateboard, right?"

"Yeah. But I'm not as good as they are."

Riley pointed to an unoccupied bench. "Do you want to sit and watch for a while?"

"Will Cari be okay?"

"She's a lazy dog at heart. She'll be fine."

"Okay."

They settled in, and Cari sprawled on the grass between their feet and rolled onto her back, offering Tyler her muddy belly to scratch. Her white paws had turned brown, and Riley was not looking forward to dragging her into the shower to clean her off when they got home.

"Woah!" Tyler's eyes widened as one of the teenagers spun around on their board. "Did you see that? They did a backside 540!"

"A backside five-what, now?"

"A backside 540. It means they went in the air and did one and a half rotations. I can only do half."

Riley still had little idea what he was talking about, but she looked impressed. "Well, a half is way more than I could do."

"I could teach you."

Riley immediately started shaking her head. "Oh, no, thank you. I'd like to keep my feet on solid ground."

Tyler grinned. "But it could be fun!"

"For you, maybe."

"How do you know if you've never tried?"

Damn. The kid could be persuasive. Did Kim have a hard time saying no to him, too? "I guess I don't."

Tyler seemed to take that as a victory. "Okay, so next time, I'll bring my board and you can try."

"Next time, huh? Who says there's going to be a next time?"

"Me," Tyler said, his smile turning cheeky.

"How about instead of you teaching me to skateboard, we can play some soccer instead?"

Pursing his lips, Tyler considered it. "Or we could do both."

"We'll see. Have you found yourself a team yet?"

"No, but we're going to go look at some soon. When's your next game? You said I could come watch."

"I did. And you still can."

Kim hadn't been thrilled. She'd probably been hoping Tyler would forget. Riley hoped Kim wouldn't be mad. "It's in a couple weeks."

"Are you top of the league?"

"We don't have a league. Not a proper one, anyway. There are four teams in the area, and we play each other a few times a year. Just for fun."

"So, it doesn't matter who wins?"

"Oh, I wouldn't say that," Riley said. "It's still competitive. But we all go for a drink together afterwards."

"As long as you don't get another elbow to the face."

"I was thinking of getting one on this side, too." Riley touched her right cheek. "To even it out. Do you not think blue suits me?"

"No. You're silly."

Riley tapped him on the nose. "That's not nice. What would your mother say?"

"Probably that it's your own fault for getting hit in the face."

"I guess you have a point there."

Chapter 5

DARREN WASN'T WHAT KIM HAD expected. While he was the guy from the photos—white, brown-eyed, and five foot nine—they'd clearly been taken a number of years ago, based on his rapidly receding hairline and the wrinkles on his face.

Kim pursed her lips.

Still, she was giving him a chance, even though their small talk since meeting at the front of the restaurant had been awkward and stilted. Their conversations on the app had gone okay, and while her photos were current, Kim had used filters. Maybe Darren was just nervous. Kim struggled with nerves herself whenever she met someone new.

As their server approached, Darren set down his menu and Kim followed suit, deciding the beef burger sounded like a winner.

"Hi, I'm Erin, and I'll be looking after you this evening," their sever said when she reached them. "What can I get you two?"

"I'll have the steak," Darren said. "And she'll have the salad." He didn't look toward Kim as he said it.

Kim blinked, astounded at the audacity. He hadn't once asked her what she was thinking of ordering. "Er, no, she won't," Kim said before Erin could walk away. "I'll have the beef burger, please."

Darren frowned. "Are you sure?"

Kim bristled. "Why wouldn't I be?"

His mouth opened, apparently before he thought better of whatever he was about to say, but he ended up grunting instead.

"And, um, any drinks?" Erin looked mortified.

"We'll have a bottle of Merlot."

Erin paused, pen hovering above the notepad, and glanced at Kim.

"You can have that, if you want," Kim said, trying not to grit her teeth, "but I'll have a bottle of Budweiser, please."

"Coming right up." After grabbing their menus, Erin scampered away.

Kim wished she could do the same, but she forced a smile. She operated a three-strike rule on a first date. Darren was already on strike two, but maybe the night could still be salvaged.

"So, Darren. How was your day?"

Eight minutes—and half a bottle of Budweiser later—Kim wished she hadn't asked. He didn't let her get a word in edgewise as he told her all about his plumbing business. Kim was regretting not spending a few more days talking to him online before agreeing to meet.

Then again, he was a quadruple texter. Maybe she should have seen this coming.

God, why did this always happen to her? Kim couldn't remember the last time she'd had a date go well enough to end with plans to meet a second time. Darren certainly wouldn't be the one to end her five-date losing streak. And that didn't include the ones she'd already sifted through on the app and decided *not* to go out with.

Kim had thought it would be good to put herself back out there now that Tyler was older and Cake My Day was more established. She actually had free time during the weeks when Tyler was with John— free time she'd much rather be spending on her couch with a bottle of beer in front of an episode of *Grey's Anatomy* than listening to Darren drone on about the best way to fix a leaky faucet.

Maybe this was a sign Kim should stop trying to meet someone. At least until the universe stopped throwing frogs her way.

Kim knew two things for certain, though.

Darren wasn't The One.

And she wouldn't be staying long enough to have dessert.

———◦⊰◦⊱◦———

Riley jabbed the elevator button for the fourth floor with her thumb. Cari sat on her haunches beside her feet, the short ride to their floor apparently not worth standing for. The doors were about to slide closed when a voice called out.

"Can you hold the doors, please?"

Riley smiled when Kim stepped inside a few moments later, a harried look on her face. She wore a black-and-white jumpsuit molded to her curves, and her three-inch heels put her close to Riley's height. Her hair framed her face in soft curls, and Riley was taken aback by her beauty.

Wow.

Riley felt underdressed in her sweats and baggy Sounders jersey, her go-to outfit for taking Cari for a quick walk around the block before bed.

"You look good," Riley said, keeping Cari close to her side—she didn't want to get any fur on Kim's outfit. "Special occasion?"

"I had a date," Kim said.

Though she had no right to feel it, Riley felt a flutter of disappointment. "Oh, nice."

Kim's face twisted into a grimace.

"Or not?"

"It was awful," Kim said.

"How awful?"

"Where do I start?" The doors opened on their floor, but Riley paused in the hall. She wanted to hear what Kim had to say.

"His pictures were ten years out-of-date, for a start. And then he tried to order for me—and a salad at that."

"Are you serious?" How disgusting. "Tell me you walked out of there straight away."

Kim sighed, leaning a shoulder against her doorframe. "I wish. Then I could've spared myself an hour of mind-numbing conversation where he only ever talked about himself and didn't ask me a single question."

"Ouch. Why did you stay?"

"I wanted to give him a chance. I thought it might be nerves. When we spoke on the dating app, things were fine. But it turns out he's just a dick. You know, he asked me if I wanted to go back to his place for a 'nightcap' after we'd finished eating and looked so surprised when I said no way. How he thought it was going well, I have no idea."

"Doesn't surprise me. He was probably too self-involved to remember to check if you were having a good time." Riley couldn't imagine being on a date with a woman as beautiful as Kim and being such an asshole. "But you're a better person than I am—I wouldn't have stayed there anywhere near as long."

"I wish I hadn't. I wish just once I could pick a decent guy. This is the fifth date I've been on in six months, and every single one has been a disaster. I'm starting to think it's a sign I should stay single." Kim shook her head and seemed to remember herself. "Sorry. The three beers I had to get through dinner must have gone straight to my head. You don't need to hear this; you barely know me."

"I don't mind. Everyone needs to vent sometimes. And I know you well enough to know you deserve better than the way you've been treated tonight."

At Riley's feet, Cari let out an indignant whine and nudged the door of 4C with her nose.

"Okay, okay, little miss grumpy pants." Riley unlocked her door, and Cari bounded inside. "Sorry. If she's not asleep by ten, there's hell to pay. Look." Riley beckoned Kim over and pointed to where Cari had already curled up on her armchair. "She'll be snoring in five minutes."

"I wish I could fall asleep that quickly," Kim said. "I won't tonight. I'll be too busy reliving the horror of my dinner date from hell."

"Hey, look on the bright side: the next one can't be any worse, right?"

"Why would you say that?" Kim groaned. "You've gone and jinxed it now. Not that I'm planning on having another one anytime soon. I think I need a break."

"Don't blame you. Seems like you haven't had the best of luck."

"That's putting it mildly. I'd love to say tonight was the worst date I've had recently, but it would be a lie."

"Sounds like a story worth hearing. Want to come in and tell me about it?"

"I'm glad my dating history amuses you." Kim gave her a teasing smile.

"I could share some of my own horror stories, if you like." Riley didn't exactly have the best dating history either. Otherwise, she wouldn't be single at twenty-eight. "The first girl I dated cheated on me with her married art teacher."

"Ouch."

"Mm. And there was the one who had fourteen cats." Riley suppressed a shudder at the memory.

Kim's mouth dropped open. "Fourteen?!"

"She lived in a one-bedroom apartment. Yes, it was as awful as it sounds. I stayed for twenty minutes before faking an emergency and leaving."

Bea had bailed her out that night, responding to Riley's SOS text with a phone call so dramatic that it could have won an Oscar.

"I'm not surprised." Kim glanced at her watch. "I can come in for a bit. Just to compare notes on whose dating history is worse."

Riley stepped inside, turning on the light and laughing when Cari cracked open one eye to glare at her for the intrusion.

"I see you've unpacked a lot more since I was in here. It's looking good."

"I've been here a month—I couldn't justify stepping over boxes any longer."

"You think a month is too long to have boxes lying around? I think it took me almost a year to get rid of all of ours when we moved in next door." Kim cast her gaze around Riley's living room. "You moved the desk."

"Yeah."

Kim approached it, now nestled in the corner of the room rather than underneath the window.

"It was facing the sun, and I got tired of squinting into my sketchbooks."

One notebook was open on the desk, and Kim seemed to be trying to look like she wasn't interested in the designs splashed across the pages.

"You can look, if you want," Riley said. "I don't mind. Though that one isn't very polished."

Kim stepped closer, and Riley heard her quiet intake of breath as she looked at Riley's latest commission. The double-page spread was filled with several hummingbirds, each drawn in a different pose as Riley tried to figure out which would work best.

"Are you kidding?" Kim said. "They're beautiful."

"Thank you. I hope my client thinks so, too."

"Do you do a lot of designing? I always thought most people would have something in mind already."

Riley shrugged. "Some do. Some come to me with exactly what they want. Some have an outline, but they let me fill in the gaps. Others—usually my regulars—will toss out a vague idea and see what I come up with, and together we'll find something they love."

Kim nodded in understanding. "Vague briefs are always my favorite. We make custom cakes as well as running the bakery—that's how Tina and I started out—and I like when people don't necessarily have something specific in mind. It gives you a chance to be more creative."

"They're my favorite, too."

"Which category does this one fall into?"

"The middle one. She told me she wanted a hummingbird on her shoulder but left the pose to me. Which do you like the best?"

Kim pursed her lips, then tapped the bird in mid flight in the center of the page, its beak buried in the middle of a flower. "This one."

"I like that one, too. But we'll see if she feels the same when I show them all to her tomorrow."

Kim's attention turned to Riley's record player, which she'd positioned beside the desk.

"Another reason for moving it," Riley said, running a loving finger over the wood. "Now, when I want to change the album I'm listening to, I don't have to get up."

"I was admiring your record collection when I saw the box in the hall that first day."

Now Riley had them displayed on a bookshelf above the record player, and Kim eagerly thumbed through them, scanning the titles.

"Oh yeah? Any you recognized?"

"A few. My dad practically raised me on *The Wall*."

"Ah, a classic. The man has good taste."

"And this is one of my favorite albums," Kim said, pulling one half of the record cover out of its shelf and lightly tapping on the cover.

It was one of Riley's most-played records, but she blinked in surprise. "You know Halestorm?"

"What?" Kim shot her a raised eyebrow. "Single moms can't like rock music?"

"No! I just don't know many people who have heard of them."

"Honestly, me either. Which is tragic because they're awesome, but I can never get anyone to go to gigs with me. John called my taste in music "horrible noise" when we were together, and Tina would rather die than let me drag her to hear anything other than a musical."

"I know the feeling. Bea hates it, too. And, believe me, I've tried to get her to like it." Riley bit her lip, considering. "You know, there's a dive bar uptown that has an open mic night every Wednesday. Some of them are terrible, but there are a lot of good ones, too. I haven't been for a while—I hate going on my own—but we could go together, if that sounds like something you'd enjoy? I guarantee I'll show you a better time than the guy you were with tonight."

It came off more flirtatious than Riley intended, but Kim didn't bat an eyelash.

"You realize that's a low bar, right?"

"Then I won't have to try very hard, will I?"

Kim smiled. "Okay. That sounds like a lot of fun."

When Kim stepped out of her apartment at seven thirty on the dot, Riley was already waiting, wearing ripped jeans, a red and white flannel with the sleeves rolled to her elbow, and the pair of beat-up Doc Martens she always wore.

She looked good, and Kim's gaze lingered on the sleeve of tattoos. Each time she looked, she noticed something different, another tiny detail. Today it was the Halestorm logo tucked in between Spider-Man and the smiley face Kim knew represented Nirvana.

Kim had dressed similarly, in her comfiest pair of gray jeans and a faded band tee, a pair of black Vans, and her favorite dark blue double-breasted peacoat draped over her shoulders to ward off the winter chill.

"Thanks for inviting me tonight," Kim said as she pressed the button for the elevator. "I don't remember the last time I went to something like this. Not since Tyler was born."

"Hopefully, there are some good bands on tonight."

"Even if there's not, it'll be fun." Kim regarded Riley thoughtfully, remembering her promise to show Kim a better time than Darren.

She hoped Riley didn't think this was a date. Riley would have mentioned it if that had been what she meant, right? Kim hadn't ever talked about dating women, after all.

"Unless, that is," she added as an afterthought, "you start talking to me about the best way to unclog a toilet."

Kim decided to brush off her uncertainty. No, she was sure Riley had invited her out as a friend. Kim could use a few more of those.

"I don't know what you're complaining about, Kim." Riley followed her into the lobby. "Darren sounds like a useful man to have around."

"Doesn't exactly make you want to jump into bed with him, though, does it?"

Riley snorted. "No, it doesn't. I ordered us an Uber." She looked at her phone. "I think it's already here."

A silver Corolla idled by the curb, and Riley led Kim over to it, opening the door for her, then going over to the other side. Sitting together in the back seat, they barely had the chance to fasten their seatbelts before the driver peeled out onto the street.

"How was your day at work?" Kim said. "Did your client pick out one of the tattoos you drew?"

"She chose the same one as you," Riley said. "Do you want to see the finished product?"

"Yes, please."

Riley's drawings had been incredible. While Kim excelled at designing cakes, her artistic ability was next to zero, and she was fascinated by people who could draw. She regretted not leafing through more of Riley's sketchbook before getting distracted by her records.

Riley fished her phone out of her pocket and opened Instagram. Kim caught a glimpse of a dozen snaps of black ink on skin before Riley clicked on the most recent one, showing Kim the hummingbird in flight.

"It's beautiful." The bird was delicate and detailed on the person's shoulder. "You're so talented."

Riley flushed, ducking her head to hide a smile. "I do okay."

"I'd say that was more than okay. I wish I could draw like you."

"And I wish I could bake like you. I'd say we should teach one another, but I don't want you to see how terrible I am."

"And you don't have the patience to teach me, so maybe we should stick to what we're good at for now."

When the car pulled to a stop, Kim took in the front of the bar with interest. The windows were filled with neon signs advertising the beers available inside the Blue Moon, and people were already milling on the street outside.

"C'mon," Riley said with a smile and started inside, looking back occasionally to see if Kim was still behind her.

A large wooden bar dominated the room. The lighting was low and the floor sticky beneath the soles of Kim's shoes. Framed photographs of musicians covered every available inch of the walls, and a chalkboard listing obscure craft beers on offer hung above the bar.

Kim had to raise her voice to be heard above the chatter. "Quite the turnout."

"Yeah, it's popular. Plus, it's a small place, but I like that." Riley paused a few steps inside the doorway. "I usually sit over there"—she pointed toward the wooden booths nestled into the back corner, all of which were claimed—"but it looks like we might have to stand."

"That's fine." Kim weaved in among groups of people to reach the bar, slipping into the first available open space she spotted. "What do you want to drink? I'll grab the first round." Kim waved to grab the bartender's attention.

"I'll have a Budweiser, please."

Deciding on a gin and tonic for herself, Kim clinked her glass against Riley's bottle once she'd paid.

They found a free space near the wall facing the stage, where a few people were setting up instruments.

With so many people crowded together, the room was warm, and Kim shrugged out of her jacket. "This is already better than my date," she said, turning toward Riley and leaning her shoulder against the wall.

"I'd be offended if it wasn't. I—" Riley's eyes widened at something over Kim's shoulder before she ducked with a whispered curse.

"What's wrong?"

When Kim turned her head to look behind her, Riley reached for her wrist, holding it tight.

50

"Don't look! My ex is over there." Riley looked over Kim's shoulder. "I don't want to draw her attention."

"I think you're doing a good job of doing that all by yourself," Kim said, amused. "You're, like, four inches taller than me, Riley. Hiding behind me isn't exactly subtle."

Straightening up, Riley sighed. "You're right. Sorry."

Riley's dejected look made Kim desperate to comfort her. "Bad breakup? Don't tell me it's the one who cheated on you."

"Not the one with the art teacher. But she did."

Kim could tell Riley was valiantly trying to keep her eyes focused on Kim, and not straying toward her ex. "Do you want me to kick her ass?"

Riley snorted. "I think that might get us banned. She realized she was poly when we were together. I didn't want to lose her, but I said I couldn't be in an open relationship. She said she didn't need that and that she could be loyal to me. Spoiler alert: she couldn't."

Sympathy flooded through Kim. Seeing the woman again couldn't be easy. "Do you want to leave?"

"No. It was months ago. I'm over it, but I didn't expect to see her. I brought her here a couple of times, but I thought she only came because of me. I guess not." Riley grimaced. "Oh no. She's seen me. Fuck, she's coming over."

"There's still time to make an escape," Kim said. "It's busy enough that we could melt into the crowd. Sneak out the back."

"No, it's fine. This is fine. Everything's—hi, Lizzy!" Riley forced a smile, and Kim turned, curious about the woman who had put Riley on edge.

She was beautiful: Kim's height, white, with sparkling brown eyes, and wearing a figure-hugging dress.

"Riley. It's so good to see you. It's been a while."

Riley folded her arms, tension visible in the set of her jaw. "I've been busy."

"You look good." Ignoring Kim, Lizzy appraised Riley with a warm smile. "Can I buy you a drink? For old time's sake?"

God, Lizzy was annoying. Kim didn't like being treated like she didn't exist, but she let Riley take the lead. Kim wasn't about to tell her ex-girlfriend to get lost, tempting as it was.

Riley waved her full bottle. "I'm good, thanks."

"What about the next one?" Lizzy pressed.

"I don't think that's a good idea. Besides, I'm already here with someone."

Lizzy turned her gaze to Kim as if noticing her for the first time. "Oh, sorry. I didn't see you there," she said with a fake smile.

Kim wanted to roll her eyes but managed to stay polite and give her a small smile in return.

"I'm Lizzy. An old friend of Riley's."

"Kim."

"Sorry. I didn't realize I was crashing a date." Lizzy glanced between Kim and Riley like she was expecting one of them to deny it.

"Yeah, well, you are," Riley said.

Surprise flooded through Kim, and she forced herself not to tense up when Riley curved a hesitant arm around the small of Kim's back. Taking a look at Riley's anxious face, Kim decided that if Riley needed this to get rid of her ex, Kim would play the part.

She relaxed into the touch, curling further into Riley's side. Heat radiated off her, and Kim was pressed so close, she could feel the frantic thud of Riley's heart.

"We're *very* happy together," Kim purred. "So, if you could just..."

Lizzy looked like she'd been slapped in the face, and her smile became more of a grimace. "Right. Of course. It was good to see you again. Have a good night."

Riley waited until Lizzy had retreated toward the bar before letting her arm drop to her side.

"Sorry." Riley's cheeks were pink as she stepped back to put some space between them.

Kim felt cold all over when Riley was gone, despite the sweat beading at the back of her neck.

"I shouldn't have done that." Riley shifted her weight from one foot to the other, her fingers plucking at the paper label on her bottle. "I just thought it would be the quickest way to get her out of here."

"Hey, it's fine." Kim reached out to touch her wrist lightly, before letting her hand drop back to her side. "I didn't mind. Though I don't know if it worked." Kim glanced over her shoulder. "She is still looking over here."

Or glowering, more accurately. Lizzy's gaze was burning into the side of Kim's head from across the room.

"So, if you still want her to think this is a date, you might not want to stand three feet away from me."

"Sorry. I don't want to make you uncomfortable."

"Will you stop apologizing? You're not." Kim stepped closer to prove her point, though she kept a few inches of space between them—she didn't want to make Riley uncomfortable, either. "I think Lizzy might be second-guessing things." There was no mistaking the way Lizzy had looked at Riley.

"Well, I'm not." Riley took a long swig of her beer, her arm brushing against Kim's as she lifted the bottle to her lips. "I don't have many dating rules, but never get back with an ex is one of them."

"Mm. Even if you can be friends with them afterwards, it ended for a reason."

Riley smiled. "Can't say I've ever managed to be friends with an ex after a breakup. Though I guess it's different if there's a kid involved."

"Yes. Although there was no animosity in mine and John's separation. We just… We married young. We were twenty-one. Neither of us knew what we wanted. Hell, John couldn't even decide on a major, but when I got pregnant, everyone told us it was the right thing to do. No wonder we grew apart after a few years and fell out of love. We started off as friends—it wasn't too hard to fall back into that."

"More mature than any of my breakups."

As the first band took to the stage, Kim grew distracted.

Riley leaned close to Kim's ear. "You have to guess before they start playing whether they'll be any good or not. What do you think?"

A thrill ran down Kim's spine at the feel of Riley's breath so close to her ear. Suppressing the unexpected feeling, she took another sip of her drink and tried to weigh up the three musicians. "I think they're going to be good."

Three notes in, Riley was chuckling as Kim grimaced. They weren't all bad—the drummer was amazing—but the rough, barely-in-tune shrieking of the lead singer did leave something to be desired.

Still, Kim enjoyed the reverberation of the beat through her chest, the lilt of a guitar riff ringing through her ears. She'd forgotten how much she enjoyed live music.

"Regretting your decision to join me?" Riley said once the short set had ended.

"No—you did warn me."

"True." Riley's eyes brightened as the next band took to the stage. "Oh, I think you'll like these guys."

"I can't tell if you're being sarcastic or not."

"You'll have to wait and see."

Surprise bloomed through Kim as the band launched into a hauntingly beautiful cover of Evanescence's "Bring Me to Life." For Riley was right—they were incredible. As Kim sipped her drink and enjoyed the dulcet tones of the lead singer, Kim couldn't remember the last time she'd had so much fun.

Kim smothered a yawn with the back of her hand and turned to make herself a cappuccino—she needed the caffeine if she was going to make it to the end of the day. It was barely ten o'clock and she was already flagging.

The open mic night had finished at a reasonable time—half past ten—but she and Riley had ended up staying for a couple more drinks, and she hadn't gotten to bed until midnight.

It had taken its toll on her.

"Late night last night?" Tina said, amusement in her eyes. She knew Kim had a glaring lack of a social life.

"I did, actually."

"Oh yeah? Don't tell me it was another date. I thought you were taking a break after the last disaster?"

Kim shuddered at the reminder of her dinner with Darren. "I am. I can't face going through that again." Kim had dealt with being single for five years; what were five more?

"So, where'd you go?"

"I went out with Riley," Kim said around a sip of the coffee warming her hands. The temperature was in the low forties today, and Kim couldn't wait for spring to arrive.

At least the heat from the kitchen ovens warded off some of the chill in the air.

"The neighbor?" Tina looked surprised. "I didn't know you two hung out."

"We have a few times," Kim said. "Tyler is a big fan of hers—and her dog. And we're friends."

"Since when?"

"Since…I don't know." Riley had crept into Kim's life, and Kim couldn't pinpoint the exact moment she'd realized she liked having Riley around. "Since I realized we have a lot in common."

"Like what?"

"Taste in music, for one. That's where we were last night—she took me to an open mic night."

"She likes the same racket you do?" Tina looked impressed. "Thank God for that. Does this mean you'll stop asking me to go with you to things now?"

"Like you ever came with me anyway!"

"I did!"

"Once. And then you said never again."

Kim could still remember the look of horror in Tina's eyes as the band had taken to the stage.

"It still counts."

Kim shook her head. "Well, you're off the hook—for now."

"Excellent. You had fun last night, then?"

Kim smiled. "Yeah, I did. It was nice to have a good night out for once." Feeling refreshed after her coffee, Kim set the cup down beside the dishwasher. "Shall we get a head start on our next birthday cake design while it's quiet? Making the *Paw Patrol* dogs out of fondant is going to take ages."

Tina sighed. "Those damn dogs. I'm sick of them—how many times have we made them now?"

"I lost count somewhere between the seventeenth birthday cake and the decorative cookies."

"Whatever happened to the simple kids birthday cakes? One tier of chocolate, cover it in candy—done. That's what I had when I was younger. None of these fondant creatures and weird flavors."

"Social media happened." Kim flashed her a wry smile. "But we shouldn't complain—it keeps us in business."

If she was being honest, Kim loved the challenge. She loved getting a brief—even a complicated one—and figuring out the best way to complete it. She loved stretching her creativity and learning new techniques—even if it sometimes took multiple attempts to perfect it.

Reaching for the white fondant, Kim took her place at the counter, ready to begin her latest creation.

Chapter 6

"Remember—first round of drinks is on Riley!" Tess said as the members of Seattle Pride filed through the doors of their usual after-practice lesbian bar.

"Yeah, yeah." As they approached the bar, Riley fished out her card. "As long as no one orders a bottle of champagne."

"There goes my plan," Jessika said with a heavy sigh, her eyes sparkling and her Black skin flawless beneath the bar's lights. Being their captain—and the oldest and wisest of the team—Riley knew she wouldn't dare.

Once everyone had a drink in hand—and Riley's bank balance was lighter—they found two tables they could push together and squeeze around. Riley sat between Tess and Jodie.

"Everyone ready for the game on Saturday?" Jessika said.

"I hope we win this time." Jodie's expression was wistful.

The last game between Seattle Pride and Tacoma Ladies had ended in a loss for them when Tacoma had scored in the last minute, and all of them had been eagerly awaiting the chance to avenge themselves in a rematch.

Not that they were competitive or anything.

"Just don't elbow anyone in the face, okay, Jodie? We don't want a red card," Tess said.

Jodie flushed scarlet. "For the last time, it was an accident! And she was fine, weren't you, Riley?"

"Uh-huh. It only took a week for the bruise to fade."

Jodie huffed out a sigh, and Riley knocked her shoulder with her own.

Relaxing back into her chair, Riley enjoyed the excited chatter of her teammates. It had taken her a while to find her place in this city, but she couldn't be happier with how life had turned out in the end.

The sound of someone tapping lightly on a bottle captured everyone's attention, and they all turned to their goalkeeper, Raven.

"So, Finley and I have an announcement we'd like to make," Raven said, fiddling with the paper label on her bottle of Coke. "I'm afraid you might have to find yourselves another goalkeeper for a while."

Finley took Raven's hand and squeezed. "We're having a baby," they said, their smile so wide, it lit up their whole face. "Raven's pregnant."

The squeals erupting around the table were enough to draw the attention of the bar's other patrons, but none of the team cared.

"Maybe we *should* get a bottle of champagne," Jessika said. "This is reason to celebrate! Seattle Pride's first baby." She headed for the bar.

The kid would be spoiled rotten by every single member of the team. Riley was over the moon for Raven and Finley—after their wedding last year, they'd been desperate to start a family. She couldn't deny, however, that a tiny part of her was jealous, too.

They weren't the only couple on the team, and seeing her friends start to settle down and have kids put into sharper focus the fact Riley was still single. It had been months since she and Lizzy had broken up, and Riley hadn't been with anyone since.

Maybe it was time she put herself back out there.

As if sensing her thoughts, Riley's gaze met that of a brunette smiling at her from close to the bar. She was cute, her hair falling in tight curls around her face, lips painted red to match the color of her dress and to stand out against her white skin.

Tess noticed the path of Riley's gaze. "Looks like you have an admirer. You should go over there."

Tempting, but it wouldn't be right for Riley to dip out of the celebrations for her teammates.

She decided, as she clinked her glass against everyone else's, that if the brunette was still there by the time things wound down, Riley would go over and introduce herself.

And if she wasn't, it wasn't meant to be.

Thump.

Startled by the noise outside her apartment, Kim sat upright, paused her episode of *Grey's Anatomy*, and listened for another sound.

There. Another thump.

Heart beating fast, Kim rose to her feet and approached the front door. She leaned on her tiptoes to look out the peephole, but she couldn't see anything. Against her better judgment, and because she knew she wouldn't be able to sleep if she didn't know what was going on outside, Kim opened her front door and stepped out into the hall to investigate.

Kim didn't know what she expected to find, but it wasn't Riley kissing another woman.

Riley had her pressed against the wall between their apartments—the source of the noise, Kim suspected—one hand fumbling for 4C's doorknob, and the other sliding dangerously high on the other woman's thigh through the slit in her dress.

Unable to look away, Kim's eyes widened as they exchanged needy open-mouthed kisses, Riley digging her nails into the skin of the woman's thigh.

God. Kim didn't know if she'd ever been kissed like that—could barely remember the last time she'd been kissed at all.

Her mouth felt dry, and Kim swallowed. What was she doing? At any moment, they could turn and see her, and what would they think if they found Kim gawking at them?

Speaking of—*why* was Kim gawking at them?

She needed to move before they saw her. And not think about how it would feel to be thoroughly kissed in her hallway, to be so desperate she couldn't make it inside her apartment.

Kim shook her head. What the hell was wrong with her?

Before the couple noticed, Kim spun around. In her haste to retreat, she tripped and stumbled, grabbing the doorframe to keep herself standing.

The noise was enough to separate the pair, Riley turning toward Kim with glazed and unfocused eyes. The woman's lipstick was smudged across her mouth.

"Kim?"

"Shit. Sorry." Kim wasn't sure how to explain how she'd come to be half-leaning into the hall while wearing her baggy pajamas. "I wasn't—" *watching*, she was about to say, but that came off as creepy. "I heard a noise. Wanted to check that everything was okay."

The woman giggled and looped her arms around Riley's neck. "Everything's more than okay."

"Right. I see that now." Mortified, Kim wanted the floor to swallow her whole. Why did she have to be so nosy? "I'll, um, leave you to it." Kim closed her door before she could embarrass herself further.

Next time she heard a weird noise, she was going to pretend nothing had happened.

Glancing at the time, Kim switched off the TV and decided to get some sleep. She had two dozen cupcakes to make for a children's birthday party in the morning, and if she started early enough, she could whip them up before taking Tyler to the skate park—their Saturday-morning tradition on the weeks he spent with her.

Only, once Kim had brushed her teeth and slipped beneath her cotton sheets, she realized she might not be getting much sleep at all.

It hadn't occurred to her before that Riley's bedroom shared a wall with hers. It hadn't occurred to her because she'd never heard a peep from Riley's apartment—other than the odd bark from Cari.

But, oh, not anymore. Riley and her friend had made it inside. Kim could hear them. Soft moans echoed through the thin walls. Kim groaned, pulling a pillow over her head.

It wasn't enough to block out a breathy, "Fuck, Riley, that feels so fucking good."

At least they were enjoying themselves, Kim thought. Too much, if you asked her.

Kim had never been loud during sex, but clearly, Riley's lover didn't share the same sentiment.

Or Riley was just that good.

Well, at least Riley didn't share Kim's propensity for terrible dates. Kim would be happy for her if she didn't have to unwillingly experience exactly *how* well it was going.

As the moaning grew louder, Kim fumbled for her headphones to block out the noise. It wouldn't feel right to listen—regardless of whether it was unintentionally—and Kim had little desire to hear for herself how it ended.

The next morning, after taking Cari for a quick walk around the block, Riley was unsurprised to return to an empty apartment.

Five minutes after introducing herself to Kayla, it had been clear the other woman was only interested in one thing—and with her hand burning hot on Riley's thigh and her breath warm on Riley's lips, Riley had been more than happy to give it to her.

Smothering a yawn with the back of her hand—she'd still be asleep if Cari hadn't woken her, whining to be let out—Riley glanced at her phone when it pinged with a message from her sister.

Wanna meet for breakfast this morning before we go out of town? We feel like we haven't seen you for ages!

In reality it had barely been a week, but considering they were used to seeing one another every day, Riley knew they were both still getting used to it. Her stomach rumbled, reminding her it had been hours since she'd last eaten.

Sure. Meet at Busby's in fifteen?

Sounds good.

Their favorite breakfast place was the halfway point between their apartments, and Riley had a quick shower before saying goodbye to Cari and stepping back out onto the sunny Seattle streets.

When she arrived at Busby's, Bea and Ash were already seated at their usual table, both pretending to look at the menu even though Riley could bet what they were going to order.

"Hey." Riley slid into the chair opposite them. A steaming mug of coffee was waiting for her, and she reached for it eagerly. "I needed this. You're a lifesaver."

Bea raised an eyebrow as Riley took a long sip. "Did you not sleep well?"

Riley hid a smirk behind the rim of her mug. "Something like that."

Their server approached, and Riley ordered a stack of pancakes.

"Don't you have a game later today?" Ash said, once their server had taken away their menus. "I don't think I could eat pancakes before running around a soccer field."

Bea lightly patted the back of Ash's hand. "That's because you don't run, babe."

"Ah, I'll be fine," Riley said. "I've got a few hours for it to digest. Kickoff isn't 'til four. Are you two all sorted for the wedding later?"

Neither Bea nor Ash were particularly thrilled to be going out of town for the night to attend, but it was Ash's boss's wedding and she hadn't known how to say no.

"I think so," Bea said. "I managed to find some matching shoes for my dress yesterday. And it'll be nice to get away for the night. Even if we do have to spend most of it mingling and being sociable."

"Please, you love being sociable." Riley couldn't help but wonder how long it would be until the two of them got married, but she wouldn't push. She knew they would when they were ready.

"Sorry we're missing your game, though."

"Oh, it's fine." They tried to come to as many as they could, but Riley had never asked them to. She didn't always make it to Bea's softball games. "I hope you have a good time."

"I'm sure we will, despite Bea's reservations," Ash said. "Are you doing anything else this morning?"

"Probably taking Cari for a long walk after we're done here and then seeing if I can squeeze in a nap before I have to leave."

Over Bea's shoulder, she spied her pancake stack and tried not to drool. Sitting there for the last fifteen minutes and taking in the smells of fried bacon, coffee and cinnamon rolls drafting in from the other tables had Riley feeling starved. She couldn't wait to tuck in.

Once her plate was set on the table in front of her, Riley reached for the jug of maple syrup, and Bea gasped as the collar of Riley's shirt shifted.

"Riley Foster, do you have a hickey on your neck?"

A memory of Kayla's mouth working on the skin where Riley's neck met her shoulder washed over her. "Um. Possibly?"

"You've been holding out on us!" Bea leaned over the table. "What's her name? How did you meet her? How long have you been seeing her?"

"Her name was Kayla," Riley said around a mouthful of pancakes.

Bea looked at her impatiently, waiting for Riley to swallow so she could hear more details.

"We met at a bar, and it was a one-time thing."

"Oh." Bea pursed her lips. "How come?"

"Because that was all she was interested in."

Ash regarded Riley from across the table, hands cupped around her coffee. "Is it all you were interested in?"

Riley shrugged. "For now. But I think I'm maybe ready to think about dating again." Riley held up a hand when Bea's mouth opened. "I'm ready to *think* about it. Don't get too excited."

"Okay, okay."

Chapter 7

KIM BIT THE INSIDE OF her cheek so she didn't yell for Tyler to be careful as he careened down the side of the half-pipe and fell from his board. He bounced straight back to his feet, not a scratch on him, and Kim sighed in relief.

Why couldn't he have picked a less dangerous hobby?

Well, at least he was having fun. And he was still acting like a kid. Soon the day would come when he would refuse to let his mom accompany him to the skate park—would refuse to spend much time with her at all. She should enjoy the time before he turned into a moody teenager.

"I nearly had it." He skated over to Kim and dusted off his jeans when he came to a stop. "Did you see?"

"Of course I saw, sweetheart."

"I'm gonna try one more time, and then we can go."

"Do you want to get an ice cream on the way back?"

It was unseasonably warm for early March, and Kim was enjoying the feeling of the sun on her skin. She was in no rush to get back to the kitchen and make the cream cheese frosting she needed to decorate the birthday cupcakes. Thanks to her unusually noisy neighbor, Kim hadn't gotten up early enough to finish them before Tyler was begging to leave.

"Okay!" Tyler sped off, and this time he managed to land the trick he'd been trying all morning.

He wore a huge grin when he returned. "Told you I'd get it."

"You did."

He tucked his board under his arm and undid the clasp on his helmet, a spring in his step as they walked side by side to the café in the center of the park. Halfway there, Tyler paused, distracted, and Kim turned to see what he was looking at.

"Isn't that Riley?" He pointed to a figure a few yards away, and Kim knew it wasn't Riley he'd recognized but the dog trotting at her heels.

"Looks like it."

Riley was alone, one hand in her pocket and the other holding Cari's leash, watching as Cari sniffed along the path. How on earth did she look more awake than Kim did?

"Can we go say hi? I'm going to Dad's tonight and I won't get to see Cari for a whole week."

"Fine."

Kim had barely finished speaking before he was off. She hurried after him. Would she be able to look Riley in the eye without thinking about that other woman moaning Riley's name?

"Riley!"

Riley turned, her face breaking into a smile. "Hey, Tyler."

"Hi." He bent to pat Cari, who tugged at her leash to get closer to him.

"Have you been skateboarding this morning?"

"Yeah." He puffed out his chest. "Want me to show you a trick?"

"Sure."

He set his skateboard on the path and redid his helmet, and Riley watched with rapt attention as he flipped his board and righted himself with the slightest of wobbles.

"Wow, well done, buddy! You'll be in the Olympics in no time."

A blush crossed Tyler's cheeks. "I'm not that good."

"You could be—but not with that attitude."

"Do you want to try?" Tyler lifted his head to peer at Riley, whose eyes widened in horror.

"Oh, I don't think that's a good idea. I have zero balance."

"I'll help you," Tyler insisted.

"I can't leave Cari."

Tyler turned to Kim with an imploring gaze. "Will you hold her?"

"I think I can manage that." Kim chuckled when Riley glared at her over Tyler's head.

"You could help me out, you know," Riley muttered when she handed Cari's leash to Kim.

"Oh, but I think this will be so much more entertaining. Perhaps you should give her your helmet, Ty."

"Like it'd fit on my massive head. And I won't need it if Tyler does what he promised."

"I won't let you fall," he said, solemn.

Gesturing for Riley to step onto the board, Tyler set one foot on it to keep it steady. He took her hands and lifted his foot to free the board, and Kim struggled not to laugh when Riley's balance went immediately. She was so tall and lanky, Kim thought it would be like if a giraffe ever tried skateboarding, and the mental image was hard to shake.

Still, it was sweet that Riley was prepared to do something she was clearly uncomfortable with just to make Tyler happy.

Riley glowered at Kim, clearly noticing her amusement.

"I thought I was bad," Kim said, "but you might give me a run for my money."

If not for Tyler, whose hands she had in a death grip as he walked them both down the path, Kim was sure Riley would be muttering some choice curse words.

"I don't think I'll be doing that again." Riley stepped off the board, her face growing in color once her feet were back on solid ground.

"That's a shame—that was entertaining."

"I'm glad it was for someone."

"Do you want to come and get ice cream with us?"

Hesitancy flashed across Riley's face at Tyler's invitation. She glanced toward Kim.

She knew Riley was asking for permission and smiled. "It's the least we can do after spending the last few minutes torturing you."

The café Kim and Tyler led Riley to was cute. It sat in the center of the park with a dozen or so tables scattered inside the large domed-shaped building with its glass walls—more greenhouse than café—and more wrought-iron tables and chairs set outside for people to lounge on.

The menu was small—just drinks, a small selection of sandwiches, and ice cream. There were only a handful of flavors, but Riley still agonized over whether to get chocolate fudge or cookie dough. She went with chocolate fudge in the end and made a face when Kim ordered vanilla.

"What?" Kim said, noticing Riley's expression.

"That's the most boring flavor."

"That's what I tell her all the time!" Tyler had a cone of salted caramel already in his hand.

"There's nothing wrong with vanilla." Kim narrowed her eyes at her son and ruffled his hair. "And I'm not sure I like the idea of you two ganging up on me."

"Maybe you should choose a better flavor." Tyler stuck his tongue out.

"How much for all three?" Kim asked the server behind the counter.

"Seven fifty."

"Let me get them," Riley said. "Considering you won't let me pay you for the brownies you keep bringing me."

Kim looked like she was going to argue, so Riley acted quickly, fishing a ten out of her pocket and handing it over before Kim had the chance.

"You didn't have to do that."

"It's fine."

"Shall we sit outside?" Kim suggested once Riley had stuffed her change into the tip jar. "It'd be a shame to waste this weather."

Agreeing wholeheartedly, Riley followed them to one of the empty tables, looping Cari's leash around her chair leg so she had both hands free.

Sitting with the sunlight warming her skin, with her chocolate fudge ice cream sweet on her tongue and sticky on her fingers, Riley listened in contentment as Tyler chattered about skateboarding and Kim about the cakes she was baking.

"Can I take Cari for a walk when I'm finished?" Tyler said.

Riley and Kim shared a look.

"Sure," Riley said.

Impressed at the speed with which Tyler polished off his ice cream, Riley handed him Cari's leash at Tyler's expectant look.

Cari leapt to her feet—apparently a walk beat drooling as she stared at Riley's ice cream.

"Don't go too far," Kim said when Tyler began to walk away, a note of caution in her voice. "Stay in sight."

"Yeah, yeah. Come on, Cari."

They wandered off, and Riley watched them for a few moments, checking if Cari was on her best behavior, then turned her attention back to the woman beside her.

"Sorry to commandeer your Saturday morning," Kim said. "I'm sure you've got much more interesting things you'd rather be doing."

"Not at all."

Surprise flickered across Kim's face. "Really?"

"What else would I be doing?"

"I don't know. Hanging out with the woman you were with last night, perhaps?" Kim sounded like she was trying hard to keep her voice casual.

Shit. Riley had forgotten all about Kim interrupting them. She felt her cheeks warm, embarrassed that she'd been caught with her tongue down someone's throat, too eager to wait until she was behind closed doors. "Ah, yeah. Sorry about that."

"It's my fault for barging out there." Kim's gaze dropped to her ice cream, avoiding Riley's eyes.

Riley tried to lighten the mood. "Coming to my rescue in case I was in danger?"

"Something like that."

Riley grinned. "To answer your question, I won't be seeing her again. It was kinda a one-time thing."

"I can't say I'm sorry to hear that—just so you know, the walls between our bedrooms are frighteningly thin."

At the implication behind Kim's words, Riley's cheeks warmed again. "You...you heard us?"

Kim grimaced.

"Shit, Kim, I'm sorry. I didn't realize." Maybe she'd been enjoying the freedom of not having to worry about Bea and Ash sleeping next door a little *too* much. "I'll try and keep it down next time."

"Thought there wasn't going to be a next time?"

"Not with her," Riley said with a wry smile. "But I can't promise there won't be anyone else—a girl has needs."

Kim laughed. "Fair enough. I'm glad you're having more luck than me."

"No more dates on the horizon?"

"No. I've deleted the app. For now, at least. I think it's for the best."

Tyler returned with Cari, handing her leash back to Riley as he flopped into his chair.

"Did she behave herself?" Riley said, even though she'd had one eye on them the whole time.

"She always does." Tyler scratched Cari's head.

"At least she does for someone." Cari shot her a baleful look, and Riley huffed. "Sometimes I swear she understands me."

When Cari settled her head in his lap, Tyler sighed happily. "Maybe she does."

"I hope not." Riley finished off her last bite of ice cream cone and wiped her hands clean with a napkin. "So, what have you two got planned for the rest of the day?"

"Mom promised we could play *FIFA* before my dad comes to pick me up."

Kim heaved a long-suffering sigh. "Yes, I did. To see if you can beat me for the one thousandth time."

"Come on, Mom. It's probably only the five hundredth." Tyler grinned at Kim when she glared at him. "You can come and play, too, if you want, Riley."

"Sounds like fun, buddy, but I'm afraid I have to go and play a real-life soccer game this afternoon."

Riley realized her mistake when Tyler's eyes lit up.

"You are?" He turned to look at Kim. "Mom, can we go watch?"

"I suppose so," Kim said, a pained look on her face. "I did say we could go. Provided it's not too far away."

"It's a ten-minute walk from our apartment block."

"Yay!"

"You could've lied," Kim said under her breath.

"Hey, look on the bright side. At least now you won't have to play *FIFA*."

"But those games only last twelve minutes. Please tell me you don't play the full ninety."

"I'm afraid I can't do that, Kim."

Kim sighed. "You so owe me."

"Look! There she is!" Tyler pointed toward where Riley was warming up with her teammates.

Her sleeve of tattoos stood out starkly against her white jersey. She looked comfortable with the ball at her feet as she passed it to another white player with a shock of blue hair.

A few other spectators milled around the edge of the soccer field, and Kim led Tyler toward the halfway line, figuring that was where they'd get the best view. It wasn't how she'd intended to spend her Saturday afternoon, but it was worth it to see the look of bright excitement on Tyler's face when Riley waved at them.

And at least it wasn't raining. The sun shone weakly on her face, and Kim shrugged out of her jacket and tied it around her waist.

"Do you think Riley will score a goal?"

"She might, sweetheart."

Riley controlled the ball smartly with her feet and sent a shot flying into the top corner of the net.

"Especially if she plays like that."

"Woah." Tyler's eyes widened. "Do you think she could teach me how to do that?"

"You'll have to ask her."

The referee, dressed from head to toe in black, motioned to her watch, and both sets of players stopped their warm-ups, gathering at the side of the field to have a drink of water before lining up on opposite sides.

Kim riffled through her bag to grab a bag of chips as the game kicked off. Tyler was absorbed immediately, his gaze following the ball, but Kim's focus was on Riley, hovering near the edge of the opposition penalty box.

From the few touches of the ball Riley had, Kim could tell she was good. Sometimes it was as if the ball was glued to her feet, and Tyler wasn't the only onlooker who groaned when Riley's first shot sailed an inch wide of the post.

It wasn't long before she had the opportunity for a second, and this time, the ball thundered past the opposition goalkeeper, the net bulging with the force of her shot. Kim and Tyler applauded as Riley was swept into a hug by her teammates.

As the game went on, Kim found herself growing more invested. The games she'd watched before had been professional men's games her father and John had put on, where the players spent more time rolling on the floor after the lightest of touches, or petulantly arguing with the referee when a decision didn't go their way, than actually playing.

This game was different. No one was playacting, and beyond a slight huff or roll of the eyes, none of the players got in the referee's face. It made things much more enjoyable, and maybe Kim could become a soccer convert.

"She's going to score again," Tyler said, leaning forward as Riley slipped between two players and turned toward the goal.

Her left foot pulled back, ready to unleash a shot—before a defender slid in with a crunching tackle that sent Riley thudding to the floor with a cry.

Riley didn't get up right away, her face scrunched in pain as she clutched her right ankle. Kim wrapped a hand around Tyler's shoulder to stop him from racing onto the field to see if Riley was okay.

Any notion of the game being as friendly as Riley had suggested was squashed as Riley's teammates swarmed around her. The blue-haired player was the first to reach her. She shoved the defender who had made the tackle, still standing nearby, sending them tumbling to the ground beside Riley.

"Tess! Don't be stupid—we've never had a red card, and we're not starting now." Seattle Pride's captain, a well-built gorgeous Black woman, grabbed the blue-haired player—Tess—around the waist and dragged her away as Tacoma's players got involved.

The referee blew on her whistle to try and command attention as arguing erupted between both sets of players.

Kim didn't envy her.

"Is Riley okay?" Tyler said.

On the field, Riley's captain and another player helped her to her feet. She winced as she put weight on her injured ankle.

"I don't know, sweetheart."

Riley's teammates helped her to the side of the field, where she sat on the grass, and a first-aider—who looked barely old enough to be out of college—bent to have a look at her ankle.

"Can we go see her?" Tyler peered at Kim with worried eyes. Riley was only a few feet away, so Kim nodded, her hand still on Tyler's shoulder as they walked over.

"Looks like a sprain," the first-aider was saying as Riley gingerly rolled her ankle. "It's already swelling. I'm going to put a compression bandage on it, but you'll need to rest it, ice it, and elevate it when you get home. And if there's no improvement after a couple of days—or if the pain gets worse—you'll have to go and get it checked out."

"Okay." As a bandage was slid over her foot, Riley bit her bottom lip. She glanced up, noticing Kim and Tyler hovering, and managed a weak smile. "Hey."

"Are you okay?" Tyler said. "Does it hurt?"

"I've had worse." Her grimace as she put her shoe back on suggested she was putting on a brave face. "I'm sorry you had to see that, buddy. Looks like I'm not going to be playing the full game today. But I'll watch the rest of it with you."

"Not a chance in hell," the captain said, her expression stern. "You're marching your ass back home right now to rest."

"Jessika, I'm fine—"

"I don't want to hear it. We've already lost Raven; I'm not having you out for weeks because you were stubborn and made it worse by standing around on it for an extra sixty minutes."

"But—"

"No." Jessika held up a hand, and Kim could see why she was the captain. "Let me get my phone, and I'll call you an Uber."

"It's a ten-minute walk, Jessika."

"You shouldn't be walking at all."

"I can help her," Kim said, recognizing the stubborn look on Riley's face. "I can order a ride and make sure she gets home okay. Without putting any weight on her ankle."

Jessika turned her gaze toward Kim, looking like she was sizing her up. "I didn't know you had a new girlfriend, Riley."

Riley coughed, her cheeks tinging pink. "I don't. Kim's my neighbor."

"Oh." Jessika looked embarrassed. "Sorry. Are you sure you can manage?" she said to Kim. "She's stubborn. And hates accepting help."

"Believe me," Kim said, remembering Riley's struggle with her desk, "I'm well aware."

"Hey!" Riley looked affronted. "I'm standing right here."

"I like you." Jessika's smile was warm. "And you"—she poked Riley in the chest—"rest. Or I'll come and kick your ass."

"Yeah, yeah. Make sure you win for me." Riley cast her eyes back toward the field, where Tess and the Tacoma defender were getting an earful from the referee before they were both brandished with yellow cards. "And make sure Tess doesn't get herself sent off for me."

"I'll try my best." Jessika clapped Riley on the back before jogging back onto the field.

Riley watched her go with a forlorn look.

"Come on." Kim already had her phone in hand. "The car will be here in five minutes, but it'll have to pick us up outside the park. Put your arm around my shoulders and lean your weight on me."

For a second, Kim thought Riley would argue, but then Riley glanced at her bandaged ankle, which must have been hurting more than she was letting on. She sighed, sliding her arm around Kim's neck.

Riley leaned her weight against Kim, who noticed how blisteringly warm she was at her side. Kim breathed in the smell of sweat and grass—Riley's lovely white shirt now had a green stain where she'd fallen.

Riley hissed when she took her first step.

"Tyler, you get on her other side," Kim said. "Put an arm around her waist to help."

Tyler hurried to comply, and together they helped her limp toward the park entrance.

Chapter 8

RILEY HAD BEEN STUPID TO think the Uber was unnecessary. After an agonizingly slow hobble into her apartment, Kim and Tyler deposited her on the couch. Her ankle was throbbing.

Kim headed straight for Riley's kitchen. "Where's your ice pack?"

Lifting her foot onto her coffee table, Riley tried not to be offended by the fact Cari was much more interested in saying hello to Tyler than her.

"I don't have one."

Kim came back into view, her arms folded across her chest and a severe look on her face. "You regularly play a contact sport and you don't have an ice pack?"

"I don't get injured often."

Her protests did little to ease Kim's disapproving expression. "You've lived next door to us for two months and I've already seen you with a bruised cheek and now a sprained ankle. That's not a great track record, Riley. I'll go and get an ice pack from next door."

"You don't..." But Kim was already gone.

At least she could tell Jessika she was being well looked after.

"Did you enjoy the game before we had to leave, Tyler?"

"Yeah." He paused his game of tug-of-war with Cari to smile at her. "You were so good! And I got to see you score a goal. Will you teach me how to shoot like that?"

"It'll have to wait until after Riley's ankle has healed." Kim had reappeared with an ice pack wrapped in a towel. "There will be no soccer of any kind until then."

The stern way Kim looked between Tyler and Riley made Riley feel like the naughty kid at school.

"Obviously, Mom." Tyler rolled his eyes. "Otherwise I'd definitely win. Riley has to have a chance."

"Fighting talk." Riley smiled faintly. Having Tyler and Kim around was distracting her from her injured ankle's dull ache. "You think you can take me, little man?"

"I think so. I know your weakness now. I'll just kick your right leg."

Riley chuckled, but Kim looked horrified.

"You will do no such thing. Here." Kim handed Riley the ice pack and two aspirins. "These will help with the pain and the swelling. Also, you do know having your leg out straight doesn't count as keeping it elevated, right?"

"It doesn't?"

"Honestly, Riley, you're a terrible patient." Heaving a long-suffering sigh, Kim grabbed a few of the cushions from Riley's couch and piled them high on the coffee table. "Use these. And keep that ice on it."

"Yes, ma'am."

Kim glared, but Riley could remember the worry she'd seen on her face earlier. It was sweet—Kim didn't have to look after her.

"How are you going to walk Cari?" Tyler said.

"She won't need to go out until later tonight. I might be better by then." Riley wasn't so sure, but she could manage a five-minute hop around the block to let Cari do her business before bed. "And my sister can probably take her tomorrow." She'd wait until after the wedding was over to tell Bea and Ash about her ankle—she didn't want to ruin their night, knowing they'd rush home even if Riley told them she was fine.

"I can take her tonight if you want," Kim said. "Save you from having to."

"Are you sure?"

"Yes. And the fact you haven't argued with me means you must be sore."

"That's no fair." A pout was on Tyler's lips. "I want to help walk her. Do I have to go to Dad's?"

"Yes, Tyler," Kim said.

He huffed, mouth opening to argue.

Riley wasn't sure if nine-year-olds still had tantrums but if they did, she was sure one was brewing. She intervened before they heard it. "You can walk her when you get back. Whenever you want."

It did little to wipe the sullen look from Tyler's face.

"Hey, I could use something to take my mind off the pain," Riley said. "Why don't you go and get your console and you can teach me how to play *FIFA*?"

Tyler bit his bottom lip. "Really?"

"Sure."

He turned his gaze to Kim.

"I did promise you we'd play it before your dad comes to get you."

"Okay!" He scrambled to his feet and held out his hand toward Kim. "Can I have the keys?" Once he had them, he bounded to the door, his earlier disappointment forgotten.

"How bad does it hurt?" Kim said when he was gone, settling herself into Riley's blue armchair. "And don't be brave about it."

"It's about a six out of ten," Riley said. "But I do think it'll be okay in a couple of days. Thank you for offering to walk Cari, though."

"Not a problem. And if you need anything else, let me know."

"Thank you."

Tyler came hurtling back through the door, his Nintendo Switch tucked under his arm and a bright look of excitement on his face. "Can I hook it up to your TV?"

"Come in!" Riley called out when there was a knock on her door at nine p.m. sharp. She paused her episode of *Grey's Anatomy.*

Kim stepped inside.

"As you can see, she's raring to go." Riley motioned to where Cari was curled up in the armchair Kim had been sitting in earlier that afternoon. "Some guard dog she is."

"Maybe she knew it was me."

"Or doesn't care if someone comes in to murder me. Do you want to sit for a little while? I don't think Cari is in a hurry to leave."

"Sure." Kim sat beside Riley on the couch. "How are you doing?"

"I'm okay. Look, the swelling has gone down." Riley lifted the ice pack. "Got an ugly bruise, though." She tugged at the bandage to reveal the blue bruise beneath. "I'm hoping it'll feel better by tomorrow. It's been a few hours, and I'm already bored out of my mind. Getting through my Netflix queue, though."

"I love this episode."

Riley blinked at Kim in amazement. "You know what episode it is from a single still?"

"I may have watched it more times than is healthy," Kim said. "I got hooked watching reruns when Tyler was a baby. I'd watch it during my nightly feeds, and then I bought the box set to watch when he wouldn't sleep at night. Haven't missed an episode since."

"Wow. Considering how many seasons there are, that is dedication. I stopped keeping up with it a few years ago when my sister got bored with it. Figured I might start catching up now that I get unilateral control of the TV remote." It was one of the benefits of living on her own.

"You miss her, don't you?"

"Am I that obvious?"

"Maybe a little. But it must be hard. How long did you live together?"

"Ten years."

"Wow. And you were only eighteen when she came to live with you? I don't know how you did it."

Riley shrugged. "I won't lie and say it was all sunshine and rainbows. We struggled. A lot. I worked two jobs just to make sure there was food on the table. I didn't want Bea to work—I wanted her to focus on school—but when she was sixteen, I couldn't make our rent payments anymore, so she started waitressing. Somehow, she still managed to graduate with a 4.0 GPA."

"Where did you work?"

"I did a bit of everything. I was a waitress too for a while. Receptionist at a hair salon. Cleaner at a hospital. Bartender at a dive bar. That was my favorite because they had a lot of live music. But I took anything I could get."

"I can't imagine what you went through," Kim said, her voice soft and her gaze full of sympathy. "You were barely an adult."

"Bea was the easiest part of it. And you're one to talk. Did you say you were twenty-one when you had Tyler? Bea was fourteen when she came to live with me—she didn't exactly need a lot of supervision. I don't think I'd be able to handle a baby even now."

Kim smiled. "I wasn't on my own, though. I had John. But, yeah, it wasn't easy. Other people were the worst. The judgment: that because I was young, I couldn't possibly be a good mother. You wouldn't believe the amount of elderly women who sidled up to me in public to offer unsolicited advice." Kim's fingers clenched at the memory.

Riley wondered if she'd ever put any of them in their place. She decided Kim had probably been good at biting her tongue. "Well, you've done a damn good job at proving them all wrong. Tyler's a great kid."

Riley's thoughts went back to their afternoon—how Kim had made sure she took care of her injured ankle while Tyler did his best to distract her with the video games.

"I'm not sure I can claim full credit for that. John has always been present in his life. And John's fiancée, Rebecca, is a good influence on him, too."

"Tyler wasn't too difficult to get ready to go to their place this evening, was he?"

"Nope, managed to pack him up in time. He did request pictures of Cari's walk, though." Kim glanced at the dog, who had yet to move. "If she ever wakes up."

"Oh, I know the perfect trick for that." Riley clambered to her feet. When Kim's mouth opened, she held up a hand to silence her protests. "I'm barely putting any weight on it. And I can't sit on my couch forever. I'm fine."

Shuffling into her kitchen, Riley reached into the treat cupboard and rustled Cari's favorite box of biscuits. Within seconds, Cari had shot upright and leapt from her armchair to the couch and over the back of it, skidding to a stop in-front of Riley and sitting, her tail swishing across the floor.

"See?" Riley tossed her a biscuit. "Works like a charm."

"Wow. Can I take some of those with me?"

Cari's designated dog-walking bag was on the table near to the front door, and Riley grabbed it. "There's some in here already. Along with everything else you should need." She reached for Cari's leash and clipped it to her collar. "She should be no trouble, but if she is, bring her straight back."

"I'm sure we'll be fine."

"I'll leave the door unlocked—let yourself back in."

Riley spent the time they were gone working on her latest design, a black-and-white moth with swirling flowers hidden within its wings. The sound of her pencil scratching against paper had always brought her comfort; her hands had been constantly smudged with charcoal in her youth.

A perfectionist, she was finishing her third attempt when the door clicked, and Cari trotted back inside with Kim in tow.

Riley tucked her pencil behind her ear. "Did she behave herself?"

"She did. Probably more than Tyler does when he's with you."

"Tyler's an angel with me."

"Makes a change." Kim glanced at Riley's sketchbook. "That's beautiful."

"Thank you."

"Is it to scale?"

The moth filled most of the A4 page.

"Uh-huh. It's going across her shoulders."

"How long will that take?"

"At least a few hours. It's always hard to tell—sometimes it can be quicker if they can handle the pain, sometimes we have to space it out over a few sessions."

Kim shuddered. "I can't imagine how many sessions that would take me."

"I bet you're tougher than you think."

"Not when it comes to needles."

The TV had been playing quietly while they spoke, and Riley noticed Kim's attention wandering toward the screen. "Do you want to stay a while?"

"Okay." Kim settled beside her on the couch, and Cari leapt to sit between them.

"Just don't spoil it for me."

"I'll try my best."

Chapter 9

KIM YAWNED, GLANCING AT THE clock with a sigh. Barely seven fifteen on a Friday night, and she was flagging. If only she didn't have a three-tier wedding cake to decorate before she could go to bed.

At least she didn't have to do it alone. Tina would be there any moment.

Sure enough, Tina announced her arrival with a sharp tap of her knuckles against Kim's door.

"It's open!"

Tina waltzed into the kitchen, a bag of baking supplies tucked under her arm. "Doesn't this remind you of the good old days? Late-night sessions trying to get our next order out around our day jobs?"

"I don't miss those days." Kim helped Tina unload onto her kitchen counter. "Though this last week has certainly reminded me of them."

They'd had a flurry of custom orders this month, and trying to fit them in around the day-to-day running of the bakery—as well as balance their home lives—had been a challenge. Hence why they were spending a Friday night making decorative fondant flowers in Kim's kitchen instead of curling up in front of the TV.

"At least all we have on next week is a batch of cupcakes," Tina said.

"Yeah, but the week after that, we have to make my parent's wedding anniversary cake." Kim shuddered. She was not looking forward to it one bit.

"Do you want to make the purple flowers or the pink ones?"

"I'll take purple." Kim grabbed a purple pack of ready-to-use fondant. Once upon a time, they'd colored it themselves, but after one too many bad batches—Kim hated food coloring—they'd settled for just buying the colors they needed.

Grabbing a rolling pin, Kim got to work. It was relaxing, if fiddly, to cut out petals and weave them together into an edible rose; that had always been Kim's favorite part. She was drawn to intricate decoration, and the trickiest cakes were the most satisfying to see go to a happy client.

"Is Tyler in his room?" Tina set a pink rose down next to Kim's purple one.

"He's out with Riley," Kim said. "She's taken him to watch her soccer practice." Kim was glad Riley's ankle had healed quickly.

"I didn't know she played."

"Uh-huh. We've been to watch one of her games."

Tina dropped her rolling pin and stared at Kim. "You? Kimberly Jackson? Willingly watching a soccer match? Who are you?"

"I only went for Tyler. And I'm coming to Sophia's game next week."

"Only because you're sick of me asking you." Tina gave her a searching look.

"Why are you acting like it's such a big deal?" Kim shifted her weight beneath Tina's gaze.

"Uh, because it is? You hate sports."

Kim shrugged. "It wasn't so bad. Better than the men's games I've seen." Kim wouldn't mind going again; hopefully to a match where Riley didn't end up limping off the field.

"You and her are getting close, then?"

Kim cut out another fondant petal and set it to one side. "I guess. We're good friends. Why are you asking?"

"Just making conversation, Kim. I'm not used to you having friends other than me."

Pretending to be outraged, Kim prodded Tina's side with her rolling pin, but she laughed and deftly danced away.

Kim was finishing her second rose when Tyler and Riley returned, Tyler wearing a huge smile and Riley looking like she'd dived front first into a puddle of mud, her white jersey stained different shades of green and brown.

"Don't tell me you fell over again," Kim said, raising an eyebrow as Riley hovered two steps inside her apartment.

"Uninjured this time, though," Riley said, her eyes twinkling. "And it was a good tackle, wasn't it Tyler?"

"Yeah. But you should stick to scoring goals instead of trying to stop them." Tyler shot Riley a wide grin.

Riley's eyes narrowed into a glare. "Are you trash-talking me, young man?"

"Is it trash talk if it's true?"

Kim shook her head at their antics and caught Tina looking between Tyler and Riley with interest. Tina usually left the bakery before Riley arrived on the days she stopped by, and Kim realized Tina hadn't seen much of Riley and Tyler interacting.

Or much of Riley at all.

Which, considering how big a part of her life both Tina and Riley were, was crazy.

"Riley, do you want to play *FIFA*?" Tyler asked Riley, leaning over the back of the couch.

"I think I'm a little too dirty to sit on your mom's couch, buddy." Riley glanced down at herself. "Don't want her to kill me."

"Then will you watch me play?"

Riley's eyes flickered to Kim, who had known her long enough now to understand that she was asking for permission.

Kim nodded.

"Sure. Maybe you can give me a few pointers so you don't destroy me next time we play." Riley toed off her shoes and padded further into the apartment. "Wow." Riley's eyes fell to the roses on the kitchen counter. "Those look amazing. You guys are so talented. How do you even make those?"

"It looks harder than it is," Kim said. "The worst thing is trying to get the petals to stick together."

"Really satisfying when it all comes together, though." Tina set down a rose with a flourish. "Where do you play soccer, Riley? A team I've heard of?"

"I'd be impressed if you had." Riley's smile turned wry. "It's just a small local team called Seattle Pride."

"My daughter's big into soccer. Wants to be the next big thing. They actually have a big state championship final this weekend."

Kim could see the pride in Tina's eyes. For all of her complaints about ferrying her girls from practice to practice, Kim knew she wouldn't change any of it.

"No way!" Riley looked impressed. "They must be good, then. I hope they win."

"Thank you. It's a big occasion—so big I've even managed to persuade Kim to come."

"Can Riley come, too?" Tyler said.

"Sure." Tina glanced at Riley. "If you'd like. The more the merrier—the team could always use more people cheering from the stands."

"That sounds fun," Riley said, her smile warm. "Just let me know the details, and I'll be there."

Knowing Riley would be there, too made Kim look forward to the weekend even more. Not that Tina wasn't good company, but... she could get very into Sophia's games. Kim remembered a swim meet when Sophia had been eight years old, where Tina had yelled encouragement from beside Kim—whose ears had been ringing for a full day afterward.

Things with Riley wouldn't be quite as intense.

—◆◇◆—

Riley fell into step beside Kim as they walked with Tyler between the buildings of Seattle University. Sophia's game was being held on the college soccer field, and the walk down was bittersweet.

How far would she have gotten if she'd stayed at Seattle University longer than a single semester? Would she have led the soccer team to the state championships? Would she have been lucky enough to be scouted and go pro?

When they reached the stands, Tina waved them over. Beside her stood a tall Black man in a turtleneck, his smile warm as his eyes landed on Kim. A younger teenage girl stood next to him.

"Glad you guys could make it," Tina said. "Riley, this is my husband, Nathan, and my daughter, Brianna."

"Nice to meet you." Riley shook Nathan's outstretched hand.

"And you. Thanks for coming along to support our girl. Tina said you play soccer, too?"

"Only as a hobby, but yeah." She watched the two teams warming up on the field as Tina drew Kim into conversation and Tyler and Brianna giggled over a video on Brianna's phone. "What number is Sophia?"

"She's number eight," Nathan said. "On the team in red. Plays on the wing and wants to be the next Megan Rapinoe."

"Sounds like she has big dreams."

"Oh, the biggest. But we've always told her as long as she works at it, nothing's impossible."

Riley wished her own parents could have been so supportive.

As the teams finished their warm-ups and scattered across opposite sides of the field, they all settled into their seats. Riley perched on the end of the row beside Kim. Tyler and Brianna sat in the middle, with Tina and Nathan on their other side.

Kim leaned close as the game kicked off. "Is everything okay?" she said. "You've been quiet this morning."

"Sorry." She hadn't meant to be. "It's just odd being back here."

Recognition flashed across Kim's face. "This is where you went to college?"

"Uh-huh. For one and a half semesters." Keeping her gaze trained on the field, Riley watched Sophia fire off an excellent pass to one of her strikers—a defender deflected the resulting shot. "I used to play for the college team. On this field."

"Oh." Kim reached out and settled her hand on Riley's knee. "I'm sorry, I didn't realize. You should have said—it must be painful being back here."

Riley met her worried gaze and smiled. "It's all good. And it's not like I've never been back. Bea works in the biology department here, and we meet up for lunch on campus all the time. But…" Riley trailed off, growing distracted as Sophia directed another dangerous pass into the penalty area that her teammate missed by inches. "I haven't been to this soccer field since I last played on it, what, ten years ago now? Just brings back some memories."

"I know what you mean. Not about the soccer field, exactly, but the nostalgia of being back here—I'm also a Seattle U dropout. For a very different reason, but still. I get it."

Riley hadn't considered that before. It was yet another thing they had in common. Maybe their shared pasts had something to do with why they were so drawn to one another. They'd walked different paths, sure, but there were commonalties, too. Both had sacrificed their education to take on the role of parent, disappointing their families in the process. Both had thrived despite their less than perfect circumstances.

"I wonder if we were here at the same time." What had Kim been like in college? Certainly more outgoing than Riley. If their paths had ever crossed, Riley would have never had the guts to approach her. "When was your last year?"

"I finished in the summer of '14."

"Just missed each other, then," Riley said. "I started that fall. What were you studying?"

"I was doing a dual major in business and marketing."

"Oh, wow." But Riley supposed that made sense. Kim wouldn't have been able to build Cake My Day into the success it was without a solid background. "Doesn't make my art history degree sound very impressive, does it?"

"Doesn't need to be impressive if it's what you wanted. Do you ever think about going back to finish it?"

Riley shook her head. "Nah. I don't need it—I'm not planning on leaving the job I have now. Would you?"

"I feel the same way. I think everything happens for a reason. And I managed to achieve everything I wanted, even without graduating."

Around them, the crowd leaned forward in their seats, and Riley turned her attention to the soccer field, where one of Sophia's teammates was surging into the box. She turned smartly and laid the ball back to Sophia.

Nails dug into Riley's knee as Sophia geared up for the shot, and she looked down. Kim's hand was still there, warm through Riley's jeans. It felt nice.

Seeming to realize it at the same time, Kim's gaze snapped back to Riley's, a flush on her cheeks as she snatched her hand back. "Sorry."

"It's all good." But Riley's words were drowned out by a cheer, and she looked back at the field to see the ball deep in the net, and Sophia being swarmed by teammates.

"Please don't tell Tina I missed that," Kim whispered.

Riley grinned. "Don't worry. Your secret's safe with me."

Chapter 10

KIM FINISHED THE LAST TOUCH on the elaborately decorated cake and stepped back to admire her handiwork. She was more critical than usual, because unlike most of her custom cakes, she was going to be present at the party for its recipients.

March 29 marked her parents' fortieth wedding anniversary.

The prospect of spending the night around her family wasn't a tantalizing one, but at least Tyler would be there to take some of the heat off of her. Kim's love life—or lack thereof—was always a popular topic.

Satisfied with the cake, Kim carefully assembled the cardboard box it would be traveling in to her parents' house around it and put on the lid.

"Are you ready to go, Tyler?"

Kim chose to take the grunted response as a yes.

After washing her hands clean of frosting, Kim went to get ready herself, cursing when she glanced at the clock. Kim would never hear the end of it if they were late, so she ordered an Uber.

It was set to arrive in five minutes. Thankfully, she'd already done her hair and makeup and chosen a dress for the evening. It was floor length, a deep green that brought out her eyes, and made of a flowy material that didn't cling too tightly to her curves.

Tyler was waiting by the door, grimacing as he fiddled with his tie, when she rushed out of her bedroom.

"Do I have to wear this?" he asked.

"Yes, because it'll be me your grandmother harasses if you don't."

Tyler sighed.

Kim gave him a gentle pat on the back. She knew the value of a good bribe. "I'll make it worth your while."

"With what?"

"I don't know. What do you want?" Kim handed him his jacket and shrugged on her own before going to grab the cake box, making sure she supported the bottom with one hand.

"I'll think about it," he said, holding open the door for her.

Kim stepped through it, nearly crashing straight into Riley in the hall outside. "Shi-oot." Kim corrected herself at the last minute, though Tyler's grin suggested he'd heard her anyway. "Sorry. That's what I get for rushing."

"It's all good." Riley steadied Kim with a hand on her elbow. "You okay?"

"Yeah."

"Here." The lid on the box had fallen open, and Riley reached out to push it back into place.

Kim prayed the cake was still intact, but she'd worry about that later.

"Woah, that's a big cake. One of your custom orders?"

"Yes. For my parent's wedding anniversary."

"I was wondering why you two looked so smart on a Friday night. Especially you, little man. I love the tie."

Tyler beamed. "Thank you!"

"I'd love to stay and chat—believe me," Kim said, "but if we're late, my mom will kill me, so we should get going."

"No problem. Have fun!"

Kim grimaced.

"...or not?" Riley corrected at the look on Kim's face. "If you need a beer and a rant when you get back, feel free to knock on my door. You know I know how family can be."

"Thank you," Kim said, grateful for the offer. And if tonight went as badly as she thought it might, she would take Riley up on it.

Kim steered Tyler into the elevator, pleased to see their Uber already idling on the curb when they emerged onto the street.

After they slid into the back seat, Kim lifted the lid off the box and breathed a sigh of relief. The cake hadn't been jostled too badly when she and Riley had collided.

Kim just had to make it through the rest of the night in one piece.

———— ❖ ————

"Oh, there you are," Kim's mother said when she walked through the door. "I thought you'd gotten lost."

Kim refrained from rolling her eyes. She could count four people in her parent's living room, so it wasn't like she and Tyler were the last to arrive.

"It's nice to see you, too, Mother."

"I didn't say it wasn't nice to see you!" She kissed both of Kim's cheeks, the scent of her floral perfume overwhelming.

"You can put the cake in the kitchen, Kimberly. Tyler! Come here, give me a big hug."

As Tyler was squished, Kim walked the familiar path to the kitchen and set the cake on the side beside a platter of fancy-looking hors d'oeuvres. No one could say her mother didn't go all out when it was time to throw a party.

"Hi, sweetheart."

Kim smiled when her father stepped through the door and pulled her into a warm hug. "Hi, Dad."

"How have you been?"

"Good. How about you? Retirement still keeping you busy?"

"Oh, very. Come, let me show you my latest project."

Kim followed him to his makeshift workshop. After spending his whole working life as a neurosurgeon, she had known he wouldn't survive a quiet retirement. It hadn't taken him long to settle on a hobby—woodworking, where he spent his time making increasingly elaborate pieces.

"Here." He showed her toward his workbench, where a half-finished wooden clock sat in the center.

"It's beautiful."

He beamed. "When I've finished this, I thought perhaps I could make Tyler a skateboard for his birthday."

"I think he'd like that."

"My only worry is the decoration."

Kim thought of the way Tyler had been chattering about Riley's tattoos for the past few weeks. "I might know someone who can help."

Hopeful eyes peered at Kim. "You do?"

"Yeah, our new neighbor is an artist, I'm sure she wouldn't mind giving a hand. Let me know what you need." Kim spent a few more moments examining the new creations lining the shelves since her last visit before deciding it was time to rescue Tyler.

Not that she should have worried—he was sitting and playing with his younger cousins when Kim returned to the living room, as happy as could be.

"Kim!"

Kim was swept into a hug by her older sister.

"It's been an age. How are you? How's that little shop of yours?"

Kim tried not to bristle at the condescending note in Ellie's voice. "It's doing well."

Kim knew she was the family disappointment. Her father, mother, older brother Alan, and sister Ellie all had advanced degrees and high-powered professions. Though she'd pursued a degree in business and marketing, it had been difficult: Kim hadn't thrived in an academic environment like the rest of them, and the only thing that had kept her going had been her desire to open her own bakery one day. She had never been interested in being rich if it meant sacrificing time with the people she loved or settling for a career she hated.

Add to that dropping out in her final year of college and having Tyler at twenty-one before she and John had gotten married, plus their subsequent divorce…well. Kim was the black sheep, and certain family members weren't afraid to let her know it. Ellie was one of them, and Kim tended to avoid her as much as physically possible.

"You made the cake for tonight, didn't you? I can't wait to taste it."

Instead of asking if that was so Ellie could criticize it, Kim plastered on a smile. "Hope you enjoy it. Where's Anthony?"

Ellie was never far from her politician husband at events like this, liking to parade him around like he was a prized pony.

Ellie pouted. "He had to work."

"Such a shame." It wasn't, though. Anthony was worse than Ellie.

"What about you? Did you bring someone tonight?"

Kim should have timed how long it took for someone to ask. "Nope."

"Oh, good," Kim's mother drawled, appearing over Ellie's shoulder as if summoned by the talk of Kim's relationship status, "because there's someone I want you to meet."

Panic bloomed in Kim's chest. "What?"

"My friend Karen's son, Henry. He's about your age, and he's lovely. He's a veterinarian. I invited him tonight."

Kim knew she hadn't had the best luck at dating, but she'd rather be single forever than date someone her mother had picked out. "Mom, why would you do that?"

"Because, Kimberly, it's about time you moved on. It's not good to be single at thirty."

"Says who?"

"Me."

Kim craned her neck, searching for a means of escape—or a friendly face. God, she should have stayed home. Maybe she could've invited Riley over for a drink and a *Grey's Anatomy* rewatch. But, no, instead she was being pushed into a blind date in front of her overly critical family.

"You must be lonely, Kimberly." Her mom's voice turned softer now. "Especially when Tyler is with John. And look at him! He's moved on. He's happy now."

"And I'm happy for him." Kim wasn't lying. She got along well with Rebecca, and she had no bad blood with John. They just hadn't worked, and Kim didn't know why that had to be such a big deal.

"Hmm." It was clear her mother thought it was a big deal indeed. "Well, I can't uninvite Henry now. In fact, there he is. I'll go and get him."

Kim groaned as her mother went toward the tall white man with bright red hair hovering on the periphery of her parents' living room.

"You know," Ellie said from beside her, looking like she was enjoying Kim's visible discomfort, "if it doesn't work out with Henry, I have some eligible bachelor friends. We could double date!"

Kim would honestly rather drop dead. Before she could open her mouth to tell Ellie so, her mother was back, a manicured hand wrapping around Kim's wrist as though she expected her daughter to bolt.

Which, to be fair, was Kim's first instinct.

"Kimberly, meet Henry. Henry, my daughter Kimberly. I think the two of you will get along wonderfully." With that, she disappeared, dragging Ellie along with her.

Kim cleared her throat as Henry's gaze slid over her figure, lingering long enough on her breasts to immediately set her on edge.

"Sorry about my mother," Kim said. "I had no idea she was planning on doing this."

"That's all right. I was hesitant—until she showed me a picture of you. Then I knew I had to come. You're even hotter in person."

Kim wished a sinkhole would open and swallow her whole. They had met barely two minutes ago—how did this guy think it was okay to say this kind of thing to a stranger?

"She said you were a baker? That's a cool hobby."

"It's not a hobby," Kim said through gritted teeth. "It's my job. I own my own bakery."

"Hey, I didn't mean any offence. Like I said, I think it's cool."

Cool didn't sum up the years of hard work it had taken to open Cake My Day. "Look, Henry, I'm sure you're great—"

"I am," he said, interrupting her with a smarmy smile, and he stepped forward to settle a heavy hand on her waist. "I can show you a good time—"

"—but I'm not interested," Kim said, continuing as though he hadn't spoken and shrugging off his touch. "I'm sorry my mother dragged you out here."

"What do you mean you're not interested?" Henry looked at Kim like she was speaking a foreign language.

"I mean you're wasting your time." Kim stalked away before he could continue to argue—she'd never hear the end of it if she caused a scene.

She needed a drink.

Kim had barely grabbed herself a beer before her mother descended on her with a furious expression.

"I hope you're happy. Henry has left."

"Good. You seriously think he and I are a good fit?"

"He has a respectable career, and he's a perfect gentleman—"

"A perfect gentleman?" Kim scoffed. "He spent most of our short conversation staring at my tits."

"Don't be so vulgar. Honestly, Kimberly, I'm just trying to look out for you—"

"Well don't," Kim said, struggling to keep her voice down, her fingers shaking around her beer bottle as she took a step toward her mother. "I'm a grown woman. I can take care of myself. Don't ever pull anything like this again."

"Why would I, when you're so ungrateful?"

"Ungrateful? Are you kidding me?"

Kim's father stepped into the kitchen, his eyes widening as he looked between the two women.

Kim rounded on him. "Did you know she was going do this?"

"Not until a few minutes ago. Or else I would have warned you. I told her it was a terrible idea."

"Well, neither of you have to worry." Kim's mother clenched her jaw. "I won't bother again."

She stormed from the kitchen, slamming the door behind her, and Kim ran a hand across her face.

It was going to be a long night.

Chapter 11

A KNOCK WOKE RILEY FROM where she'd been dozing on the couch, and she blinked in sleepy surprise before she remembered her conversation with Kim earlier that night. She hadn't expected Kim to show up, but when she opened her door, Kim stood on the other side, looking exhausted.

"Were you being serious before?"

"When I offered beer and the chance to rant? Yeah."

Kim looked like she needed it, her shoulders tense and her mouth set in a thin line. She'd had her hair up when Riley had seen her earlier, but now it was loose and messy, like she'd run her fingers through it a dozen times.

"Do you mind coming over to my place? I know Tyler will be fine, but I don't like leaving him for too long."

"No problem. Let me grab some bottles."

"You can bring Cari too, if you want."

Riley glanced toward Cari's bed, where she was splayed out and snoring. "Nah, she'll be grumpy. She'll barely notice I'm gone."

Riley grabbed the six-pack she'd bought at the weekend and slipped her keys into the pocket of her sweats before following Kim next door.

Riley liked Kim's apartment. The layout was the same as hers, though Kim's apartment looked much more lived-in. The walls were painted blue, and they had photographs of Kim, Tyler, and John plastered all over them. As Kim led her over to her brown leather couch, Riley spotted baking supplies scattered all over the kitchen counter, and an array of Tyler's drawings hung on the refrigerator.

"Your place is more homely than mine."

"But a lot messier."

"Isn't that a given when you have a kid?"

"It is when you have my kid. And he's only here half the time—who knows what it would look like if I had full custody."

"You wouldn't know any different."

"True." Kim twisted the top off her beer and brought her legs to her chest, something dark in her eyes as she took a long sip.

"So"—Riley relaxed against the couch's arm as she turned more toward Kim—"how bad was your night on a scale from one to ten?"

"Eleven. My mother tried to set me up with some asshole named Henry."

"Oh, wow. Worse than Darren?"

Kim pursed her lips, considering. "I think he might've been, you know. At least Darren was so self-absorbed, he didn't ask me enough about my job to say that baking was a 'cool hobby.' And Darren didn't spend the whole time we were talking staring at my chest. This guy was so obvious about it as well. Like, did he think I wouldn't notice?"

"I don't think guys like that care if you do." Riley was disgusted on Kim's behalf—and could hardly believe Kim's own mother had arranged the whole thing. "They probably think it's a compliment."

"Well, it wasn't. It was creepy. And after he left, my mom got all huffy because 'Henry's a nice guy. Why can't you give him a chance?' She called me ungrateful for not being overjoyed she'd sprung this on me. And implied that it's unseemly to be unmarried over the age of thirty."

No doubt conscious of waking Tyler if she raised her voice, Kim's words were hushed, and her cheeks were flushed scarlet. "Meanwhile, at dinner, when I was being quizzed *again* about my lack of love life, my cousin Kevin—who is older than me, by the way—sat opposite me, smug as fuck."

Riley had never heard Kim swear before—not properly. Her family must have really gotten under her skin.

"But no one cares if Kevin's single and has never brought a date to a family event," Kim continued. "Because Kevin's got a dick and he's going into law, so he's too *busy*, and oh, poor hardworking Kevin. Like I don't have my hands full as a single mother running my own business? A business I built myself. But no one gives a fuck because it's not doing something they think is worthwhile."

It was a miracle her beer hadn't sloshed over the lip of the bottle with how wildly Kim was gesticulating.

She took a deep breath and ran her fingers through her hair. "Sorry. That was a lot."

"No need to apologize."

Riley was content to let her rant. It was nice to get to know a new side of Kim. And Riley could definitely commiserate on the shitty family front, though she wished Kim wasn't suffering.

"But, for what it's worth, I think what you've managed to do is amazing," Riley said, her voice soft.

"Thank you." Kim patted Riley's knee and left her hand there, her fingers warm through the thin material of Riley's sweatpants. "It's just frustrating that none of them think so."

The words came out so bitter, it made Riley's heart ache. She hated that Kim's family made her feel that way.

"I'll never measure up because I'm not smart enough. Because I chose something different. Because I'm good at something they don't approve of. Because I got married and had a kid too young and—according to them—let my marriage fall apart." Kim drew a shaky breath. "They'll never think I'm good enough."

"Hey." Riley covered the back of Kim's hand with her own and squeezed. "You *are* good enough." She waited until Kim turned to look at her. "I know we haven't known each other long, but you are. You're kind and funny and an amazing mom. And you're really fucking good at baking. Like, it would be a crime if you had ended up doing something else. I mean it."

She'd wanted to make Kim laugh, and it worked, a chuckle escaping as some of the darkness on her face lifted.

"I wish I was as strong as you were. To cut them out of my life. But...I get along with my dad. And I don't want to take Tyler away from them."

"That doesn't make you weak. In fact, I'd say that makes you strong—because you keep standing up to them."

To Riley's horror, tears shimmered in Kim's eyes.

"Oh, please don't cry. I'm sorry."

"No, don't be. I'm the one who should be sorry." Kim met Riley's gaze. "Look at me—a sobbing mess because someone said something nice to me."

"Well, it's all true. You're pretty awesome. And if your family can't see that...well, fuck 'em."

Kim's eyes were still on Riley's, and Riley felt trapped beneath the weight of her gaze. The hand on her knee felt like it was burning through the fabric of her pants, and Riley swallowed. Had the temperature increased?

"Thank you," Kim whispered. She shifted, her head falling onto Riley's shoulder and an arm wrapping loosely around her waist.

Riley froze, drowning in the scent of shampoo, Kim's lips dangerously close to Riley's bare collarbone. Kim's weight should have been comforting—they were supposed to be friends—but Riley felt like she was suffocating.

Because she'd meant everything she had said. Kim was kind and funny and amazing, and Riley liked being around her. And with Kim leaning close, her breath warm on Riley's skin—Riley realized she might like Kim a little too much.

Fuck.

Kim hiccupped, and Riley felt hot tears on her skin. She pulled herself together enough to wrap an arm around Kim's back and hold her close, to offer some of the comfort Kim was clearly craving. She tried to ignore the pounding of her heart, praying Kim couldn't hear it—or feel it, with her cheek pressed against Riley's chest.

After a few minutes, Kim's crying subsided, but she didn't move away. In fact, Kim was relaxing further into Riley's embrace, and Riley realized with horror that Kim was falling asleep, her weight trapping Riley against the back of the couch.

Riley didn't know whether she should wiggle free, wake Kim, or let her sleep.

In the end, it didn't feel right to stay. Not when all Riley could think about was the fact she'd managed to fall for someone she'd never be able to have.

Inch by inch, Riley moved out from beneath Kim. She needn't have worried—Kim barely stirred, and Riley wondered how much she'd had to drink. By the time Riley was standing in the living room, Kim was stretched out on the couch, chest still rising and falling steadily.

A blanket hung over the back of the couch, and Riley wrapped it around Kim. Figuring Kim might need a drink when she woke, Riley fetched a glass of water from the kitchen and left it on the coffee table before she crept to the door and returned to her own apartment.

Once inside, she groaned, closing her eyes and tilting her head back against her front door. She could still smell Kim's perfume, still feel Kim's breath on her skin, the warm weight of her arm around Riley's waist.

She couldn't believe she'd let this happen.

Couldn't believe she'd managed to blur the lines of friendship and fall for her neighbor.

This was a huge, huge problem.

One she had no idea how to solve.

———— ⊷⊷⊶ ————

Kim woke disoriented and nearly rolled out of bed and onto the floor.

Wait.

Kim rubbed a hand over her eyes and glanced around the room, realizing she wasn't in bed. She was lying on her couch, the soft woolen blanket she and Tyler snuggled under when they watched movies wrapped around her body.

The clock on the wall read two fifteen, and Kim groaned. She didn't remember falling asleep, let alone why she hadn't made it into bed.

Her head swam when she sat, and Kim reached gratefully for the glass of water sitting on the coffee table in front of her.

Memories came rushing back then, cutting through her weariness—dinner at her parents', Henry, an embarrassing number of beers, and knocking on Riley's door once Tyler had gone to bed.

Kim went cold all over when she remembered sobbing in Riley's arms, her worn T-shirt soft against Kim's cheek. And then… Oh, God, had she fallen asleep on her? Had Riley been the one to tuck her in and leave her the water?

"I'm such an idiot," Kim said to herself as she climbed to her feet. Her cheeks felt hot, embarrassment sinking deep into her bones as she padded to her bedroom, the wooden floor cool against her bare feet.

What had she been *thinking*, dumping everything on Riley like that? They were friends, but they hadn't known each other long. Riley didn't need to know all of the skeletons in Kim's closet, especially considering the nonexistent relationship Riley had with her own parents. Kim hoped she hadn't brought up any painful memories.

She scrubbed a hand across her face. Kim was a mess, and she must have made Riley feel so uncomfortable. Why did she have to ruin everything? Someone had said something nice about her, and she was so touch starved that Kim's reaction was to have a breakdown and throw herself into their arms.

Kim didn't remember the last time she'd fallen asleep beside someone else—let alone *on* someone else; it would have been nice if it weren't so mortifying. Kim wouldn't blame Riley if she didn't want to be alone with Kim again, lest she start ugly-crying on her shirt.

And that sucked because Kim liked having Riley around. She liked having another friend, and, oh God, if Kim had ruined things, Tyler was going to kill her. He worshipped the ground both Riley—and Cari—walked on.

With a sigh, Kim forced herself to her bathroom. Maybe in the morning, after a decent night's sleep, things wouldn't seem so bad. Maybe she'd be able to laugh it off and not want to die of mortification the next time she saw Riley.

Kim supposed there was no point worrying about that now. Hopefully, her hangover wouldn't be too bad. That was the last thing she'd need for a long shift in the bakery.

Kim stared at her reflection in the mirror. Even after a nap, her cheeks were flushed, her eyes red and puffy. Kim hated that she let her mother get to her so much. But she'd always been able to get under Kim's skin, ever since she was a kid.

At least it had given her a blueprint of things not to do with Tyler.

Chapter 12

Bea poked Riley in the cheek with a french fry. "Shouldn't you be happier? Your team won four-nil."

"And you scored two goals," Ash said.

Riley's return to action following her ankle injury would have been a much better match for Tyler and Kim to watch than the disaster they'd witnessed. It was a shame he was at John's.

"What's wrong?" Ash continued, looking at Riley with concern.

Riley was glad the rest of her teammates were dotted around the bar with their friends and families. She didn't want them hassling her, too.

"I'm fine."

"Liar," Bea said.

At the same time, Ash scoffed, "You are so not fine."

Riley sighed.

Much as she denied it, she knew they were right. She hadn't been herself since Friday night, unable to stop thinking about Kim.

Kim, whom Riley hadn't seen since she'd left her fast asleep on her couch.

Kim, who was there whenever Riley closed her eyes, remembering the warmth of her arm around Riley's waist and the smell of her perfume.

Kim, her straight neighbor and *friend,* who Riley shouldn't be thinking of as anything more than that.

"It's nothing."

Now it was Bea's turn to scoff. "Bullshit."

"Fine. It's Kim, okay?"

"What about Kim?" Bea looked increasingly annoyed at having to pry Riley's answers out of her.

Giving herself a moment before she answered, Riley glanced around the brightly lit bar they sat in. It was busy, with both teams scattered around the place for their customary after-game beer and lunch, the sound of raucous laughter echoing off the beige walls.

Bea called her attention back to their table. "Riley, what happened?"

"Nothing happened. I just…" she sighed. "I think I like her. As more than a friend."

"Oh, shit." Bea leaned back in her chair. "I know I've joked about it before, but I didn't realize you actually liked her."

"Neither did I until the other night."

"Are you going to tell her?"

Riley was shaking her head before Bea finished speaking. "Why would I? It wouldn't change anything."

"So you're going to suffer in silence and hope it goes away?"

"Yep."

Ash wrapped an arm around Riley's shoulders and pulled her into a hug. "I'm sorry, Riley."

Riley leaned her head on Ash's shoulder. "Thank you. I haven't seen her since, which doesn't help. I'm worried I won't know how to act around her."

"Have you been avoiding her?"

"Our paths haven't crossed. Unless she's avoiding me." Riley didn't know why, though. Kim had nothing to be worried about.

"I'm sure she's not," Bea said. "She's probably busy."

"And so are you." Ash nudged Riley with her shoulder. "Scoring goals and winning player of the match."

Again, a part of Riley wished Kim and Tyler could have been there to see, and she shoved the thought down deep. There would be other games—hopefully, ones where they would see Riley play more than twenty minutes.

"Hey." Tess approached them and looped an arm around Riley's shoulders. "Can I steal this one from y'all? We're being challenged to a game of pool by the other team."

"And you want Riley?" Bea had a teasing glint in her eye. "Why?"

Riley gave her the finger, and Bea laughed.

"Well, she's better than most of us, so she'll have to do."

"Wow." Riley turned her glare on Tess. "Maybe I'll sit this one out."

"Please. You're way too competitive for that." Tess was already tugging Riley, trying to pull her to her feet. "Come on. I'll buy you a drink if we win."

Riley dug in her heels. "And if we lose."

"Okay, fine. Happy?"

"Yeah." Riley linked her arm through Tess's. "See you later," she said to Bea and Ash before letting Tess drag her away.

Tess had one thing right—Riley was competitive, and she wouldn't go down without a fight.

———◈———

Kim took a deep breath, steeling herself as she knocked on Riley's door, a box of apology brownies under her arm.

Cari barked from within Riley's apartment, so Kim hoped she was home.

A few moments later, Riley opened the door, looking surprised to see Kim standing there. Sweatpants hung low on Riley's hips as she stretched out a leg to keep Cari from escaping, and with her arms left bare by her tank top, Kim could see more of Riley's tattoos than ever before. Ink swirled over her shoulders, her hips and her waist, even the top of her sternum. Riley's hair was damp from a shower, and Kim watched a droplet of water slide down her neck and over the snake tattoo at her collarbone.

Realizing she was staring, Kim cleared her throat and hastily looked away.

"Hey. I, um, I brought you these." She held out the box of brownies. "To say sorry."

"You're sorry? For what?" Riley frowned.

Kim couldn't stop a brittle laugh. "I was a drunken mess the other night. I shouldn't have dumped everything on you. And I'm mortified I fell asleep on you."

"It's okay." Riley shrugged. "Clearly I'm terrible company." She gave Kim a teasing smile.

Kim was still quick to shake her head. "You are not. I'd just had six beers too many."

"Family can do that to you."

"They sure can." Kim sighed before thrusting the box toward Riley again. "Please take these. I'm sorry I couldn't bring them sooner—the bakery has been busy. We had four birthday cakes go out today."

"Four? You must be exhausted."

"You have no idea." Kim leaned her shoulder against Riley's doorframe.

"This wasn't necessary, but I will never say no to your treats." Riley opened the box, face lighting up when she recognized the toppings inside. "Are these salted caramel? And Nutella?"

"I know they're your favorites."

"Thank you. Do you want to come in? I won't be offended if you're too tired, though. Wouldn't want you falling asleep on me again." Riley's eyes shone with mirth.

Kim groaned. "You're never going to let me forget about that, are you?"

"Nope."

"Then maybe I'll go back to my place."

"What about if I promise not to mention it again? For tonight, at least."

"I suppose that's acceptable."

Riley moved aside, and Kim stepped over the threshold, bending to greet Cari. She was relieved Riley had accepted her apology, and glad she hadn't ruined things between them. "But don't tell Tyler. He'll never forgive me for coming over and hanging out with you and Cari without him."

"Your secret is safe with me," Riley said as she crossed to the kitchen to put the brownies in the refrigerator. "You can send him over when he gets back from his dad's next weekend, if you want. I feel like I haven't seen him in a while."

"I'll tell him he can. I appreciate everything you've done for him, by the way. I know hanging out with a nine-year-old isn't always fun."

"Are you kidding? He's great. And the best part of hanging with other people's kids is you get to send them back at the end of the day."

Knowing she had enjoyed doing the same with Tina's kids when they were younger, Kim laughed. "Well, thank you anyway."

"Honestly, Kim, it's not a problem. Do you want a drink?"

"Could I have a glass of water, please?" A beer would definitely have her falling asleep.

"Sure." Riley filled two glasses and led Kim to the couch.

As Kim was becoming accustomed to, Cari curled up between them, and Kim threaded her fingers through her short fur.

"Want to watch another episode of *Grey's Anatomy*?" Riley reached for her TV remote.

"Sure." Kim settled back against the couch cushions as Riley pressed play on Kim's favorite show. "Did you do anything nice today? Or were you working?"

"I worked the morning shift. And I had a soccer game this afternoon."

"And I thought I was tired." Kim couldn't imagine spending ninety minutes running around a field after a work shift.

Then again, Kim didn't run.

For anything.

"It wasn't so bad." Riley smiled. "We won, so that helped."

"And I'm assuming you didn't injure yourself this time."

"I did not."

"Maybe Tyler and I are bad luck."

Riley was quick to shake her head. "I don't think so. But if I get wiped out again the next time you go, maybe you have a point."

"Next time, huh?"

Riley's cheeks turned pink as she ducked shyly. "Yeah. If you want to."

"Like it's even a question," Kim said. "Tyler must have asked me a hundred times since if we can go again. He must have pestered you, too."

"Maybe a little. But I don't mind. It's cute. And it's nice having someone think I'm good at soccer."

Sometimes, she still couldn't believe how well the two of them got along. Riley had endless patience with him and genuinely enjoyed the time they spent together. And Kim knew Tyler treasured it, too—they were lucky Riley had moved in next door.

Kim had no idea how Riley had managed to fit into their lives so effortlessly, but, watching her mouth drop open in outrage as she watched the show's scene play out on her TV, Kim couldn't imagine a life without her in it.

Chapter 13

The next Sunday, Riley offered to take Tyler to the skate park while Kim finished baking a cake for a client. Riley hadn't spent much time with him lately, and she'd missed him.

She soon regretted her decision, though, grimacing every time Tyler rolled down a ramp, the wheels of his skateboard screeching on the concrete.

She sat watching him skate from a nearby bench with Cari settled at her feet.

Riley didn't know how Kim did this—Tyler wasn't even her kid and she was stressed about him hurting himself. When he tumbled off his board, Riley leapt up—only for Tyler to scramble back to his feet, unperturbed.

"Are you okay?" Riley said when Tyler skated back over to her.

"I'm fine." He came to a stop, brushing dust off his knee pads. "I do that all the time."

Riley refrained from telling him how that didn't make her feel any better. "How about you try and keep yourself on your board for the rest of the morning? I don't want to return you to your mom broken."

"That doesn't sound fun."

"Not being broken?"

He stuck his tongue out at her. "Staying on my board."

"Okay, let's make a deal—you don't fall off again, and I'll take you out for dinner one night this week. Anywhere you want."

His eyes lit up. "Really?"

"As long as your mom is okay with it, yeah."

"Okay." Tyler held out his hand. "Deal," he said when Riley shook it. He skated off more slowly than usual.

Her plan worked perfectly—even with the occasional trick, Tyler didn't take another tumble, and he crowed with victory when he joined her on the bench, having decided to call it a day.

"Can we get pizza?"

"If that's what you want."

"Pizza's my favorite."

"Pizza it is. You ready to head back?"

"Okay. Can I have Cari again?"

"Sure." Riley handed over the leash, and Tyler beamed.

They took a circuitous route back to their building to tire her out, and Cari was as good as gold, trotting along at Tyler's side—not pulling his arm out of his socket like she did to Riley sometimes. Riley was concerned she'd been replaced as Cari's favorite person.

"Do you think I could take Cari to my school dance next week?" Tyler said as they turned back toward their apartment building.

The mental image of Cari in a gym full of preteens made Riley chuckle. "I don't think she'd make a good date, buddy."

"I think she'd make the best date."

"Is there not anyone you want to ask?"

Tyler made a face. "No."

"You could go with friends," Riley said. "That's what I did when I was at school. In fact, I never took a date to a dance." Though she had only attended two. Dances were her idea of hell—and she definitely wouldn't have been brave enough to take a date to one.

"You didn't?" Tyler peered at her. "Didn't you have a boyfriend?"

"Uh, no." Riley tucked her hands into the back pockets of her jeans. "I've never had a boyfriend—and I never will. I'm gay."

"Oh. Cool. So, why didn't you take a girlfriend?"

Riley didn't understand why people thought it was hard to explain sexuality to kids—Tyler had barely blinked. "I didn't have my first girlfriend until I was twenty."

"Do you think it'd be okay if I didn't have my first girlfriend until I was twenty?"

"Yeah." Riley wasn't sure she was equipped to be giving out life lessons to her neighbor's kid, but he was asking. "You don't ever have to have one if you don't want to."

"But I can't take Cari?"

"Sorry, buddy."

Tyler sighed, but it was good-natured.

When they arrived back on their floor, Riley let him say goodbye to Cari, leaving her in her apartment. Then she waited in the hall with Tyler until Kim answered his knock.

"Hey." Kim looked less flustered than she had earlier that morning, out of her apron and in a cozy sweater. "Did you have fun?"

"Yeah! And now Riley owes me pizza." Tyler kicked off his shoes and wandered inside without any further explanation. As he flopped onto the couch, Kim turned to Riley with a raised eyebrow.

"We made a bet. I lost."

"What was the bet?"

"If he didn't fall off his board, I'm buy him dinner of his choice—provided you were fine with it."

"I don't see why not. Am I invited?"

Riley would love nothing more than another evening with Kim. Would it make it easier for Riley to stop her heart skipping a beat whenever their eyes met? Would she be able to stop thinking about how nice it would be to go on a proper date with Kim?

No, but Riley had always been a masochist. "Of course. Just let me know when's good."

"Okay."

Over Kim's shoulder, Riley caught a glimpse of the cake she'd spent most of the morning making. It was several tiers high with smooth white icing on the outside and swirls of rainbow frosting piped on top. "That cake looks incredible."

"I'm not sure it was worth the effort, but thank you. At least the next few weeks are quiet."

"So, if I wanted to order a cake from you, would now be a good time? My boss's fortieth is coming up. It's fine if you can't, though. I can get one from the store."

Kim looked outraged. "No! I can make one. What kind of cake? What flavor? What do you want it to look like? What's your budget?"

"Um…" Riley had not thought this through. "I must confess my knowledge of cake types is chocolate or vanilla. And I have no idea what these things cost."

Laughing, Kim beckoned Riley inside her apartment. "Come in. Let me show you a few ideas."

The kitchen was warm with heat from the oven, and her mouth watered at the smell of freshly baked cakes and sweet icing. Riley whistled when Kim produced a thick binder from one of the cupboards. It was split into sections separated by purple tabs—Riley could read *styles* and *decoration* on the two nearest to the front.

Behind them in the living room, Riley recognized the sound of *FIFA* as Tyler made himself comfortable.

"For a standard one-tier cake, we charge thirty dollars," Kim said. "Two tiers costs more—but how much more depends on a few different factors."

"One tier will be more than enough."

"Okay. What type of cake?"

"What's the easiest for you to make?" She didn't know where else to start.

"A sponge cake can be done in around an hour. And there's still a lot of scope for what you can put in or on it. And you can flavor it however you like—what kind of things does he like?"

"I know his two favorite things are coffee and whiskey."

"A coffee cake would be simple enough. And I've never tried to make whiskey frosting, but I could give it a go. I'm always looking for new things to try."

"Okay, I'm happy to be your experiment. As for decoration...I think *Happy 40th Birthday* will be enough."

"That's all?"

"Yeah. I know what Stephen's like—he won't want too much fuss."

"How long have you worked together?" Kim stretched on her toes to put the binder back on the shelf.

"Around seven years." Riley leaned back against the kitchen counter, curling her hands around the gray marble. "Started out as his apprentice. I owe him a lot; I don't know where I'd be if he hadn't taken a chance on me."

"And how does one go from being a waitress-slash-bartender-slash-cleaner to a tattoo artist's apprentice?"

Riley was impressed Kim had remembered all of Riley's odd jobs. "We actually met at one of the bars where I worked. It was a gay bar, and Stephen would come in a couple times a week and sit at the bar, too timid to talk to anyone."

Riley smiled at the memory. Coming out later in life had been hard for him, but knowing him now, that was hard to believe. "I was doodling on a napkin one night—just a silly little design—and he asked me about it."

"So you'd always wanted to be a tattoo artist?"

"I always liked to draw," Riley said. "For a while, I wanted to work on comic books or be an illustrator. And I'd always wanted tattoos—loved the look of them, but couldn't afford them at the time—but I'd never considered it as a career until I met Stephen. He told me I'd be good at it. Asked me if I wanted the chance to learn. At the time, he felt sorry for me, I think, but he swears he saw something in me. He taught me everything I know. And to work somewhere like I do—somewhere that celebrates the LGBTQIA+ community, somewhere that's a safe space—that's all I've ever wanted."

Riley shifted her weight from one foot to the other and cleared her throat. She wasn't used to talking about herself so much. Especially about her history. People always tended to feel sorry for her, and Riley loathed that.

"Well, he sounds like a great guy." Kim seemed to sense Riley's discomfort and changed the subject. "I'll be sure to make him the best cake I can. When is his birthday?"

"Two weeks from Tuesday—but could I pick it up the day before? I think he's taking the actual day off."

"No problem." Kim made a note on the calendar hanging beside the refrigerator. "I'll keep you updated."

"Thank you. I'll leave you two to the rest of your day."

"Okay. Thanks again for taking Tyler."

"Anytime," Riley said, meaning it, as she made her way to the door. "Bye, Tyler!"

He waved at her over the back of the couch, too into his game to turn around, and Riley chuckled as she stepped into the hall.

Kim wiped the front counter in the bakery, smiling as she listened to Riley help Tyler with his homework. It was math again, and better Riley than Kim, she thought. She dreaded him going to high school: Tyler was smart, and it wouldn't be long until she couldn't help him anymore.

The bell above the door jingled, and Kim glanced up, ready to greet her customer with a smile. It slid from her face when she recognized the woman striding through the door, shaking off her umbrella as she stepped inside.

"Mom!" Kim said with enough alarm in her voice to have Riley raising her head. "What are you doing here?"

"I can't come and say hello to my daughter?" She bustled behind the counter like she owned the place to press a kiss to Kim's cheek.

"Well, yes, but…you don't usually drop by unannounced." *Or ever.* In the two years that her bakery had been open, Kim could count on one hand the number of times her mother had set foot inside it—one of her more subtle ways of letting Kim know she disapproved of her chosen career venture.

"I was in the neighborhood. I had my hair done." She fluffed it with a manicured hand.

"Looks nice," Kim said, though she could see no discernable difference from her mother's usual style.

"I wanted to see how you were getting along." Her mother cast her gaze around the place. "It's quiet, isn't it?"

Kim gritted her teeth.

"In fact, my grandson seems to be one of your only customers."

"Because it's not peak hours." Kim didn't know why she bothered to explain. "It's half an hour until closing—we're busiest in the mornings and at lunchtime."

But Kim's mother wasn't listening—her gaze had zeroed in on Riley, and Kim could read the judgment on her face.

"Who is that with Tyler?"

"Riley. She moved in next door a few months ago."

Her mother emerged from behind the counter, stalking toward Riley and Tyler with her nose upturned.

"Hi, Tyler." She bent to kiss his cheek, and Kim laughed when he scrunched his nose in distaste.

"What are you doing, munchkin? Math homework? Do you need your grandmother's help?"

"Thanks, but I think Riley's got it covered," he said without missing a beat. "She's smart. Well"—his grin turned cheeky—"smarter than me, but I am only nine."

"Ouch!" Riley pressed a hand to her heart. "You cut me deep, kid."

Kim's mother turned to Riley, and some of the color drained from Riley's face.

"Perhaps Riley has other things she'd rather be doing."

"Nah. I'm good with staying right here."

Kim had to give Riley credit for not quailing beneath her mother's withering glare. Most would cave the second her mother had them in her sights.

"You can't go," Tyler said. "You owe me a pizza."

"Well, that's true. A bet is a bet."

Kim's mother looked horrified. "A...bet?"

"Yeah! I didn't fall off my board at the skate park on Sunday, so Riley has to buy me a pizza. We're going out after mom closes."

"All three of you?" Her mother looked between the three of them.

"Yes." Kim met her mother's gaze head-on.

"Kimberly, can I have a word with you? In private?"

Kim sighed, knowing it wasn't a conversation she wanted to have, but leading her mother to the kitchen anyway. Kim closed the door behind them, not wanting Tyler—or Riley—to hear whatever was coming next.

"Kimberly, what on earth are you thinking, letting your son spend time around...someone like *that*?"

Kim bristled. "Someone like what? Someone who cares about him? Someone who takes time out of her day to hang out with him? Who helps him with his homework?"

"All those tattoos! Is she in a gang?"

"Jesus, Mom! No."

"Still. She looks like a bad influence."

"Because she has tattoos?"

Her mother ignored her. "And is she...you know."

Kim chose to be purposefully obtuse. "What? Kind? Funny? Great with Tyler?"

"A *lesbian*." She whispered it—as if it were a bad word.

Kim rolled her eyes. "Why does that matter?"

Her mother's mouth opened, then closed as she searched for a response that didn't make her look like an absolute asshole.

"Exactly. It doesn't. Look, I'm done talking about this, okay? I have things to do before we close."

Hoping that would be the end of it—but knowing it wouldn't—Kim shooed her mother out of the kitchen, listening in as she said goodbye to Tyler and then flounced from the bakery without a single look back. Kim breathed a sigh of relief.

———— ❦ ————

"I don't think my grandmother likes you," Tyler said a few moments after the door shut behind Kim's mother.

"I think that might be an understatement, buddy."

The woman was even more intimidating than Kim had described. The temperature of the room felt like it had dropped ten degrees, and Riley understood completely why Kim had been such a wreck after her parents' anniversary dinner.

"I don't know why."

Riley had a good idea, but she wasn't going to tell Tyler his grandmother was probably a raging homophobe.

"You're pretty awesome," he continued, his view meaning so much more to Riley than Kim's mother's. From what Kim had told her, Riley didn't have a high opinion of the woman—and after meeting her, it had lowered even further.

"Thanks, Tyler. You're pretty awesome, too."

He beamed, returning to his homework, and Riley glanced at Kim over Tyler's head. Kim looked shaken, a crease between her brows, face more drawn than Riley had seen it before. Riley didn't like it.

"Are you okay, Kim?"

Kim nodded, managing the ghost of a smile, and Riley vowed to cheer her up fully before the day was done.

"Let me help you close." Riley got to her feet—Tyler was almost finished—and joined Kim at the counter. "Give me a job to do."

"You don't have to."

"I want to."

Kim bit her lip for a second, then nodded. "Okay. You can start stacking the chairs on top of the tables so I can sweep the floors."

"You weren't kidding when you said your mom was a piece of work, huh?" Riley said as they tidied the bakery, keeping her voice low so Tyler couldn't hear.

"Nope." Kim grimaced.

"Hey, welcome to the club," Riley said. "Do you want to talk about it?"

"She was being her usual judgmental self. She can't help putting everyone down."

Riley hadn't missed Kim's mother's pointed barbs about the bakery. "What you've built here is amazing—and if she can't see that, then that's her problem."

"Thank you."

"Anytime. Like I've said before—I know how you feel." Riley avoided talking about her past whenever possible—she was a firm believer in looking forward, never back—but she had a feeling Kim would benefit from having a shoulder to lean on. "I still remember everything my mother said to me the last time I spoke to her. That she was ashamed of me. That she thought she'd raised me better. That if I chose my degenerate of a sister over her and my father, I was dead to them."

Kim sucked in a harsh breath. "She said that to you? Because you wanted to look out for Bea? I can't imagine what kind of parent could do that to their child. Never mind both of them."

"Bigots. That's who."

"I am so sorry you had to go through that."

She shrugged. "I know we're better off without them." It had been hard to accept that at first, struggling on her own after always knowing her parents were there to support her if anything went wrong. But ten years on, she sometimes went weeks without thinking about them.

"Still. It can't have been easy."

"No, but I survived. And you can, too." Riley reached out and squeezed Kim's shoulder. "You're stronger than you think."

"Thanks, Riley." Kim covered Riley's hand with her own.

As Kim's thumb brushed the back of Riley's knuckles, Riley struggled to keep her breathing steady. She was supposed to be comforting Kim—not being affected by the gentle swipe of a thumb against her skin.

"Anytime." Thank God her voice was even. "Always happy to be your cheerleader."

Chuckling, Kim dropped her hand back to her side.

Riley followed suit.

"Where are your pom-poms?" Kim reached for her broom. "And ridiculously tiny skirt?"

"Sorry, this cheerleader's uniform is ripped jeans and a flannel shirt."

It wasn't long before Kim was ready to close, and Riley helped Tyler gather his things while Kim did her final kitchen checks, making sure everything was in its rightful place and all the switches were turned off.

"Ready to go?" Kim said when she returned, looking amused as Riley tried to attach a leash to a wriggling Cari.

"Yep." Riley handed the leash over to Tyler as soon as Cari was attached. "Lead the way."

Chapter 14

RILEY'S FAVORITE DOG-FRIENDLY PIZZERIA WAS a half-hour walk away, but neither Kim nor Tyler seemed to mind an evening stroll through Seattle's busy streets.

The rain had stopped, the clouds starting to clear, and Riley was grateful—she and Cari had gotten drenched on their afternoon walk too many times already that month. April sure was full of showers.

Tyler walked a few steps ahead, and Riley kept a careful eye on him and Cari as she and Kim followed, their shoulders brushing as they did. Kim was quiet, and Riley wondered if she was still thinking about what had happened with her mother.

"I had an interesting client today," Riley said to get Kim's mind off it. "She came in for a tattoo cover-up—can you guess what she was covering up?"

"An ex's name?"

"Yeah, like always. But that's not the interesting part—as I was tattooing her, she was ranting about what he'd done, and you wouldn't believe it. He worked away a lot—or told her he did—and he'd been sleeping with someone else practically the entire time they'd been together, living a double life. They got married, and less than two months later, he and this other woman had a kid together."

"Wow. How did she figure it out?"

"She had a hunch and looked through his phone and found dozens of videos of him and this other woman together."

Kim shook her head. "How do people do that? Lie to someone they're supposed to love?"

"Hell if I know." Riley would love to ask some of her ex-girlfriends the same question. "But it made me glad I'm single."

"Do you get a lot of your clients' life stories?"

"It depends on the client. Some want to talk to distract from the pain, and others are the opposite."

"Which do you like best?"

Riley pondered the question as they crossed the street, the sign for the pizzeria visible in the distance. "Honestly, I like both. With the quiet ones, it's easier to concentrate on what I'm doing, but I find it interesting to learn about people's lives, too, so long as they don't ask me too many questions back."

"How come?"

"I'm much more comfortable listening than talking."

They reached the pizzeria, and Tyler chose an outdoor table close to a patio heater; Cari immediately stretched out in front of it—she loved nothing more than warming herself beside a fire. No one else was willing to brave the outdoors, so it was just the three of them, illuminated by the heater's orange light.

"How big are the pizzas here?" Kim glanced over the menu. "Is trying to eat a full one going to kill me?"

Riley grinned. "Big. We could get two to share between us all? I think that should be enough."

"Only if one is pepperoni," Tyler said.

"I'm okay with that." She glanced at Kim. "Is there one you'd like?"

"What's good?"

"The meatball and ricotta pizza is my favorite."

"Then we'll have that." Kim closed the menu after one more brief glance.

"Do you not want to see if there's something else you'd like better?"

Kim's eyes were bright and her words soft. "I trust your judgment."

Riley staunchly ignored the warm feeling flooding her stomach in response.

———◦✦◦———

Kim glanced down the long alleyway, hoping she was in the right place as she made her way toward an unmarked door.

The sign at the front of the building for Space Needle Tattoo Studio was promising, but Riley's instructions for Kim to meet her at the back entrance of the studio had been vague at best.

To Kim's relief, the door swung open, and Riley stood smiling on the other side. Cari looked out from behind Riley's legs, her tail wagging when she recognized Kim.

"Let me take that," Riley said, reaching for the cake box Kim held in her hands, "before Cari tries to knock you over."

"Thank you." Kim bent to greet Cari as soon as Riley had taken the box.

"I could have come and picked this up, you know. You didn't have to come over here."

"I know, but it wasn't far. Besides—you've seen where I work. It's only fair to return the favor."

Riley's smile widened. "Okay. Let me show you around. I'll put this in the break room first before Stephen sees it. Follow me."

Kim stepped into a narrow hallway, letting the door shut behind her. As Riley disappeared into a door at the end, Cari trotted along beside Kim. The break room was small but cozy, a large round table taking up most of the space. Riley set the cake box in the center and lifted the lid to take a peek inside.

"Is it okay?" Kim couldn't help but feel a flicker of nerves whenever she presented a cake to a client, terrified they'd hate it.

"Are you kidding? It's amazing! Thank you so much."

Kim's cheeks felt warm. "It was no trouble."

Riley replaced the lid and handed Kim her payment. "He's gonna love it. I—"

Behind them, the door opened, and Riley jumped, pressing close to Kim's side to conceal the box from view. The woman who stepped inside glanced between Riley and Kim with raised eyebrows, and Riley let out a sigh of relief.

"Oh, it's just you."

"Ouch," she said with a Southern drawl, pressing a hand to her heart. "That hurts."

As she stepped closer, Kim recognized her electric-blue hair. She was one of Riley's soccer teammates.

"I didn't mean it like that." She leaned away from Kim. "I didn't want Stephen to see the cake."

"Ooh, let me see." She bustled over to the table to examine Kim's handiwork. "Does that mean you're the famous baker I've heard so much about?"

Kim glanced at Riley, who had the faintest of flushes on her cheeks.

"Yes, she is. Kim, this is Tess. She's my most annoying coworker."

"She says *most annoying*, but what she means is *favorite*," Tess said. She squinted at Kim. "Have we met before?"

"I came to watch you play once, with my son."

"The time I sprained my ankle," Riley said. "Though you were preoccupied at the time with trying to punch the woman who took me out."

"Ah, yes." An amused smirk crossed Tess's mouth as she puffed out her chest.

"Well, it's nice to officially meet you," Tess said. "The cake looks incredible."

"Thank you."

"Can you keep Stephen out of here while I give Kim a quick tour?" Riley said.

"Sure. He's still with a client, so that should be easy. Did you get candles?"

"What do you think I am, an amateur? They're in the cupboard."

"I'll set them up so we can do the cake before he leaves."

"Thank you!" Riley turned to Kim. "Come on—though it's not as exciting as your work—there's nothing edible here."

"No, but the art is much cooler."

The walls of the hallway Riley walked her through were covered in framed photographs of impressive tattoos—Kim assumed they were the work of the studio's artists. Her favorite tattoo was that of an array of vivid and brightly colored jungle animals, a magnificent roaring jaguar serving as the centerpiece on the person's back.

"Is this one of yours?"

Riley shook her head. "That was Stephen. He's the best for tattoos like that—hyperrealistic ones, and ones with a lot of color. He did most of the cartoon-like ones, too." Riley pointed to the superhero characters in her sleeve. "Including this one of mine."

"What's your specialty?"

Curling her grip around the handle of one of the three doors, Riley said, "I'll show you."

Inside the room sat a large black leather chair, the table beside it littered with tools. A desk was tucked into the corner. Riley's leather jacket was slung over the back of the office chair in front of it. A dog bed and two metal bowls sat beside it, and Cari trotted over for a drink of water.

"Welcome to my office." Riley splayed her arms wide. "Everything on these walls is one of mine."

Kim could see her style right away. Most of the designs were black and gray, but that didn't mean they were lacking any details. Some of them were tiny but unbelievably delicate. Kim traced her fingers over a tiny rose inked on the back of someone's hand. "These are beautiful. Do you have a favorite?"

"I don't know if have a favorite, per se, but this is one of my proudest." Riley pointed to a photograph of a sleeve where the arm was fully inked from shoulder to wrist with a number of different clock faces and cogs. "It was the hardest one I've ever done. It took days. But it was worth it."

"Have you been busy today?"

"It's been quiet so far. I had one appointment this morning, but it was a quick one. My next isn't for another hour. I've mostly been bothering Tess in the meantime."

"You two seem close."

"She's like another sister to me," Riley said. "Though I think she might annoy me more than Bea."

"Is it just the two of you and Stephen who work here?"

"We have another guy—Marty—who works here part-time during his kid's school hours. And our receptionist, Anna, fields phone calls and arranges all our appointments. So, it's a small team, but I like that."

"Has Tess worked here as long as you?"

Riley shook her head. "She's been here about four years."

"And how did you end up playing on the same soccer team?"

"Tess got me into it when she started working here. She was already part of the team. As you know, I used to play when I was in college, but I stopped when I dropped out. When Tess said she was part of a queer soccer team, I couldn't turn down the chance to join. And four years later, I still enjoy it."

Kim was about to ask more when there was a knock on Riley's half-open door, and Tess peered around the frame.

"Hey. Stephen's nearly finished with his client—you ready to do the cake?"

"That's my cue to leave," Kim said. "It was nice to meet you, Tess. And I'll see you around, Riley."

Kim left the way she came, sneaking out the back entrance before Stephen spotted her, and made her way back to the bakery to finish her own day at work.

"She was cute," Tess said once Kim had left, turning to Riley with a thoughtful look on her face. "Y'all together?"

Riley shouldn't be surprised Tess had asked. In four years, the only people who had come to visit Riley at work—aside from Bea and Ash—had been her girlfriends.

"She's straight." Riley was waiting for the day when she'd stop wishing that wasn't true.

Still, it was nice to have the chance to show Kim around her little corner of the world and introduce her to the people in her life. Even if it would only ever be as a friend.

"That's a shame. A pretty woman who can make a damn good cake? That's my dream."

Tell me about it, Riley thought, but she didn't say that out loud. She didn't need Tess piling on with Bea and Ash, asking her about her stupid crush.

"Aren't you seeing someone?" Riley knew Tess had a much more active love life than she did.

"I called it off last week."

"What flaw did you find this time?"

Tess made a face. "She started talking about us moving in together after we'd been on three dates. Way too fast for me."

"Did you tell her that? Or did you break up with her and not tell her why?"

"Does it matter?"

Riley chuckled. "The latter, then. You're terrible! You always bail at the first sign of trouble."

"At least I'm putting myself out there! Unlike someone in this room." Tess threw Riley a pointed glance. "When's the last time you went on a date, little miss judgmental? And, no, one-night stands with cute brunettes you meet after soccer practice don't count."

"You sound like my sister."

"We're just looking out for you."

"Well, I don't need you to."

Tess held up her hands. "Okay, okay. But if you want to come with me next time I go out, let me know. We could wing-woman each other."

The door opening saved Riley from answering, and Anna joined them in the kitchen.

"He's on his way," she said, so Riley lit the candles—carefully arranged so as to not destroy the *Happy 40*th *Birthday* written in neat, cursive writing on the cake.

When the door next opened and Stephen walked in, the three of them burst into a loud round of "Happy Birthday."

"Aw, thank you all," Stephen said once he'd blown out the candles, a wide smile on his face as he pulled them all into a tight hug. "You didn't have to. I didn't need a fuss."

"You deserve it," Riley said, and Tess and Anna nodded in agreement. "And here's to forty more years, old man."

"Watch it, young lady, or you might not last until my next birthday." Stephen's eyes glinted as he wielded a knife to cut them slices of cake.

"Please," Tess said, "we all know Riley's going to be taking over this place when you retire."

"Who says I don't want you two to run it together?" Stephen handed out pieces of cake.

"We'd kill each other!"

"Only if you didn't listen to me," Riley said.

"Well, I'm not going anywhere for a while yet," Stephen said, "so let's not worry about that now, hmm? Let's eat cake."

"Cheers to that." Tess lifted her plate in lieu of a glass. "Oh my gosh," she gushed after her first bite. "This thing is amazing."

Riley had to agree. The cake was crumbly and soft, the whiskey frosting complimenting the coffee sponge perfectly. Considering Kim had never made it before, Riley thought it was perfect.

"I assume I have you to thank for this?" Stephen leaned close to Riley's side as Tess and Anna chatted away. "Much as I adore them, Tess wouldn't be this organized, and Anna hasn't been here long enough to know I have a penchant for whiskey."

"Guilty."

"Well, thank you." He wrapped an arm around her back to pull her into a warm embrace. "I appreciate it."

"You're welcome. Like I said, you deserve to be spoiled every now and again."

"Can you tell my husband that, please?"

Riley shook her head. She knew Christopher doted on Stephen. "The same husband that's taking you for a weekend away?"

"Ah, semantics." Stephen flashed her a wry grin. "You must tell me where you got this cake because it is delectable."

Licking frosting off her fingers, Riley had to agree. "My neighbor made it."

"Your neighbor, you say?" Stephen looked interested. "Do you think you could persuade her to make us a new one every week?"

Chapter 15

FROM BEHIND CAKE MY DAY'S counter, Kim heard Riley helping Tyler with his homework.

"Are you two doing anything nice this weekend?" Riley said once Tyler had set his pencil down with a flourish—his signal that he was done and ready to take Cari for a walk.

"I'm at my dad's. I think him and Rebecca are taking me to another hockey game."

"And I'm going to my sister's birthday dinner," Kim said with a groan.

"And you're excited to go?"

"Can't wait," Kim said, heavy on the sarcasm, and Riley grinned. "It's only been three weeks since I last saw them; I've barely recovered. Especially because at my parents' anniversary dinner, Ellie threatened to start setting me up with her 'eligible bachelor friends'." Kim shuddered to think of who her sister would consider a good match.

Based on her smile, Riley seemed to find amusement in Kim's pain. "Can't you lie and say you're seeing someone to get them off your back?"

"I wish, but they wouldn't rest until they knew every last detail, and I don't think I'm that good of a liar."

"You could take Riley," Tyler said, shoving his books into his backpack.

Riley's smile slipped.

"What?" Kim said, sure she'd misheard.

He met her gaze. "Take Riley. Say she's your date. Then you won't have to lie, and you might have more fun. Plus, I think the look on Grandma's face would be funny."

Kim couldn't argue with that logic—her mother might have an aneurysm—but it sounded like a recipe for disaster. Kim liked Riley, but she wasn't interested in dating her or any woman, for that matter. And her family would no doubt question Kim hard about it, considering she'd only ever shown an interest in men.

Not to mention the impact that pretending to be girlfriends could have on their friendship.

"I don't think that's such a good idea, Tyler."

"Okay." He shrugged. "I'm gonna go pee."

He disappeared to the bathroom, and Cari followed at his heels, sitting outside the door when it closed. Kim realized Riley was watching her closely, teeth worrying at her bottom lip.

"I..." Riley took a breath. "I wouldn't mind being your pretend date. If...if you wanted me to be, anyway."

"Why? You've met my mother. Why on earth would you want to put yourself through that?" Kim barely wanted to go and she was related to them all. For Riley to volunteer...she couldn't understand it.

Riley shrugged. "Cause the kid's got a point. Plus, I still owe you after you saved me from Lizzy that night at Blue Moon, not to mention the soccer game. And I'd like to see the look on your mother's face. If it'd make things less miserable for you..."

"Got a high opinion of yourself, don't you?" Kim said to hide the sudden tightness in her throat, how touched she was that Riley would want to do this for her.

Riley grinned. "Think about it."

Kim did. She thought about how nice it would be to have someone by her side—someone who was *on* her side—to guard against her mother's acerbic words. Someone she could turn to and laugh with, or whisper about her ridiculous family with.

Someone who wouldn't ogle her or put her down.

"Okay."

"Just let me know so I can mentally prepare myself."

"No, I meant, 'Okay, come with me.'"

Surprise bloomed across Riley's face. "Wait, really?"

"Yeah." Kim took a deep breath. "What's the worst that could happen?"

"I can't believe you're doing this." Bea sat at the end of Riley's bed.

"Honestly? Me either."

Riley should have kept her mouth shut after Tyler had skipped off to the bathroom. Kim wouldn't have brought it up again. But Riley hadn't been able to resist having an excuse to spend more time with Kim.

So, on a night where Riley should have been relaxing on the couch in a pair of worn sweats and a loose tank, she was pawing through her closet, trying to find an outfit that wouldn't look out of place in front of Kim's family.

"Do you think it's a good idea?" Bea asked.

"No." It was a terrible idea, even though she'd been the one who convinced Kim to do it. "But it's too late to back out now."

"I'm sure we could think of an excuse."

"Like what? Fake an emergency?"

"Sure." Bea lay back against Riley's pillows and draped a hand over her forehead. "I think I'm coming down with something—I'm feverish. I couldn't possibly be left alone."

"You are ridiculous."

"So is this plan! You can't seriously think pretending to be the girlfriend of the girl you like is a good idea!"

"I already told you I don't think it's a good idea, but it's happening." Riley pulled out the suit she'd worn to Bea and Ash's graduation—and hadn't had a need to wear since. "So, are you going to help me or not?"

Bea leaned up on her elbows. "I guess."

"Thank you." Riley laid out the dark blue suit on the bed beside a pair of black dress pants and a shirt and tie. "Which of these outfits will offend a homophobe the most?"

Bea tilted her head. "Both are solid choices. Do you know how fancy the restaurant you're going to is?"

"They serve caviar."

"Then I think the suit is a solid choice. If you want to fully scandalize her, don't wear a shirt underneath the blazer."

Riley bit her lip. "I can't pull that off. And I don't want them to kick me out of the restaurant." She reached for a white shirt and inspected it for creases.

Bea glanced at her phone. "Do you need me for anything else? I'm supposed to be meeting my softball team for drinks in ten minutes."

"That might be the most lesbian thing you've ever said. And, no, I think I'm good."

"Okay." Bea climbed to her feet and pressed a kiss to Riley's cheek. "I'll speak to you later. Let me know how tonight goes."

"I will."

As the door closed behind Bea, Riley swallowed a flicker of apprehension. She'd be lying if she said she wasn't nervous about what might unfold when she met Kim's family. And just the thought that there might be any sort of PDA with Kim made her heart beat faster.

Shaking off her nerves, Riley stepped back into the suit. Even though it had been two years since she'd last worn it, it fit perfectly—and the sleeves of the blazer covered most of her tattoos, so Kim's mother should be pleased by that, at least.

Knowing she didn't have much time, Riley styled her hair and fastened a skinny black tie around her neck. Looking in the mirror, she smoothed her hands down her sides. Riley had to admit she looked good—and well-dressed, which was the most important thing.

Shoving her phone into her deceptively large pants pocket, Riley said goodbye to Cari before knocking on Kim's apartment.

"Wow," Riley said, when Kim opened the door. "You look...you look nice." *Beautiful* was what Riley had almost said.

Kim's dress was a deep purple, tight to her waist, with a skirt ending above her knee. Strapless, its neckline showed off a hint of cleavage, and Riley swallowed. She wasn't blind—she'd always thought Kim was attractive, but like this—her hair pinned in an elaborate updo, her eyes gleaming, and her lips painted a deep red—she thought Kim looked perfect.

"Thank you. So do you. I like the suit."

Riley tugged at the lapels of her blazer, trying to force herself to act regular while standing in front of an actual goddess. "I thought a suit would be most likely to irritate your mother."

Kim laughed. "You would be correct. I've ordered an Uber—it'll be here in two minutes."

"Lead the way."

———— ✦ ————

"Are you sure you want to do this?" Kim said, glancing at Riley across the back seat of their ride.

Judging from the way she was constantly fiddling with the buttons on the her blazer jacket's sleeves, Riley was nervous.

And she wasn't the only one.

Kim wondered if it was too late for her to ask their driver to turn around. "I know it's not the ideal way to spend a Saturday night."

"I don't mind, honestly. I'm happy to spend time with you."

Riley was too kind. Kim was certain her company wasn't a great enough reward for what her family was about to put them both through.

She'd be sure to drop some salted caramel brownies off at Riley's next time she made some.

"Thank you," Kim said.

They met each other's gazes, and Kim was swept up in the depth of Riley's eyes. After a few seconds, she forced herself to look away, glancing instead out the window.

"So, give me the lowdown on who's who," Riley said, a look of determination on her face. "Mom and Dad?"

"Martha and Edward—though I wouldn't call my mother Martha to her face."

Riley grinned. "God, no. Wouldn't want to give her a reason to kick me out."

"My dad will insist you call him Edward—he hates being called Dr. Jackson now that he's retired."

"He was a doctor?"

"Neurosurgeon. And my sister Ellie is a pediatrician. Can you see why I'm the family disappointment?"

Riley took Kim's hand and squeezed it. "Don't say things like that."

"Just getting it out of the way before everyone else starts later."

"I think they'll be more focused on you and me to talk about your job." A flicker of apprehension appeared in Riley's eyes. "So, Ellie—it's her party? Anyone else I should know about?"

"Yes, it's Ellie's party. And her husband is Anthony. I think my older brother will be there, too—he's Alan, and his wife is Claire."

"Okay, got it. Any kids?"

Kim shook her head. "None will be there tonight. It's a child-free zone."

"How upper-class of them."

"That's one way to sum them up." Kim grinned.

"And if anyone asks—how did we meet?"

"I guess sticking as close to the truth as possible? You moved in next door, we became friends, and…"

"Fell madly in love?" Riley asked, her thumb caressing Kim's hand, which she hadn't let go of.

Even if they were just fake dating for the sake of irritating her parents, Kim had to admit that it was nice to have someone's hand on hers again. "Sure."

"And should we talk about…" Riley hesitated. "How touchy-feely do you want to be?"

The thought hadn't even crossed Kim's mind. "I don't think it will come as any surprise to you that my family aren't tactile. If we don't do more than hold hands, no one will bat an eye."

As the car eased to a stop, Kim took a deep breath. "Last chance to back out."

"I'm not going anywhere," Riley said, her voice soft and sure.

Swallowing, Kim looked away from her face. She didn't have many friends, and to have Riley say that—and know she meant it—made Kim's heart warm.

"Well," Riley continued, "that is, unless you tell me to. If your family gets to be too much, we can have a giant fight and you can break up with me and claim it was all a phase."

Smiling, Kim thanked their driver and stepped out of the car. Riley pressed close to her side as they approached the restaurant door, one comforting hand resting at the small of Kim's back, her fingertips burning through the thin material of Kim's dress.

The place was busy, the low hum of chatter reaching Kim's ears. Her family was easy to spot—Ellie and Claire stood talking to her mother around a long row of tables in the rear, well away from any of the other patrons.

Kim's father sat talking to Anthony and Alan at the table and smiled warmly as Kim approached. He glanced at Riley curiously, which was a lot more polite than the open-mouthed gaping from Kim's mother.

"Hi, Mom. You remember Riley?"

"Yes. What is she doing here?"

"She's my date," Kim said, watching her mother's face turn ashen. "We're dating."

"You're…what?" Ellie blinked.

"You're always telling me I need to put myself out there more and find someone after John, so I took your advice."

"It's nice to meet you all," Riley had plastered on a megawatt smile. "I've heard so much about you."

And all of it terrible went unsaid, and Kim bit the inside of her cheek to smother a smile.

"Is this some kind of joke?" her mother demanded.

"Why would I joke about something like this?"

"Is this why your marriage didn't work out? Why you scared away Henry?"

She couldn't believe her mother was still bringing him up. Was Kim being alone so much worse than her being with a misogynistic asshole?

"I didn't scare Henry away," Kim said, her words clipped. "And this has nothing to do with my marriage."

Her mother probably wished it did, though. She'd never been able to understand the divorce, had tried to convince Kim to reconcile with John for years despite there never being anything to reconcile.

"Can't you just…be happy for me?"

Her mother pursed her lips.

"There's no need to make a scene," Ellie said. "Though it would have been nice if you could have given us a heads-up beforehand."

"I told you I was bringing someone."

"But you didn't say…"

"That Riley wasn't a guy?" The only thing keeping her voice from rising was Riley rubbing soothing circles on her back. God, this was a terrible idea. Kim never should have brought her here. She didn't deserve to be put through this. "Did you give everyone a heads-up the first time you brought Anthony over?"

"Well, no, but…"

"But?"

"It's different! You can't blindside us like this and expect no reaction."

"Let's all sit and have a nice meal, hm?" Kim's father, ever the voice of reason, spoke. "Riley, you sit here next to me. I want to hear all about you, seeing as Kim's told us nothing."

Kim felt her first flash of guilt for lying but was quick to push it away. She followed Riley to the table and sat beside her as her father drew Riley into conversation.

Her mother's disapproving gaze bore into Kim. She ignored it as best she could.

"You're a tattoo artist?" Kim's father said. "How interesting!"

No doubt wondering if her father was being sincere, Riley glanced at Kim.

"Dad, do you remember I said I knew someone who might be able to help you design Tyler's skateboard? Riley's an incredible artist."

Her father looked overjoyed. "Oh, excellent! Could I show you the design I'm making?"

"Uh, sure. You're making a skateboard from scratch?"

"For his birthday, yes. It's one of my projects now that I'm retired. I like to make things." He reached for his phone. "Like this clock."

"Oh, wow. That's beautiful."

He beamed. "Thank you. This is what I have for the skateboard so far." He showed Riley another picture, of the outline of the board. "Making it isn't a problem—but when it comes to being creative, I'm not so good. And I have no idea what he'd like on it. Do you think you'd be able to help?"

Riley studied the photograph with a thoughtful look on her face. "Do you have a pen?"

"Kim." Ellie waved at Kim from across the table, tearing her attention away from Riley. "How did you two meet?"

"Riley moved into the empty apartment next door."

"How do you go from new neighbors to becoming a lesbian?"

"Ellie," Alan said, "don't be rude."

"It's fine," Kim said, forcing a smile. "And it just sort of...happened." Kim figured keeping things vague was the best policy.

"Well, you look happy." Claire raised a glass of wine toward her. "So, good for you."

"Thank you." Kim glanced at Riley, who was doodling a design on a cocktail napkin and engrossed in conversation with Kim's father. "I am happy."

Not romantically, like they all thought, but otherwise? Kim was more content than she'd been in a long time. And having Riley in her life was a big part of that.

Riley let out a long breath once she and Kim were safely on their way home. Feeling much more relaxed, Riley loosened her tie.

"So," Kim said, "on a scale from one to ten—how bad was that?"

"You know, it wasn't bad at all. Your dad is cool."

"He liked you. But he's not going to stop pestering you about that skateboard."

Riley thought Edward's idea was so sweet, and she knew Tyler would love it. "I don't mind. It'll be worth it to see the look on Tyler's face when he gets the board."

"Thank you for helping him."

"It's not a problem. Your mom wasn't so bad tonight, either." Mostly because she hadn't said much, but still. "I think she took it well."

"I think she was in shock."

"Did you see the look on her face when she recognized me?"

"I wish I'd taken a picture." Kim laughed. "But, no, it was much more bearable than usual." Kim stretched out across the empty seat between them and squeezed Riley's hand. "Thank you. I don't know how to repay you."

"How about suffering through another soccer game with Tyler this weekend?"

Kim smiled. "I suppose we could arrange that."

"If it makes you feel any better, it'll be the last one for a few months. We have a break between May and July. We start back up again in August."

"Do you still practice in the meantime?"

"Yeah, but every other week instead of twice a week."

"So you don't lose all your skills?" Kim's smile was teasing. She looked beautiful, her eyes bright in the darkness.

Not for the first time, a part of Riley wished that things between them were real. "Please. Like I'd ever lose any of my skills."

It's not like that, Riley reminded herself sternly, realizing she'd leaned into Kim's space. She shifted away to press closer to the car door. She needed to stop blurring the lines between them before someone got hurt.

Because that someone would be her.

They arrived back home, and Riley smothered a yawn with the back of her hand as they waited for the elevator.

When they reached their floor, Kim paused outside her apartment. "Thank you again for tonight. I really appreciate it."

Kim pressed a kiss to Riley's cheek, and Riley felt it all the way to her toes. Her heart pounded as she breathed in the scent of Kim's perfume. She swallowed thickly, her throat tight.

"S-see you soon," Riley said with the faintest of trembles in her voice. Once she was safely inside her apartment, she sagged back against the door and tilted her head toward the heavens.

She sighed.

How the hell she was going to get over Kim?

Chapter 16

TYLER'S GASP WHEN THEY ARRIVED for Riley's game, at the soccer field was loud enough that Kim looked around in a panic—then she saw Cari.

She sat near the halfway line, her leash held by Riley's sister, who stood talking with the woman with the buzz cut Kim had seen the day Riley had moved in.

"Can we go say hi?" Tyler said, like he wasn't already tugging Kim toward them.

"Okay."

When she spotted Tyler, Cari leaped to her feet and lurched toward him with enough force to nearly send Bea tumbling to the ground.

"Woah, Cari, what—ah." Bea noticed Tyler as Cari pounced on him, tail wagging at light speed. "I'm guessing you're Tyler. Riley said you were coming." Bea's blue eyes—the same shade as Riley's—flickered in Kim's direction. "It's nice to properly meet you. I'm Bea, and this is my girlfriend, Ash."

"It's nice to finally meet you both. I'm sure Tyler thinks so, too, but something about being around Cari makes him forget his manners." Kim cast an exasperated glance toward her son. "I've heard a lot about you."

"Ditto," Bea said. "How's the bakery? I confess I've stolen a few of the brownies you've gifted Riley, and they are to die for."

"Thank you. And it's good. Crazy, which is great for business, but also tiring."

"It must be a lot of pressure to run your own business," Ash said. "I could never do it myself."

"It's not so bad. It was my dream, so even though it's hard sometimes, it's all worth it. Plus, I'm not on my own—I have a wonderful business partner. What is it you both do?"

"I'm an elementary school teacher," Ash said.

"And I'm a research scientist in cell biology," Bea said. "I got all the brains in the family—but don't tell Riley I said that."

Tyler giggled, obviously paying more attention to their conversation than Kim had thought.

Bea pointed at him, expression grave. "That includes you, young man," she said.

"I won't!" Tyler shifted to sit cross-legged on the ground, laughing when Cari tried to squeeze herself onto his lap.

"Don't forget why we're here," Kim said, ruffling his hair. "What would Riley say if you were too distracted by Cari to watch her play?"

"I can do both." Tyler shifted to face the field where both teams were finishing their warm-ups.

"Here," Bea said, holding Cari's leash toward him. "You may as well take her. Something tells me that's what she'd prefer anyway."

"Thank you!" Tyler took the leash, his eyes falling to Bea's wrist and the splash of bright color against her pale skin. "I like your tattoo! Did Riley do it?"

"She did. It was the first one she ever did at her tattoo studio."

"That's so cool! What is it?"

"It's a transgender pride flag."

"What does that mean?"

Bea glanced toward Kim.

"Like your friend Remi from school," Kim told him.

"Oh yeah! He was born in the wrong body—he used to be a girl, but now he's a boy like me."

"Yes, exactly like that. Except the opposite—I was born a boy, but I always knew I was a girl."

With a stab of sympathy, Kim realized that that was probably the coming out that had resulted in Bea being kicked out at such a young age. She'd always assumed it was because of Bea's sexuality—Riley had never specified, but it probably wasn't Riley's story to share. She couldn't ever imagine tossing Tyler aside, and she was glad Bea and Riley at least had each other.

Tyler nodded to himself. "Cool. I'm going to tell Remi about your tattoo at school on Monday. Maybe he'll want one, too."

"I think he'll have to wait a few years, sweetheart," Kim said. "You have to be eighteen to get a tattoo."

"That's only eight years away."

"Please don't say things like that." It was bad enough he was nearly ten. Kim didn't want to think about him heading off to college. "What grade do you teach, Ash?"

"Kindergarten."

Kim shuddered. "I don't know how you do it. I remember how hard it was keeping Tyler entertained when he was that age—I dread to think what it must be like in a room full of them."

"Oh, I love it. They're the best at that age. So curious to learn about the world—and not old enough to act up too much. It's nice to be their first experience of the classroom and watch how much they grow in a year."

Kim could never have the patience.

The sound of a whistle brought them all to attention as the warm-ups were called to an end. Instead of joining her teammates straight away, Riley jogged over to them for a brief hello.

"I hope you're behaving yourself, Bea," she said.

Bea pressed a hand to her chest. "Don't I always?"

"Absolutely not." Riley's gaze moved to Kim. "Glad you could make it."

"Just don't get hurt this time." Kim wasn't sure she could go through watching that again.

"I'll try my best," Riley said.

"And you have to score a goal again!" Tyler said from his position on the floor.

"I almost didn't see you there, buddy. You comfy with Cari sitting on you? She's heavy."

"No, she's not." Tyler acted affronted. "She's fine."

"But you're not going to be able to see me play."

Tyler peered around the side of Cari's body. "I can."

"Riley!" A voice called from behind her. Tess was looking toward them, waving her hands. "Get your butt over here! We're talking tactics."

"I can give you some tactics," Bea said as Riley jogged away. "Score a goal! Don't fall over! Don't get sent off!" She lowered her voice. "She would so be giving me the finger if Tyler weren't here."

"I think Tyler has the right idea." Ash lowered herself onto the grass next to him. "Why do we normally stand?"

"Because it's usually rained the night before and the grass is soaking," Bea said, but she threw herself down next to Ash, and Kim followed suit, sitting on Tyler's other side.

"Do you two watch Riley's games often?" Kim said as the teams kicked off.

"We try to," Ash said. "Whenever we can—typically, the one where she needed us to be here, we weren't. Thank you for looking after her, by the way."

"It was no trouble. As long as it doesn't happen again." Despite knowing the chances of Riley getting hurt again were slim, Kim couldn't help a flicker of worry every time someone went to tackle Riley.

"She's so good." Tyler watched Riley turn neatly to take her first shot at a goal—it was kicked away, behind the goal, by a player on the opposing team. "I want to be as good as her one day."

"Well, keep practicing and you might be," Kim said.

"Riley mentioned you've started playing, Tyler. She said you skate-board, too." There was a flicker of mischief in Bea's eyes. "Have you got her to try it yet?"

"Once." Tyle turned a wide smile wide onto her. "She wasn't good."

"Good thing she's better at this," Bea said as Riley's next shot was saved. "She's playing like she's possessed today. Must be trying to impress someone."

Bea's eyes mysteriously lingered on Kim.

Surely Bea was referring to Riley impressing Tyler.

Kim sucked in a breath when an opposing player bundled Riley over on the edge of the penalty box.

Riley bounced straight back up, dusting off her shorts as the referee blew her whistle to give Seattle Pride a free kick. Riley set the ball down, a look of concentration on her face as she took three steps back.

"She's going for goal." Ash leaned forward. "Come on, Riley!"

When the ball curled into the top corner of the net, past the goalkeeper's open hands, Kim didn't know who cheered the loudest—Tyler, Bea, Ash, or her.

The restaurant slash bar Kim and Tyler were bustled into by Bea and Ash was busy, all of Riley's teammates and their friends and families crammed inside. Kim even spotted some members of the opposing team queueing to order a drink from where she sat at the back.

Seattle Pride had won four-nil, and Riley had three goals—known as a hat trick, or so Tyler had reliably informed Kim—to her name. It meant that Kim had yet to see her since the game had kicked off, since Riley had been swarmed by her teammates at the full-time whistle.

She stood by the bar with Tess's arm slung low across her back and Jessika pressing a beer into her hand.

"She'll come over soon." Bea, who sat with Ash on the opposite side of the table, seemed to have noticed the path of Kim's gaze. "She hates all this stuff. Being in the spotlight. Won't take her long to slink away."

"Why does she play as a striker, then? They always get all the glory." Tyler was chewing on the end of his paper straw.

Kim was glad Bea and Ash had rushed them over here before the others had arrived—they'd managed to order drinks before the place got too busy.

"You saw her today, little man," Bea said. "If you were her manager, where else would you play her?"

Kim couldn't argue with that logic. Riley had been in her element throughout the game. She'd made her goals look effortless and, most importantly, hadn't had to limp off at any point. Watching Riley glide across the field, looking like the ball was glued to her feet, Kim had been unable to look away. She'd been magnificent—athletic as she leaped for every ball, the muscles in her calves pronounced as she raced across the field.

As Riley ducked her head to avoid the cheers of her teammates, her cheeks flaming red, it was hard for Kim to reconcile this version of Riley with the confident persona she'd seen on the field.

Riley hadn't showered after the game, was still clad in her kit, the back stained with mud and grass, and had a light sheen of sweat on her skin. Kim didn't know why, but she liked that look on her.

A server walked past with a burger, and Kim noticed Tyler eyeing it with interest. "Hungry, Ty?"

"Sorry. It's been ages since lunch."

It had barely been two hours, but Kim wasn't going to argue with a growing boy. Soon, he'd be eating everything in sight.

Kim handed him a menu from the table. "Let me know what you want; it looks like you order at the bar."

Tyler's eyes lit up as he perused the menu. "Can I get a burger and fries, Mom?"

"I suppose. We are celebrating, after all." Kim reached for her purse. "Do you two want anything?"

"We have dinner plans this evening so probably shouldn't," Bea said. "Don't want to spoil our appetite."

"You okay here for a minute, Tyler?"

"Uh-huh." He didn't spare Kim a glance.

"We'll keep an eye on him." Ash smiled.

Kim could see why she was a kindergarten teacher. She had a warmth about her that was reassuring. "Back in a sec, then."

Kim made her way through the throngs of Seattle Pride players and weaved her way toward the bar. She ended up waiting a few feet away from Riley, who was engrossed in conversation with some of her friends. Kim didn't want to intrude.

It was Tess who noticed Kim in the end, waving at her just after Kim had given her order.

As Kim waved back, Riley turned, her face brightening when she spotted Kim.

"Hey there, hat trick hero," Kim said when Riley made her way to Kim's side. "You weren't showing off for me and Tyler, were you?"

"Me? Showing off?" Riley scoffed, but her cheeks were pink. "Doesn't sound like me." She was forced to step closer to Kim when someone squeezed behind Riley to place an order. "Sorry," she said, raising her voice to be heard over the chatter. "I'm all gross and sweaty."

"Oh, it's fine," Kim said. "Sign of a job well done, right?"

Riley smiled, her eyes sparkling in the bar's low light. She was glowing—victory looked good on her.

"Did you enjoy the match?"

"Much more than last time," Kim said. "Did you?"

"Well, I always like to win. But yeah. It was good. And it didn't rain." She glanced down at her dirty kit with a grin. "Not that you can tell."

"You did still manage to spend a lot of time on the ground."

"Rude."

Kim poked at a grass stain just below Riley's heart, feeling the points of her ribs beneath her fingertips. "But true. Does diving on the floor usually help you win?"

"Did today, didn't it?"

Riley's joy—and that of her teammates all around them—was infectious. She'd never expected she could ever get so invested in a soccer game that didn't involve Tyler.

Kim was about to ask Riley if she'd be joining them at their table when a hand clapped around Riley's shoulder and jerked her backward. Kim recognized the colors of Seattle Pride's goalkeeper.

"If it isn't the woman of the hour. Can I buy you a drink?"

"I'm already on my fourth, Addie." Riley waved the half-empty bottle. "I need to eat something first."

"Let me buy you a snack, then." Addie's gaze lingered on Kim. "Unless I'm interrupting something?"

Kim was quick to shake her head. "Not at all. I'll leave you to it. Just come over and say hi to Tyler soon, okay? He's waiting to gush all over about how wonderful you were today."

"I'll be right over," Riley said. "I promise."

Three days later, an out-of-breath Riley rushed to make it to the diner where she and Ash had agreed to meet. It was rare for the two of them to hang out without Bea, but Ash had texted Riley the day before and asked her not to tell Bea about it.

Riley was doing her best not to be worried.

"Hey, Ash." Riley slid into the booth and shrugged out of her jacket. "Is everything okay?"

"Everything's fine," Ash said, but the way she fiddled with the rings on her fingers suggested she was lying.

Riley used her big-sister tone of voice that Bea loved to tease her for. "Spill," she said.

"Okay, so you know Bea and I have been together for a while."

"Yeah…"

"Well…" Ash paused. "I'm thinking of proposing."

Riley smiled widely, suddenly understanding Ash's nerves. "You are?"

"I am, because I really, really want to make her my wife. And I know the whole asking for permission thing is misogynistic and outdated, and I know you're not her father, but you're the only family she has, and I wanted to know if I had your blessing."

"Ash, are you kidding? 'Course you have my blessing!" All Riley had ever wanted was her sister's happiness, and she knew she couldn't have asked for a better partner than Ash. "Come here." Riley rounded the table to yank Ash into a tight hug. "Have you thought about how you're going to do it?"

"I think something low-key while we're at home. And I was hoping maybe you'd be there?"

"Do you not want it to be just you guys?"

Ash shook her head. "No. You've been such a big part of both of our lives. And you mean everything to Bea. I think she'd want you there."

Riley was touched. "I'd love to be a part of it. And what about rings?"

"I wanted your input on that." Ash pulled out her phone. "I've been looking, but I'm not sure what style she'd like. Can you help me look? And maybe come with me to pick out the ring?"

"I'd love to."

Feeling like a proud parent, Riley knew it was going to be a struggle to keep the secret from spilling out the next time they were all together. Bea had always been able to read Riley like a book.

She hoped Ash popped the question sooner rather than later.

———— ⋄⋈⋄ ————

"What's wrong?" John was lingering by the door after Tyler had said goodbye and gone to his room. It might have been years since they'd been together, but Kim could tell if there were things on his mind. "Did something happen this weekend?"

"No, nothing like that. I just… I wanted to say I'm happy for you. And if you're seeing someone, you don't need to keep it a secret from me."

Kim frowned, confused—and wondered for one awful second if her mother had messaged him after Kim had taken Riley to Ellie's birthday dinner. "I'm not seeing anyone."

It was John's turn to frown. "You're not?"

"Why would you think I am?"

John ran a hand through his hair. "Because…well, Tyler's been talking all about your new boyfriend, Riley, so—"

"Tyler's been what?"

"Don't be mad at him," John said. "I think he's excited. He's smitten with him."

"Tyler said Riley was my boyfriend?" Kim repeated, feeling like she'd stepped into an alternate dimension.

"Well, not technically…" John looked unsure. "But he's been talking nonstop about this Riley guy for a few weeks now. 'Riley's so cool; Riley took me to the skate park the other week; me, Mom and Riley went for ice cream; we watched Riley's soccer game this weekend.' I connected the dots."

Kim couldn't help but laugh. "Riley's not my boyfriend. Riley is my neighbor." Kim waved toward next door. "You know, the one with the dog? The woman you met a few months ago?"

"Oh." A beat then: "Are you sure?"

"Am I sure Riley's not my boyfriend?"

"It sounds like you've been spending a lot of time together."

"We're friends." Kim paused. "Well. Unless my mother asks."

"I feel like I need to hear this story."

"I…may have taken Riley to Ellie's birthday party. Partly to get everyone off my back about still being single and partly because I knew it'd piss her off if she thought I was dating a woman."

John's eyebrows climbed toward his hairline. "So there is something going on between you two."

"No. Riley did it as a favor to me."

John didn't look totally convinced. "Okay, then. Oh, before I go— let me know what you need me to grab for Tyler's birthday party next month. I know you've probably already got a list."

"Several," Kim said with a smile. "Thank you for hosting it."

"You know I don't mind."

"Even if it means putting up with my mother for a few hours?"

"She's much less scary now that we're not together," he said. "And we're still on for the zoo on his actual birthday, right?" he asked.

One of the perks of Tyler's birthday being in the summer was that he always had it off from school. They always made sure to spend the day together as a family—even after she and John had separated.

"Uh-huh," Kim said.

"He...he mentioned wanting Rebecca to come this year too," John said. "Is that okay?"

"Absolutely." It had been five years—if she couldn't accept that John had moved on by now, she needed to go back to therapy. "You know I like Rebecca."

"Great," he said. "We'll sort the details closer to the time."

"See you soon!" Kim waved him off and closed the door, wondering if Tyler would be up for a movie night.

Chapter 17

"I'm sorry, but this is bullshit." Riley had an adorable frown on her face as the episode of *Grey's Anatomy* unfolded. "They clearly belong together!"

Having known this moment was coming, Kim patted her shoulder in sympathy. Riley had made it no secret she was a huge fan of the characters Callie and Arizona, and Kim had tried not to wince whenever Riley had asked if they were still in the latest episodes.

"Why can't anyone be happy on this damn show?"

Kim snorted and reached for another handful of popcorn. "To make us feel better about our own lives?"

"But I don't! Now I'm sad they're not together anymore. Unless"—Riley looked at Kim with hopeful eyes—"they get back together and live happily ever after?"

Kim stared back, unblinking. "You told me not to spoil it."

"You can make an exception for this."

"I don't think I can. I promised."

"I could google it."

"You could, but you won't." Kim's voice left no room for uncertainty.

"How do you know?"

"Because you hate spoilers. And you like being surprised."

Riley huffed. "I'm not sure."

"Well, I a—" Kim's phone rang, and she answered without checking the caller ID—it was around the time Tyler usually called to say good night. "Hi, sweetheart."

"Hello Kimberly."

Kim nearly dropped the phone. "Mom? What's wrong?"

Riley turned away from the TV to look at her, worry on her face.

"Does something have to be wrong for me to call?"

"Well, no. But you usually don't."

Kim's mother sighed. "Yes, well, I am now. And nothing's wrong. I was calling to ask if you'd like to come over for dinner tomorrow night. With your…girlfriend."

For one long moment, Kim couldn't do anything but blink in surprise.

"Are you still there?" Impatience lined her mother's voice.

"I… Yeah, I'm still here."

"So? Will you come?"

"Um…" Kim glanced at Riley. "Why?"

"It was pointed out to me that I didn't make much of an effort to get to know her at your sister's birthday," her mother said. Kim suspected the words were coming through gritted teeth—and at the behest of Kim's father. "And perhaps I ought to, if she makes you happy."

"Oh. Well, that's nice of you, but—"

"No buts. Be here at seven. I'm making a chicken pot pie." With that, her mother hung up the phone and Kim was left staring in shock.

"What happened?" Riley asked.

Kim tore her gaze away from the device in her hand. "She invited us to dinner tomorrow night." She'd be seeing her mother three times in two months. It was unheard of.

And she'd have to spend another night pretending Riley was her girlfriend. Which wasn't a hardship, exactly, but she was sure Riley would soon grow tired of being dragged along to Kim's family events.

The last thing Kim wanted to do was drive Riley away.

Riley looked the way Kim felt. "She what? Us? Why?"

"So she could get to know you better." Kim ran a hand through her hair. "She framed it as a choice, but it wasn't. Don't worry, though—I'll find a way out of it."

"I'll go if you want me to. This whole thing is kinda all my fault anyway—I was the one who talked you into it. And my plans for tomorrow night involved eating pizza in my sweats, so..." Riley squeezed Kim's hand when she didn't smile. "Why does she want to get to know me better, anyway?"

"I think it's my dad's doing. I don't think he was happy with the way she treated you. Which would be sweet, if this were real, but..."

"It's not." Riley pulled her hand back. "Well, it's up to you. If you want to go, I can be the world's most perfect girlfriend and get her off your back for good. But if you want to stop the charade, tell her we broke up already."

"She'd be so smug." Kim could imagine it already and hated she'd managed to put them both into a lose-lose situation. All because Tyler had had to open his big mouth.

"Then it's settled. Besides, last time wasn't so bad. And your dad's great. Getting to see the workshop he told me all about would be cool, too."

Kim couldn't believe they were doing this.

Again.

"Okay. But if you change your mind..."

"I'll let you know."

⁕

Sitting in the back seat of another Uber on the way to Kim's parents' house, Riley couldn't believe she'd managed to talk herself into another dinner pretending to be Kim's girlfriend.

Butterflies swirled in the pit of Riley's stomach. Beside her, Kim tapped her leg in a nervous rhythm. This felt different than the last time, more intimate, if they were going to be one-on-one with Kim's parents.

And there was an intimacy in being invited into Kim's childhood home, too—the place where she grew up, where she'd formed into the incredible woman she was today despite her mother's best efforts to drag her down.

Riley took a deep breath as the car pulled to a stop outside a charming two-story house. The house had decking along the front with a swinging chair nestled into the corner, and Riley imagined Kim curling up there with a book after a long day at school.

"Ready?" Kim's fingers curled tightly around the handle of the car door.

"Yup."

Gravel crunched under the heels of her Doc Martens as Riley followed Kim to the front door. Kim had assured Riley she could dress much more casually this time—though Riley had still put on her newest pair of black jeans and carefully ironed her flannel shirt before leaving.

Edward opened the door before they reached it, a big, beaming smile on his face. "Hi, sweetheart." He swept Kim into a fierce hug, and Riley was surprised when he did the same to her. "Nice to see you again, Riley."

"And you, Dr. Jackson," Riley said, the words muffled.

"What did I tell you?" He stepped back and settled his hands on Riley's shoulders. "You call me Edward."

"Sorry." Riley had never done well with other people's parents—a consequence of having no relationship with her own—and she reminded herself she wasn't really there to make a good impression.

It was all pretend.

And she needed to keep focused on that.

"Come in, come in. Martha is in the kitchen." Edward waved them inside, and both Riley and Kim kicked off their shoes by the door before following Edward deeper into the house.

Riley couldn't help but look around. The walls were a mixture of wooden paneling and brilliant white paint, and artwork was interspersed with photographs at regular intervals. Riley spotted Kim and her siblings with their families in some of the frames and was disappointed she couldn't see any of a younger Kim.

They followed the sounds of clanging pans, and Riley's eyes widened as they stepped into the kitchen. It was huge, a marble island in the center, the stove twice the size of the one in Riley's apartment.

Martha stood beside it, and even barefoot and wearing a pink apron, the woman managed to be intimidating.

"Kimberly." Martha kissed both of Kim's cheeks before turning her attention to Riley. "Riley." Martha made no move to step toward her, and Riley was grateful. Simply inviting Riley into her home was big enough progress, based on how she'd reacted at their first meeting.

"Thank you for having me, Mrs. Jackson." Unlike Edward, Martha didn't correct her. "The pie smells delicious."

"Yes, well, Kimberly had to get her culinary skills from somewhere."

"It certainly wasn't going to be from me." Edward smiled. "I could burn a pot of water."

"Remember that movie night when Mom was out and you tried to make us microwave popcorn?"

"How could I forget nearly burning the house down?" Edward shook his head at Riley. "I didn't know it could catch on fire."

She grinned back. "Sounds like you could rival me in the kitchen."

"Well, it's a good thing we've got these two to look after us, isn't it?" Edward said.

Riley forced the smile to stay on her face. "It sure is."

"How long until dinner's ready, dear?" Edward looked hopefully toward the pan of bubbling broccoli.

"Fifteen minutes."

"Excellent—long enough to show Riley my workshop." The look in his eyes as he turned toward her reminded Riley of Tyler whenever he wanted to show her a new trick. "Come, see what I've been working on since we last spoke."

"Kimberly can stay and help me."

Riley shot Kim a look, not wanting to leave her alone with her mother—but Kim waved her off.

"Go. Let him talk your ear off."

"But don't be too long!" Martha called after them. "I know what you're like, Edward."

"Yes, yes, we'll be back before dinner." He took hold of Riley's elbow to steer her out of the kitchen. "It's down here. Used to be the garage, but I converted it a few years ago."

It was spacious, the center dominated by a large wooden table. Tools were dotted around: saws, sanders, chisels, vices, and all manner of other things Riley wouldn't know how to start identifying. The walls were covered in shelves, most showcasing things Edward must have made, including the beautiful wooden clock he'd shown her a picture of.

"Oh, wow," Riley said.

At the table's center sat a skateboard deck (Riley had only realized the actual board wasn't called a skateboard when Edward had told her at their last dinner together). The wood gleamed where it caught the light.

"This is beautiful." Riley paused at the table's edge, not daring to touch the deck, lest she mark it. "How did you make this?"

"Oh, it wasn't so hard. Making the molds was the most difficult bit." He nodded to the corner of the room where a few sections of wood had been joined together and sanded. "It took a few tries to get the right shape."

"I wouldn't know where to start." Give Riley something to draw, no matter how dainty, and she was fine, but ask her to try and make something with her hands and she was useless. "You're incredibly talented."

Edward beamed. "I'm hoping it'll be ready for your design by the end of the week."

"It's all done." Riley had been working on it in every spare moment she could. It had been surprisingly easy to sneakily get Tyler's opinion on things by doodling in the café while hanging out with him. "And I've found a graphics company who can print it."

"Excellent. I hope he likes it."

"He'll love it." Riley didn't see a world in which Tyler wouldn't. "Especially because of how much thought has gone into it."

Riley's own grandparents had never put so much effort into a birthday present for her or Bea. The most they'd ever gotten was a twenty-dollar bill, contingent on an extracted promise to spend it on something nice. The money had been great at the time, but to be given such a tangible reminder of how much she was loved? Something hours of labor had gone into? Riley would have loved to have something like Edward's creation hanging around to remember her grandparents by, now that they were long gone.

Edward glanced at the clock. "Shall we get back? I don't want to get told off for keeping you too long."

A part of Riley wished he'd keep her all evening, but that wouldn't be fair to Kim. And, besides, Martha hadn't been too terrible.

Yet.

⁕⸻⟨⟩⸻⁕

The kitchen was eerily silent once Riley had left with her father, and Kim stood at the counter, drumming her fingers against the marble as her mother busied herself at the stove.

Her shoulders looked tense, and Kim wondered what was running through her mother's mind, what words were bubbling beneath the surface, desperate to escape.

"How can I help?" Kim said when it became clear her mother wasn't going to provide her with any instruction.

"You can set the table and fetch me the plates. Use the nice china."

Kim knew that was usually reserved for special occasions. "Riley won't care if we use the regular plates."

"She's a guest, Kimberly. I'll treat her as such."

Kim couldn't tell whether that was a good thing or not but did as her mother said—that approach usually served her well. She returned, carrying her mother's finest china plates. "You didn't have to invite us over, you know."

"I know." Her mother wiped her hands on her apron before turning to study Kim with shrewd eyes. "I won't pretend to understand it—and I certainly don't know where it's come from, or what you see in her—but you do seem happier. I know you don't believe me, Kimberly, but all I've ever wanted was the best for you. And if that's her...I suppose I'd better get used to it. It just might take me some time."

Kim swallowed, barely able to believe a word she was hearing. Never in her wildest dreams, after how her mother had reacted when she'd first laid eyes on Riley, had Kim imagined this as a possibility.

How had Riley managed it? She'd won over Tyler instantly—though Kim suspected Cari had given her a helping hand—and Kim's father in less than ten minutes. And now her impossibly-high-standards-and-a-little-homophobic mother?

"I... Thank you, Mom. That means a lot."

"Yes, well, no need to get emotional about it." She turned back to the stove.

Kim smiled. That was more like it.

When Riley and her father returned from his workshop, Riley went straight to Kim's side.

"Everything okay?" She kept her voice too low for Kim's parents to hear.

"Weirdly? Yes. You seem to have a charming effect on people," Kim whispered.

Riley grinned. "What can I say? It's a skill."

"What do you two want to drink?" Edward opened the refrigerator.

"Do you have any beers that aren't obscure craft brands?" Kim said.

"We have Budweiser. But you're missing out if you don't try this new one I've found. It's strawberry and mango flavored."

Knowing from experience that his craft beers often tasted nothing like their flavor names, Kim said, "I'll stick with a Budweiser, please."

"I'll try the craft beer."

Kim glanced at Riley. "You're brave."

"How bad can strawberry and mango be?"

"You might be able to answer that for yourself in five minutes."

"Oh, don't listen to her, Riley. She had one bad experience and now she won't touch the stuff." Her father handed them both their chosen bottle.

"It was not one time—it was at least five. And they were all horrible."

"All beer is horrible," Kim's mother said, scrunching her nose. "I don't know how you all drink the stuff."

"We feel the same way about wine," Kim said.

Her mother shook her head. "You're all so unrefined."

It was almost a joke, and Riley looked surprised for a moment.

"I told you," Kim said, escorting Riley to the dining room after her mother ushered the two of them out so she and Kim's father could serve their plates. "You've had quite the effect on her."

"Or your real mother has been abducted by aliens. That is not the same woman I met at Cake My Day."

"She's trying," Kim said, taking her usual seat at the table. "I don't know what exactly happened to inspire the change, but…I'm going to enjoy it while it lasts."

Watching her mother engage Riley in—albeit occasionally stilted—conversation, a part of Kim felt bad for lying. Riley was only there because Kim had been trying to get a rise out of her mother, and yet, there she was, asking how Riley had ended up becoming a tattoo artist.

It was all a façade, but Riley fit in so seamlessly, it was maddening. Kim had expected it to last for one dinner, and now it had already spiraled. Kim couldn't tell her parents she and Riley had called it quits anytime soon—not after the effort her mother had made.

Kim should have known the whole thing would backfire—but she hadn't imagined it would be because everything was going so well.

Chapter 18

THE WHEELS OF TYLER'S SKATEBOARD screeched over the concrete path running through the center of the park as he skated along beside Riley and Cari. Sunlight streamed through the trees, warming Riley's skin. June brought with it warmer weather, and it hadn't rained for days. She loved their walks, loved hearing Tyler chattering all about what he'd done at school that day, loved seeing his wide-eyed excitement every time he landed a trick he'd been trying to learn for weeks.

"Are you looking forward to the end of the school year?" Riley knew he only had one more week left.

"Yeah! Although it sometimes gets boring hanging out in the bakery all day." His nose wrinkled. "Could I come hang out with you some days?"

"I don't know, buddy. A tattoo studio isn't the best place for a kid."

"But it would be so cool!"

"You know some tattoos take hours, right? You'd be bored!"

"I wouldn't. I'd—woah!"

An unleashed dog raced out in front of them. In his shock—and haste to avoid hitting it—Tyler leaned back too far on his board and toppled over, crashing hard to the concrete and lying in a crumpled heap.

His scream as he landed would haunt Riley.

Cari whined. Riley crouched beside him. Tyler's eyes were filled with tears, his face pale as he cradled his left arm. His wrist was already swelling—Riley was no doctor, but it looked broken.

"Shit, Tyler, come here." Riley helped him shuffle to the edge of the path. With guilt churning in her stomach, Riley reached for her phone. "I'm going to call your mom, okay?"

He nodded through the little sobs he was making, and Riley rubbed a hand across his back as she lifted her phone to her ear. As it rang, Cari sniffed Tyler's face and licked away a tear, and Tyler turned his head to bury his face in her fur.

"Hey, Riley. Everything okay?"

"No, I... Tyler's had an accident in the park," Riley said, and Kim drew in a sharp breath. "I think he might have broken his arm. I don't know what to do."

"I'll be right there. And I'll call John—he has a car; he can drive us to the hospital. Where are you?"

Riley glanced around for an obvious landmark. "We're near the café where we had ice cream."

"Okay, I won't be long." She hung up.

"Your mom is on her way," Riley told him. "Can I have another look at your arm?"

It was bruising. And fast. It was going to hurt when he moved. Riley needed to stabilize it somehow. "I'm going to try something, okay, Tyler? It might hurt now, but I think it'll help in the long run."

"O-okay."

Riley shrugged out of her jacket and, as gently as she could, maneuvered Tyler's injured arm into the hood. He whimpered, and it sent a dagger straight into her heart. Riley found herself fighting tears, too. "I know, Tyler. I'm so sorry."

She tied the arms of her jacket over Tyler's right shoulder to finish her makeshift sling and was inspecting her handiwork when Kim reached them, panting like she'd sprinted all three blocks.

"Oh, sweetheart." Kim dropped to her knees beside her son, worry painted across her face.

Guilt ate further into Riley, though she knew she couldn't have done anything to prevent the accident. The dog had come out of nowhere and disappeared as quickly. Riley hadn't even seen its owner—they certainly hadn't bothered to come over to see if Tyler was okay.

Kim turned to her. "Will you help me get him to the parking lot?"

"Yeah."

"Wait," Tyler said, sniffling, as he was helped to his feet. "Don't forget my skateboard."

"Your—" Exasperation was in Kim's voice as she turned to look for it.

Riley bent to scoop it up and tuck it beneath her arm.

"You'll be lucky if I ever let you skate again, young man," Kim said, wrapping her arm around Tyler's back to help support him and motioning for Riley to do the same.

Together, they made it to the parking lot as a silver sedan was screeching to a halt, parking haphazardly over two spaces. Riley recognized John scrambling out of the driver's seat, and she assumed the blonde woman with him was Rebecca, his fiancée.

Feeling like she was intruding, Riley took a step back as they approached. They were a family, and she was on the outskirts—she'd let this happen—and it felt uncomfortable to watch.

"Come on, Tyler. Let's get you to the hospital." John and Rebecca helped him to the backseat.

"I'm sorry," Riley said, her voice choked when Tyler's face contorted in pain as John put on his seatbelt. "I didn't...I should've watched him more closely. Grabbed him as he fell."

Kim turned to her and settled a warm hand on Riley's arm. "It wasn't your fault. It could've happened while anyone was watching him."

The words did little to make Riley feel better. "Will you let me know how he is?"

"Of course." Kim gave her arm one last squeeze before slipping into the back seat beside her son, smoothing his hair away from his forehead.

John shut the door behind her and gave Riley a nod before climbing behind the wheel.

Riley watched them drive away, with Cari pressed close to her shins and Tyler's skateboard still under her arm.

———— ⋈ ————

Kim rubbed her eyes as John's car pulled up outside her apartment block. After spending five hours in the hospital—waiting for Tyler to be seen, waiting for X-rays, and getting his cast—she was ready to crawl into bed.

It had all gotten to be too much for Tyler, too, who had passed out as soon as they'd gotten into the car, the pain meds kicking in.

"I'll carry him upstairs," John said when he pulled to a stop at the curb outside. "I don't want to wake him too much."

Kim didn't argue, and they left Rebecca running the engine as they made their way upstairs.

"Would you mind putting him to bed?" Kim said as they reached her floor. "I'd like to let Riley know he's okay." Kim had sent Riley a text earlier, but she knew seeing Kim in person would put Riley more at ease.

Riley had looked so panicked—almost as panicked as Kim had felt—and Kim wanted to reassure her.

"Sure."

Kim let John into her apartment and left him to it before she knocked lightly on Riley's door. She might already be in bed—it was late.

But Riley opened it after a few seconds. "Again, I'm so sorry," was the first thing she said, her face drawn.

"And, again, it wasn't your fault." Kim handed back the jacket Riley had used to make a sling.

"I gave your kid a broken radius."

Shattered was the technical diagnosis the doctor had given, but Kim had chosen not to burden Riley with that level of detail. She already felt guilty enough.

"Technically, he gave it to himself. And now that the shock of it has worn off, he's doing well. He's excited to show you his cast, and his biggest disappointment is that he's not going to be able to play for his soccer team until later in the summer."

She still wouldn't look Kim in the eye, so she reached out to cup Riley's cheek and guided her head up, refusing to let her look away. "I swear to you, Riley, he's fine. I'd let you see it for yourself if he weren't currently passed out. But come over in the morning before you go to work."

"So I'm not banned from seeing him again?" Riley leaned into Kim's touch.

Kim laughed, caressing Riley's check with her thumb. "No! You didn't do anything wrong." But her words did nothing to soften Riley's face. "Besides, do you think he'd ever let me ban you? He loves you."

That earned Kim the flicker of a smile.

"Please don't feel bad, okay? Like I said—it could've happened at any time, there was nothing you could do, and, most importantly, he's okay."

A throat cleared from somewhere behind them, and Riley reared away from Kim as if she'd been burned.

Kim turned to find John standing in the hall. Remembering her last conversation with him there—John thinking she and Riley were a couple, and Kim's staunch denial—Kim hated the way her cheeks warmed, like she'd been caught doing something she shouldn't.

"I'll let you get back to your night," Kim told Riley.

"Okay. I'll see you tomorrow." Riley closed her door.

John's lips curved into an amused smile, and Kim narrowed her eyes. "What?"

"Nothing."

"Something."

"You two looked very…cozy. For just friends. Are you sure you're *fake* dating and not for-real dating?"

Kim bristled. "I told you. We're just friends."

"If you say so. Regardless, it's good to see she cares so much about Tyler. She looked spooked earlier."

"Yeah. I think the guilt will take a while to fade." Kim remembered every scraped knee from Tyler's childhood. She'd always looked at the cuts and bruises and chastised herself for not catching him before he fell.

"Make sure she knows it's not her fault."

"I'm trying my best."

"All right. I'd better get back to Rebecca. I'll see you at the weekend—let me know how Tyler gets on."

"I will. Thank you for being there tonight."

"Anytime." He drew Kim into a fleeting hug. "You know that."

Kim watched John stride toward the elevator before going to check on Tyler. John had managed to wrangle him into a pair of pajamas, but he'd soon fallen back asleep, his chest rising and falling steadily. His cast was balanced on a pillow, and Kim hoped he'd sleep through the night without pain.

⁂

Riley smiled when Tyler opened Kim's door the next morning.

He was paler than usual, but he looked a lot better than the last time Riley had seen him.

"Riley! Look!" He brandished his blue cast toward her. "Do you like the color?"

"I love it."

"It matches my favorite pair of shoes." He pointed to a pair of sneakers beside the door.

"How are you feeling? Does it hurt?"

"No."

"You don't have to lie to me, you know. It's okay to say yes."

"A little," he said. "But it's not so bad." Hopefully, he peered around Riley's legs. "Where's Cari?"

"I didn't want her to knock your arm if it was sore."

Tyler looked disappointed, but he nodded. "Okay. Do you want to come in? Mom's in the shower."

"And you opened the door?"

"She said you were coming over and that I could invite you in. I checked the peephole before I answered."

"Good to see you have some sense of self-preservation. If only you could have that when you're skateboarding, too."

He stuck his tongue out at her, and Riley was glad she could joke about it—even if she had had one too many nightmares about Tyler's scream.

She followed Tyler inside, and he led her to the dining table and the bowl of cereal he'd clearly been halfway through when Riley had knocked.

"You know, since you won't give me a tattoo," Tyler said as they sat, and Riley was wary of what he was going to say next, "will you decorate my cast?"

"I can do that." It was the least Riley could do. "What do you want me to draw?"

"I don't know. Something cool."

"I'm going to need you to be more specific than that, Tyler." She chuckled. "Tell you what: why don't you think about it today, and then I can make you a design like I would for a real tattoo."

"What's he asking you for this time?" Kim walked into the room wearing sweats and an oversized tee. With wet hair curling around her shoulders, all dressed down and casual, she took Riley's breath away.

"She's gonna decorate my cast!"

"Is she, now?" Kim settled a hand on Tyler's shoulder, a sparkle in her eye as she looked at Riley.

Riley swallowed the lump in her throat as their eyes met, and she forced herself to speak. "As long as you don't have a problem with that."

"Not at all."

"Great. You guys could swing by the studio tonight if you're free? My shift finishes at five, so any time after that will work."

"Will Stephen be okay with it?"

Riley smiled. "Stephen hasn't stopped raving about your cake since he took his first bite—he would be more than okay with it."

"Okay. Then I guess we'll see you tonight."

Tyler beamed.

"I'll leave you to eat your breakfast in peace, Tyler. I'm glad you're feeling better."

Kim waved goodbye, and Riley returned to her apartment to grab Cari. She had a busy day of appointments, but she already knew Tyler was going to be her favorite one of them all.

Chapter 19

TYLER HAD BEEN TALKING NONSTOP about Riley since getting home from school, and Kim was relieved to let him drag her down the street to the tattoo studio. This time, she used the front entrance, stepping into a charming reception area filled with plush leather armchairs. From behind the large desk, a Black man with a bald head and kind eyes smiled at them.

"Kim, I presume?" he said. "I'm Stephen. Riley said you'd be coming—with a special VIP customer, no less." Stephen glanced over the edge of the desk at Tyler. "Have you decided what you want on your cast?"

"I think so." Tyler clutched tight to his chest the notebook he'd doodled in while he'd been waiting for Kim to finish things up at the bakery.

"Good. Don't tell Riley this, because her head is already big enough"—Stephen lowered his voice to a whisper—"but Riley is my best artist. You'll have the coolest-looking cast in town when she's through with it."

Tyler smiled so wide, Kim wouldn't be surprised if his cheeks hurt.

"I'll take you through to the back." He came around the side of the desk. "Riley's just tidying up."

"Thank you." Kim lifted the box she held toward him. "I, um, I brought cupcakes. As a thank-you for letting us come tonight."

Stephen's eyes brightened. "Cupcakes, you say? I can take those off your hands. Put them somewhere safe."

"Somewhere you can eat them all without anyone else knowing, you mean?" Riley appeared in the hallway Stephen had been about to take them through.

"Would I do such a thing?"

Riley grinned. "Probably. But you can keep them. Though if Tess finds out, she might never forgive you."

Stephen looked thoughtfully at the box. "I guess I could share one. Or two."

"I'll leave that decision to you." Riley glanced at Tyler and Kim. "You two ready?"

"Yeah!" Tyler scampered toward her, and Kim followed a few steps behind as Riley led them to her room.

Cari was curled up in the dog bed, but when she saw Tyler, she raced over to him, her tail wagging. Kim received a less enthusiastic greeting, but she didn't mind.

"Okay, Tyler. Have you thought about what you want me to draw?"

He presented Riley with his notebook. "I have some ideas."

"Wow, buddy, these are amazing! Come over here." Riley led Tyler over to her desk. "Let me draw some things, and you can decide if you like them, okay?"

Tyler nodded, watching with rapt attention as Riley sketched out a design.

Leaving them to it, Kim perused the photographs on the walls, letting herself take in the details in a way she hadn't had time to before.

"You asked me last time what my favorite was, but I never asked you," Riley said when Kim came to a stop beside her desk.

"I like the dragon." She pointed to the outline on someone's thigh, the black dragon's mouth open wide, ready to spit fire.

"I could design you a similar one, if you wanted."

"I think it I was ever going to get one, I'd be better off starting with something small."

"Nah." Riley's eyes were twinkling in the bright lights of her studio. "Better to throw yourself in at the deep end before you talk yourself out of it."

Kim wasn't so sure she agreed.

"Mom! You haven't looked at what Riley's going to draw."

Kim glanced at the notebook on Riley's desk. The roughly sketched scene was a mishmash of superheroes, skateboards, and Tyler's favorite fictional characters—and sitting front and center was a cartoon-style dog that was unmistakably Cari.

Not for the first time, Kim was in awe of the lengths Riley was willing to go to for Tyler. Some would say she was doing this because she felt guilty about Tyler's accident, but Kim knew better.

Riley was doing this because she *wanted* to. Because even after a long, hard day at work, nothing made her happier than spending a couple of hours letting a nine-year-old talk her ear off. Because Riley cared about Tyler, more than Kim could have ever imagined possible.

Both she and Tyler were so lucky Riley had stumbled into their lives.

"Wow, Riley, that's incredible. How long will it take?" Kim was no expert, but it didn't look like the easiest of designs—especially to draw onto a cast.

Riley bit her lip. "I'm not sure. An hour? Two, max? Which I appreciate could be boring for you, so if you want to go back to your place, I can drop Tyler off later."

Tempting, but... "I'd like to see you work." As someone with no artistic ability whatsoever, seeing Riley transform the sketch from the page onto the cast would be fascinating.

Riley seemed touched. "Okay. Before we get started, is anyone hungry? I could order some takeout."

Tyler's stomach rumbled, and Riley grinned.

"I'll take that as a yes."

Kim munched on a slice of pepperoni pizza and relaxed into Riley's desk chair.

In the middle of the room, Tyler lay reclined in Riley's leather tattooing chair, his cast supported on its arm. Cari had her head in his lap, giving him puppy dog eyes as he ate his own slice of pizza.

Riley had her head bent over his cast, careful not to jostle him as she drew over the plaster with a fine-tipped black marker. Her tongue poked between her lips as she concentrated, the tiny frown between her eyebrows suggesting she wasn't as happy with it as she wanted to be.

"It's a lot harder to draw on this than on skin," Riley said, seemingly more to herself than anyone else.

Tyler didn't seem disconcerted. "It'll still look awesome."

Riley's lips curved into a smile. "Thank you, buddy."

"I can't wait to show everyone at school tomorrow. They're gonna be so jealous!"

Kim was relieved the break wasn't bothering him too much. It was a good thing it was his left hand.

"Mom, do you think they'll let me keep the cast when they take it off?"

"I'm not sure, Tyler, but we can ask."

"You might not want to keep it." Riley leaned back and traded her pen for another slice of pizza. "You've got to keep it on for, what, eight weeks? It'll be gross by then."

"I don't care—I want to keep it."

"Okay, if you want to keep your gross and stinky cast, you go right ahead."

"It won't be stinky!"

"How do you know?"

"Because I'm not stinky."

Riley wiggled her eyebrows. "Are you sure?"

"Yes!" Tyler looked affronted, and Riley's face split into another grin.

Kim loved seeing the two of them together.

"I don't know, kid. You can't get that cast wet, right? So how are you gonna keep your arm clean?"

"By not getting it dirty."

"Maybe we should get you a plastic bag to keep wrapped around it." Riley tossed the last of her crust to Cari—who devoured it in record time—and picked her pen back up.

"But no one will be able to see the drawings."

"Saran wrap?"

"No!" Tyler giggled. "You're silly."

"You're the silly one, mister broken arm."

"It's not a big deal."

"Not a big deal? You scared the crap out of me." Riley glanced toward Kim. "And your mom."

"Are you really never going to let me skate again?" Tyler turned his best imploring gaze on Kim.

"We'll see." But Kim already knew she would. She couldn't keep him wrapped in cotton wool his whole life—she didn't want to be one of those helicopter parents who smothered their children, and she couldn't take one of Tyler's favorite hobbies away from him. "But it's not something we need to worry about yet, is it? You'll have to get your cast off first."

"I guess."

Tyler's attention turned back to what Riley was drawing, so Kim's did, too. She climbed to her feet for a better look. It was coming along nicely, and Kim didn't know what Riley had been complaining about—it looked incredible, and she could tell Tyler was already over the moon.

Riley finished off drawing the whiskers of Cari's face. "What do you think?" she asked Kim.

"It doesn't matter what I think," Kim said, her voice soft, "but for what it's worth, I think it's wonderful. You're incredibly talented."

Riley's cheeks were tinged pink, and she ducked her head back over Tyler's arm. "Thank you."

Kim returned to her seat, smiling at Riley's bashfulness. She didn't think it would be too much longer before Riley was finished, and she stretched out, content to watch her complete her artwork.

———◇———

Riley turned the key in the lock of her old apartment, a sense of nostalgia immediately engulfing her.

It had been her first place, after all, where she and Bea had struggled for those first few years until Riley had landed on her feet. She loved it, and even though she loved her new place, too, this apartment would always have a special place in her heart.

It helped that inside, things had all been changed since Riley had moved out. Bea and Ash had upgraded most of the furniture—including the blue leather couch they both waved at her over the back of—and had rearranged things to make it their own.

"Hey. I brought wine." Riley brandished the champagne she'd picked up from the liquor store on her way over.

Bea raised her eyebrows. "That looks fancy. Are we celebrating something?"

Over Bea's shoulder, Ash shot Riley a warning look, and Riley knew what she was saying.

Do not ruin this.

"You think I'd splurge on you guys?" Riley brushed off Bea's question and headed to the refrigerator as she unclipped Cari's leash. "I just know how to buy bottles that look fancy."

In fact, it was the most expensive bottle Riley had ever bought, but Ash and Bea deserved the best.

"How was work?" Bea said when Riley joined them.

"Nothing special. Did you get your grant application finished?" Riley didn't know how Bea had gotten to be so smart, but she was so proud of her—even if she had no idea what she was talking about sometimes.

"Yup."

"And how does it feel being free for the summer, Ash?"

"Great."

"I don't know how she's going to keep herself occupied, though." Bea turned to Ash with a fond look. "She's been restless all evening."

Ash managed a laugh, and Riley hoped Bea couldn't tell how forced it was. Ash was wracked with nerves, but she didn't need to be. Bea wasn't going to turn her down.

"How's Tyler doing, Riley?" Ash was clearly desperate to change the subject.

"He's fine. Kim said he's been showing off his cast to everyone he meets."

"That's cute. It sounds like he idolizes you."

"And Riley idolizes his mother," Bea said.

Riley tossed a cushion at her. "I do not."

"Does anyone want a drink?" Ash's hands were trembling faintly as she climbed to her feet and brushed some of Cari's hair off her shirt.

"No, thanks," Riley said, pulling out her phone and trying to angle it toward Bea as surreptitiously as possible—she needed to get this moment on video.

When Ash returned, she was going to pop the question.

"Could I have a water please?" Bea turned her attention to Riley, frowning. "Why are you looking at me like that?"

"Like what?"

"I don't know. But can you stop it? You're freaking me out."

"I'm not doing anything!"

"You are! What's the matter with you?"

"Nothing! This is my usual face."

"Thank you," Bea said as Ash set a bottle of water on the coffee table. "What are you doing?" she said as Ash fell to one knee and pulled out the ring box she'd hidden behind her back.

"Bea," Ash started, tears already shining in her eyes as she opened the box. Inside, the beautiful diamond ring Riley had gone with her to pick out sparkled as it caught the light. "You are the most wonderful woman I've ever met. I count my lucky stars every day I get to wake next to you. I knew the first moment I laid eyes on you that you were special, and I couldn't believe my luck when you let me take you out for that first coffee. The last three years with you have been the best years of my life, but I want more. I love you so much, and I want a lifetime with you.

"So I have another question to ask, and I hope you say yes to this, too—Bea Foster, will you marry me?"

"Yes." Bea launched herself off the couch and into Ash's arms, throwing her arms around her neck. "Yes, yes, yes, yes."

Riley decided to give them a moment of privacy as they kissed and grabbed the bottle of champagne and three glasses in the kitchen. She had to wipe a few tears of her own away, filled with so much happiness, she could burst.

"It *was* a fancy bottle!" Bea said when Riley returned. She and Ash were relocating themselves to the couch. "You liar."

"Well, I couldn't give the game away, could I? Ash would never forgive me."

"How long have you been keeping this a secret?"

"I've been planning on asking you for months, but I only told Riley a few weeks ago. I didn't want her to have to keep it from you for too long in case she caved."

"Rude," Riley said.

At the same time, Bea said: "Makes perfect sense."

Twisting the cork off the bottle, Riley tossed it to Cari for her to chew as she poured them all a glass. "Cheers," she said, raising hers toward them. "I'm so happy for you." She cleared her throat, tight with tears. "I can't wait to see you get married."

They all clinked glasses, and as the two of them cuddled on the couch together, Riley's heart ached at the way they looked at one another, wishing she had someone who looked at her like she held the stars in her hands.

Unbidden, Riley thought of Kim and took a gulp of champagne, washing the thought away. She and Kim would never be like that, and the more Riley reminded herself of that, the better.

Chapter 20

As a customer approached Cake My Day's front counter, Kim hopped off her stool, eager for something to do. It was around two and still quiet, before they would start to get dribs and drabs of parents on the school pickup run.

"Hi," Kim said as the Black man stopped to admire the display cases. They were filled with white chocolate and raspberry cupcakes, gooey chocolate brownies, and a handful of salted caramel cookies, the only treats remaining after a busy morning.

"What can I get for you?"

"I was actually hoping to see someone—does Tina work here?"

Kim eyed the man with renewed interest. Tall—at least six foot two—his hair was shaved short, stubble covering his sharp jawline.

"I'll just go and get her." Kim spun on her heel and moved toward the kitchen.

Inside, Tina was singing along to the radio as she whisked a bowl of chocolate buttercream for their latest cupcake batch.

"Hey Tina, someone's here to see you."

"For me?" Tina frowned as she set down her bowl and dusted off her hands on her apron. "Who?"

"No idea." Kim followed Tina back out to the front of the bakery.

"Aaron!" Tina screeched when she saw him.

Well, that answered that question. Kim watched with interest as Tina swept Aaron into a tight hug.

"Tina, it is so good to see you."

"And you. It's been, what, fifteen years?"

"At least!"

Kim cleared her throat, and Tina glanced between her and Aaron. "Aaron, this is Kim, my business partner. Kim, this is Aaron. We went to high school together."

"Many years ago," he said. "I moved to Atlanta for a job a while ago, but I just came back. I thought I'd see if Tina was still around, and she said I should come check out this place. She always talked about opening something like this one day. I'm so pleased for you both."

"Thank you," Tina said. "Can I get you a drink?"

"I wouldn't say no to a cappuccino."

"I'll make it," Kim said. "You two sit, catch up."

When Kim delivered the coffee, Aaron thanked her and smiled at her with warm brown eyes. He was handsome, with a sprinkling of gray in his hair.

She returned to the counter, letting them chat as she served the next few customers who came through the door.

"Nice to meet you," Aaron called out as he was leaving, lifting a hand to wave goodbye to Kim after hugging Tina.

"You, too." Once Aaron had left, Kim turned to Tina. "He seems nice."

"He is." Tina looked at her thoughtfully. "He's single, too. He and his wife divorced a couple of years ago."

"And you're telling me this because…?"

"Because he's a decent guy! And I think the two of you might have a lot in common. Plus," she paused, "he asked me to put in a good word for him. He said he thinks you're gorgeous."

Kim felt her cheeks warm. "He did?"

"Yes. Look, no pressure, obviously, but if you were interested, I could set the two of you up. Think about it."

Kim did, as she went about the rest of her day. Whipping up a batch of brownies, Kim thought about Aaron's warm smile, and how she hadn't been on a date since the disaster with Darren. Aaron had seemed nice enough—and Kim knew Tina wouldn't have suggested they go out if he wasn't—and he was cute.

What was the worst that could happen?

"Okay," Kim told her as she transferred the brownies to the glass counters at the front of the shop. "I'll go for dinner with him."

Tina squealed in excitement. "Yay! Oh, Kim, you're going to love him, I swear. I'll give him your number?"

"Yeah, sure."

"I'm sorry, Kim," John said over the phone. "Rebecca's mom has been rushed into the hospital—I can't watch Tyler tonight."

"No problem," Kim said even though her date with Aaron was rapidly approaching, and she was already nervous enough without having to worry about someone keeping an eye on Tyler for the night. It had been a mistake to schedule it for a week when Tyler was with her. But Aaron was out of town the following two weeks, arranging to move the rest of his things back from Atlanta, and Kim hadn't wanted to wait that long.

"I can find someone else," she told John. "I hope she's okay—let me know if you need anything."

John thanked her and hung up.

Kim turned to Tina, who was wiping the counter before leaving for the night. "You're not by any chance free to watch Tyler later, are you?"

"Sorry, darling, I can't. Nathan's work is throwing some kind of fundraiser, and he hates going to those things alone. What about Riley? I'm sure she'd watch him. She loves the kid."

In truth, after John, Riley should have been at the top of Kim's list of people to ask. And the only reason she hadn't already her was because…well, Kim hadn't told Riley she was going on a date.

She didn't know why—it wasn't like it was a secret she needed to keep. But Kim hadn't known how to bring it up, so she hadn't, and then it was the day of the date and she still hadn't said anything.

"Yeah. Yeah, I could do that," she replied absently.

Tina scrutinized her face, eyebrows drawn. "What's the matter?"

"Nothing. I just… I haven't told her I'm going out with Aaron tonight."

Tina's frown deepened. "What? Why? I thought you two were close."

"We are. It just hasn't come up."

"Sure."

Kim whirled around to face Tina. "What's that supposed to mean?"

"I dunno. Maybe the reason you didn't tell her was because you didn't want her to know."

"Why wouldn't I want her to know?"

"You tell me." Tina's gaze was glued to Kim's face.

"It slipped my mind, okay? You don't need to read anything into it." Kim's voice had turned unintentionally sharp.

Tina raised an eyebrow. "Have I touched a nerve?"

"No."

"You know I can always tell when you're lying. Are you… Did something happen between you two?"

Kim hadn't told Tina about Riley pretending to be her girlfriend, and she was glad about that now. "No! Why would you ask that?"

"Just curious."

"Well, can you go and be curious somewhere else?"

Tina scoffed and walked away. Kim knew she'd have to apologize later—she'd just been a brat—but she couldn't handle Tina any longer.

Her reaction to Tina's pressing didn't have to mean anything.

Sighing, Kim pulled out her phone and opened her message thread with Riley.

Hey, I know this is super short notice, but is there any chance you'd be free to watch Tyler tonight? From around 6?

Kim pressed send, having no idea what she'd do if Riley already had plans. But it was her own stupid fault for not asking Riley in the first place. She should have told Riley about Aaron. Sure, they'd only arranged the date three days ago, but Kim had seen Riley since. They were supposed to be friends, and wasn't that something you told friends? They'd even bonded over Kim's terrible dating history when they'd first met.

Kim didn't know what was wrong with her.

Her phone buzzed with Riley's reply, and Kim breathed a sigh of relief.

Sure. I'll be at your place at 6. You doing anything nice?

Thank you, you're a lifesaver. I have a date.

There. She'd told Riley. And Kim had no idea why she'd made it into such a big deal.

I hope this one is better than the last one.

Kim didn't know what she'd been so worried about.

———— ✦ ————

Even though her stomach was roiling, Riley knocked on Kim's door at six on the dot.

The last thing she wanted was to see Kim dressed to the nines, ready for her date.

It stung that Kim hadn't mentioned it until the last minute. Maybe they weren't as close as Riley had thought.

And it stung, too, to send Kim off into the arms of a stranger, when Riley wished more than anything it was her taking Kim to dinner. Riley was trying her hardest to push her feelings for Kim down deep, but it was hard when she saw her nearly every other day.

"You'll have to be on your best behavior," she told Cari when she heard footsteps coming. "No sitting on couches that aren't ours."

It was Tyler who opened the door, bending to give Cari a huge hug. "Hi, Riley. You can come in—Mom is still getting ready. She's stressing about what to wear."

Riley understood that feeling. She kicked off her shoes by the door and followed Tyler over to the couch. "What do you want to do tonight, buddy? You want to watch a movie?"

"Yeah! We have popcorn."

"I think you'll need to have proper food first. Can't have your mom thinking I'm a terrible babysitter."

"I'm not a baby."

"But *child sitter* sounds so much more sinister." Riley reached out to tickle him. "You can choose the movie. I hate making decisions."

"I want *Into the Spiderverse*."

"Tyler, you've seen that movie so many times, I swear you must be able to quote it from start to finish." Kim emerged in a blue and white jumpsuit that rendered Riley speechless. Her hair was down, curled to frame her face, and Riley thought for the thousandth time that she was beautiful.

"It's my favorite!"

"Yeah, yeah." Kim ruffled his hair, and Tyler ducked away, curling into Riley's side. "Are you going to behave yourself tonight?"

"I always do."

"Hm." Kim turned her gaze to Riley. "Thank you again for doing this."

"It's no trouble. We're gonna have fun, right, Tyler?"

"Yeah."

"Help yourself to whatever you need, Riley. There's leftover lasagna in the refrigerator or pizzas in the freezer for you two to eat—or feel free to order something if you want. I trust Tyler to show you where everything is."

"We'll be fine." Riley might not be an expert babysitter, but Tyler wasn't exactly high-maintenance. "Go, have fun on your date. You look beautiful."

Kim's cheeks turned pink as she glanced at herself, fiddling with the zipper of her jumpsuit. "You think so?"

"Yeah." Riley swallowed around the lump in her throat. "He's a lucky guy, whoever he is."

"Thank you." She glanced at her watch. "I'd better go. I'll see you both later." Kim kissed Tyler atop his head—she had to lean close to Riley to do it, and her cheek brushed Riley's. Riley's face burned, remembering the feeling of Kim's lips pressed to her skin.

She was in trouble.

Real big trouble, and she had no idea how to drag herself out of it.

Kim threw a blazer over the jumpsuit and headed for the door. Riley breathed easier when it had closed behind her.

"You hungry, buddy? Should I put some food in?"

"Okay."

Riley tossed him the TV remote as she climbed to her feet. "You can find the movie." Opening Kim's refrigerator, Riley's mouth watered at the sight of the lasagna. Pasta dishes were her weakness, and it looked incredible. If Kim was as good a cook as she was a baker, Riley needed to try it. "Does lasagna sound okay with you?"

"Yeah."

After putting it in the oven, Riley returned to the couch. To her surprise, as soon as she sat, Tyler was back by her side, burrowing under her arm and wrapping his own around her waist, resting his cast in her lap. Riley was careful not to jostle it.

He'd hugged her before but never like that, and it made her worry. "Is everything okay, Tyler?"

He let the question sit for a minute, and Riley waited, trusting that if he wanted to talk to her, he would when he was ready.

When he did speak, the words were muffled against Riley's shoulder. "I don't want my mom to go on a date."

"Oh." Riley tried not to think about the fact they were talking about a woman *she* would like to date if things had worked out differently. "How come?"

"I dunno. It's weird."

"Your dad has moved on, though." Riley kept her voice gentle, feeling like she was out of her depth.

"Yeah. And I like Rebecca. I guess it's hard to think of my mom with someone else. I never have before. And I thought…I thought maybe you and her would end up together."

He peered up at her, something hopeful in his eyes, and Riley swallowed, her throat feeling tight.

Maybe a part of me was hoping for that, too. But instead, she said, "Why would you think that, Tyler?"

Tyler bit his lip. "Because you make her happy. Happier than I've ever seen her. She's always smiling when she's with you or after she's seen you. She talks about you when you're not around. She went to *two* soccer games to watch you, and she hates soccer."

Riley didn't know what to say. If she had felt out of her depth a moment ago, it was nothing compared to having Tyler's expectant gaze on her face.

"She came to those games because of you," she told him.

He shook his head. "She could've had my dad bring me. He loves soccer. He goes to games all the time. But she didn't. She went because she likes you. And she took you as a date to Aunt Ellie's birthday dinner because she likes you."

"Your mom and I are just friends, Tyler," Riley said, though she wished more than anything they could be more. "I'm sorry."

Tyler looked away, a pout on his mouth. His next question made her heart ache.

"If my mom gets a new boyfriend, will you still hang out with us?"

"Of course I will."

Would it hurt? Yes, but Riley was no stranger to having her heart broken. And she needed to move on sooner rather than later. Maybe the existence of a boyfriend would help her brain finally get the message.

"I'm not going anywhere," she said.

"Promise?"

Riley squeezed him close. "I promise."

"Will you promise me something else?"

Riley looked at him, wary. "Depends what it is."

"Will you come to my birthday party next Saturday? I already asked my mom, and she said I could ask you. She said I had to warn you my grandmother will be there, though."

Riley chuckled—and wondered what her and Kim's dynamic would be if her date went well. Surely, she'd want to tell her family she'd met a nice man. Martha would probably throw another party.

But that wasn't something for Riley to worry about yet. And she'd love to see Tyler's face when Edward gifted him the skateboard. She'd worked on the design for weeks before she'd been happy with it.

"I'd love to come."

"Yay! And on my actual birthday, I'm going to the zoo with my mom, dad, and Rebecca. Will you come then, too?"

Honored to be on that exclusive list, Riley smiled.

"I wouldn't miss it for the world."

Chapter 21

"SO, TELL ME ABOUT HOW you and Tina went about opening Cake My Day."

Aaron smiled at Kim from across the table while they waited for their entrees to arrive.

The Italian restaurant was bustling—Kim was impressed Aaron had managed to get a reservation on short notice. The low chatter of voices mixed with the clanging of cutlery and the soft music playing in the background.

"It's a long story."

Her nerves had eased, somewhat, when she'd met Aaron outside the restaurant. He was sweet, had pulled out her chair, and hadn't tried to commandeer the conversation—or order for her. He was a great guy, and he was doing all the right things, but Kim couldn't shake the feeling that something was missing.

Still, Kim was powering through because this was still the best date she'd had in ages. Maybe ever.

"We met at a cake-decorating class." Kim fiddled with her glass of beer, twisting it between her fingers. She needed to shake this off. What was wrong with her?

Glancing across the table, Kim realized that Aaron was looking at her expectantly, waiting for her to elaborate.

"Most people were there for fun, but not me and Tina." Kim smiled, remembering that time of her life fondly, even if juggling a toddler, a full-time job, and a cake class had been one hell of a challenge. "We took it so seriously—and were so competitive with one another when it came to any of the activities. We got to chatting one night after class, went for a drink, and figured out we had a lot in common."

"You are similar," Aaron said. "I can see why you're such good friends."

"After that, we were inseparable. I was working in a day care, and she had an office job, and both of us were miserable. I'd always wanted to run my own place, make my own cakes, and be around people. And I think Tina was the same. So, we started saving money and drafting business plans. Six years down the line, we found the perfect storefront to rent."

Kim knew she'd been doing most of the talking. "What about you? Why did you move back from Atlanta?"

"It wasn't for work," Aaron said. "My mother was diagnosed with dementia a few weeks ago. My father isn't around, so I decided to move back to help take care of her. And to spend more time with her before she forgets who I am."

Flooded with sympathy, Kim stretched a hand across the table to cover Aaron's. "I'm so sorry. It's a horrible disease."

For a moment, she let her touch linger. His skin was soft and warm, but his hand felt too big beneath her own, and she soon pulled it back and settled it in her lap. The last time she'd held hands with someone had been at her sister's birthday dinner—Riley's hands were slight, the same size as Kim's, and had never felt wrong in her own.

"It is. But she's still lucid at the moment, so I'm going to enjoy it while it lasts. And I'm privileged enough to be able to work three days a week."

Forcing herself to concentrate on Aaron, Kim pushed thoughts of Riley away. "What's being a mechanical engineer like?"

"It's fine. I don't love it like you love what you do, but I'm good at it, and it pays the bills. It's allowed me to live the kind of life I've always wanted. Although there are some things missing. Like, I've always wanted kids, but it never worked out between me and my ex-wife. Do you have kids?"

Relieved her status as a mother wasn't going to be a dealbreaker, Kim smiled. "I do. I have a son, Tyler."

"Tell me about him," Aaron said, sounding genuinely interested and not like he was asking because he knew he should.

"He's nine, and he's the greatest thing that's ever happened to me." Kim could talk about Tyler all day long. She wondered what he and Riley were up to—*Into the Spiderverse* must be nearly over. He'd probably have Riley watching another Marvel movie next. "His favorite things are superheroes and skateboarding—even though he broke his arm falling off his board last week."

"Oh no! Is he okay?"

"He's fine. He loves his cast—I'm half-worried he's going to try and break something else when he gets it off so he can get another one."

"I broke my leg when I was a kid. I loved getting everyone to sign it."

"I don't think there's any space left on it for anyone to sign. He had a friend of mine draw all over it."

"Are they an artist?"

"She's a tattoo artist." Again, Kim's mind drifted back to Riley and Tyler. Tyler hadn't been his usual self all afternoon, and Kim hoped Riley had been able to cheer him up. He'd looked more content when Kim had left him, at least, snuggled into Riley's side with Cari sitting at his feet.

"I never saw the appeal of tattoos. Like when people are covered in them? I think that's a bit much."

Kim thought of Riley's arms, the intricate patterns swirling over her skin, and had to disagree. "It's not harming anyone."

"No, you're right. That was judgmental of me; I apologize."

Kim couldn't think of a single other man she'd been out with who would have been big enough to admit they were wrong and apologize instead of doubling down, but Kim still didn't feel a spark.

Part of her wished she was with Tyler and Riley, eating popcorn and hearing about Riley's day, not on a date—even with a handsome guy who was making all the right moves and saying all the right things over a bowl of expensive pasta. It couldn't be going better, and yet, Kim wanted it to be over.

Aaron realized the same thing when they were halfway through their meal. "You don't want to be here, do you?" he asked.

Kim was mortified. "No! I do. I'm sorry, I haven't been at my best tonight."

"Would you like to reschedule?"

"I…"

Kim's hesitation was the killing blow, and Aaron smiled through a grimace. "Look, it's okay. I can handle it. Did I do something wrong? Was it what I said about tattoos—you have a lot of them hidden under your lovely outfit, and I've offended you terribly?"

"No! Nothing like that. It's all on me—and, yes, I know that sounds like a line, but it's not. I'm so sorry. I didn't mean to waste your time."

"It's all good." Aaron stayed as genial as ever. "Let's get the check."

He hailed the server, and when they set the bill on the table, Kim was the first to grab it.

"Please, let me," she said. "It's the least I can do."

Aaron didn't argue, and Kim ordered an Uber, relieved that it was two minutes away as they stepped together onto the street outside.

"I don't know what happened tonight," Aaron said, his hands in the pockets of his jacket, "but if you change your mind about me, give me a call."

"I will. I'm sorry."

"Hey, no harm done." He offered Kim one last smile before walking away.

Was she making a terrible mistake? Aaron was amazing—a world away from the men she was used to dating—and she'd ruined things.

But, slipping into the back seat of her Uber, things started clicking into place: why Kim hadn't told Riley about Aaron, why she hadn't been able to stop thinking about Riley all night, why things had felt so easy when Kim had pretended Riley was her girlfriend around her family.

Maybe all this time, it was Riley who Kim should have been dating—for real.

Except...Kim had never had feelings for a woman before. She'd kissed one, once, when she'd been drunk in college, but she hadn't felt anything.

Closing her eyes, Kim thought about what it would be like to kiss Riley. Casting her mind back to when she'd stumbled across Riley kissing her one-night stand in the hallway, Kim imagined what it would feel like to have Riley pressing her against the wall, to have Riley's hand, hot and heavy, on her upper thigh.

She imagined wrapping a hand around Riley's neck and pulling her close, running her fingers through her hair, tracing over the ink staining Riley's skin...and flushed as heat flooded through her.

Okay.

That was not nothing.

Groaning, Kim pressed her overheated forehead against the car window and tried not to scream.

Because this? This was a problem.

How had this happened? How had Riley undone her so thoroughly, without Kim even noticing?

And how had it taken Kim this long to realize that Riley might have been the person she'd been searching for this whole time?

A key clicked in the door, and Riley frowned.

It was early—so early, they had barely finished the movie. Kim hadn't even been gone two hours.

Despite obviously knowing Riley was going to be there, Kim looked surprised to see her when she stepped into the living room. In fact, Kim looked out of it, her cheeks pink. Riley's stomach flipped because was that from her date? Was Kim blushing because he'd kissed her good night downstairs?

Riley wanted to be sick.

"Hey." Riley forced herself to speak. "Did you have fun?"

"It was fine."

Could've fooled me.

Kim's voice was strained, her shoulders hunched, and her eyes firmly focused on the floor. Riley had rarely seen someone look less fine.

"Hi, Mom. Want to play Uno with us?" Tyler waved his handful of cards—much smaller than Riley's after he'd made her draw four times twice in a row.

"Shouldn't you be in bed?"

"In bed?" Tyler frowned. "Mom, it's not even eight yet."

"It's not?" Kim glanced at her watch. "Oh, that's true. Excuse me for a moment."

As Kim disappeared down the hall, Riley and Tyler shared a glance.

"What's wrong with Mom?" Tyler said.

Riley had no answer for him. "I don't know. I'm going to go and see if she's okay."

Tyler nodded, and Riley padded after Kim. The bathroom door was half-open, making light spill out onto the wooden hallway floor. Through the gap, Riley could see Kim leaning over the sink. Her hands were curled around the edge of the basin.

"Kim? Are you okay?"

She jumped at the sound of Riley's voice and whirled around to face her. "I'm fine."

"You're not fine." Riley stepped closer to the door but didn't push it further open. "What's wrong? Did something happen?" Riley's voice trembled, and she curled her hands into fists, fearing the worst. "Did he try something? Do something? Because I'll—"

"He didn't do anything. He was…he was great."

"Oh." Riley deflated. "So what's the problem?"

"There isn't one. I told you, I'm—"

"If you say 'fine' once more…" Riley left a note of warning in her tone. "You're clearly not."

"I just…don't think he's the guy for me. That's all." Kim's voice was firm.

Riley felt like she wasn't going to get anything else out of Kim. She let it go. "Okay."

Riley retreated to the living room and back to her and Tyler's game of Uno.

When Kim joined them a few moments later—after Tyler had thrashed Riley yet again—Kim had changed out of her jumpsuit and into a tank top and a pair of low-hanging sweatpants. Riley didn't know which of the two outfits she preferred on Kim; the woman looked amazing in anything.

"Should I deal you in?" Riley said as she shuffled the cards.

"Sure."

They played three more games, and Kim's gaze strayed Riley's way more than once; it lingered on her skin. There was something different in Kim's eyes, and Riley had no idea what to do with the way it made her stomach churn.

She wanted to ask Kim why she was staring, ask Kim what was wrong, why she'd come home so shaken, but her attempts to find out had already gotten her nowhere.

Whatever it was, Kim didn't want Riley to know, and that was the thing that stung most of all.

"What the hell is wrong with you?" Tina rounded on Kim the second she stepped into the bakery, her hands on her hips and her face twisted into a frown. "Aaron is perfect for you!"

Kim knew she should have been prepared for Tina's irritation, but she'd had a sleepless night, tossing and turning and thinking of Riley's blue eyes whenever she closed her own.

"Clearly not," Kim said, shrugging out of her coat and into her apron.

"What the hell happened? What did he do wrong?"

Kim sighed. "Nothing."

"Then what's the problem?"

"I just don't think we're a good match," Kim said, using the same excuse she'd used with Riley last night. But, unlike Riley, Tina didn't buy it—or wasn't polite enough to pretend, at least.

"Are you kidding? He's smart, well-mannered, good-looking, family-oriented, and loves children," Tina said, ticking them all off on her fingers. "All of which are qualities I know you look for in a guy."

Kim tried hard not to think about the fact that those were all qualities Riley had, too.

"I don't believe you think he's not a good match for you. There's something on your mind. And don't you dare lie to me, Kimberly Jackson. Talk. Now."

Kim bought herself a few moments by wiping the already pristine counter, but when she turned around, Tina was staring at her, eyes narrowed.

"Okay, fine! You…might have been onto something yesterday."

"I need more than that."

"Riley." Kim groaned her name. "Aaron was an amazing guy, and he did everything right, but he…he wasn't Riley."

"Oh, shit." Tina looked floored. "I know I said what I said yesterday, but I didn't…I didn't realize it was true. You like her?"

"Apparently." Kim covered her face with her hands. "I think I have for a while," she said through her fingers, "but I only realized it last night."

Tina settled a hand on the small of Kim's back, and Kim dropped her own to her sides.

"What am I supposed to do?"

Before Tina could answer, the bell above the door jingled, and Kim froze when Riley walked inside, coming for her coffee with Cari in tow.

"Good morning," she said, wiping her feet on the welcome mat. Hearing no response from Kim—who had apparently lost the ability to speak—Riley glanced between Kim and Tina, her eyebrows rising toward her hairline at the look on both their faces. "Is everything okay?"

"Morning!" Tina said, her voice too loud. She sharply elbowed Kim's side.

"Your usual?" Kim said through the sudden tightness in her throat.

"Yes, please."

"I'll make it," Kim said before Tina could move, because she didn't know if she could look Riley in the eye.

She'd tried last night, knew her gaze had lingered—knew Riley had noticed—but Kim hadn't yet figured out how to pretend nothing had changed.

As she made Riley's coffee, Tina and Riley were making small talk behind her, but Kim couldn't focus on a word they were saying.

"Here you go," she said, voice too bright when she set the to-go cup onto the counter.

"Kim, are you okay?" Riley's brows were creased in concern.

She hated making Riley worry. "Yes."

Clearly not believing Kim, Riley pursed her lips before she shook her head and picked up the coffee, leaving three dollars in its place. "See you later."

As soon as Riley left the bakery, Tina smacked Kim's shoulder.

"Ow! What was that for?"

"Are you kidding me? What was *that*? If she didn't already know something's up, she sure as hell does now."

"I know, okay? But I...seem to have forgotten how to act around her."

"You are hopeless. And as for what you're supposed to do now—I guess that's up to you. But you'd better figure it out fast after that performance."

"But I don't know what to do!"

"Do you want to be with her?"

Kim bit her lip, pondering the question that had been at the forefront of her mind all night. "I don't know. I like her a lot, and she's amazing with Tyler. But that worries me, too—he's already so attached. What if we don't work out? What if I realize I'm not into women like that? I don't want to mess either of them around. Besides, I don't know if she feels the same way. She's never given any indication she does. How awkward would it be if I confessed and she said, 'Thanks, but no thanks'?"

"Maybe that's a risk you have to take."

"I think I need some time."

It had been less than twenty-four hours since her universe had turned upside down, and Kim was spiraling. But she'd never been one to make quick or rash decisions—and she sure as hell wasn't going to do it with so much on the line.

She didn't want to jeopardize her friendship with Riley, or Riley's relationship with Tyler.

Not when she wasn't sure what she wanted.

And not when she wasn't sure Riley would want her back.

Chapter 22

A FEW DAYS LATER, RILEY knocked on Kim's door. When Kim answered, wearing pajamas—a white tank top and a pair of black shorts—she looked surprised to see her.

Riley made a conscious effort to keep her gaze away from the long expanse of Kim's bare legs.

"Riley? Is everything okay?"

"Yeah," she said, even though it wasn't. It hadn't been ever since Kim went on that stupid date. And while they still saw one another all the time, it was *different* somehow. Kim had been careful to avoid being alone with Riley, and Riley couldn't for the life of her figure out why.

She'd given up asking. She hated seeing Kim lie to her.

"I wanted to check if you still want me to come to Tyler's birthday party tomorrow. And to the zoo on Sunday."

Kim frowned. "Why wouldn't I want you to come?"

Because it feels like you can't stand being around me anymore. "I dunno." If Kim didn't trust Riley with the truth, Riley didn't owe it in return.

"Do you still want to come? I know my family aren't easy to be around." Kim scrutinized Riley's face. It was the first time Kim had properly looked at Riley in days.

"They weren't too bad. I just thought—I don't know—that maybe you'd want to tell them we'd broken up."

"Oh." Kim's teeth worried at her bottom lip, and Riley ached to know what was on her mind. "I wasn't planning on it. If I told them we'd broken up, they'd wonder why you were there. And you have to be there—Tyler would be upset if you weren't."

Riley didn't know why that hurt. It was Tyler's birthday, after all. Of course that was what Kim should focus on.

"And...I want you to be there," Kim said, so softly that Riley barely heard it.

The quiet admission—the knowledge that Kim still wanted her around—was almost enough to make Riley forget about everything else. "Then I'll see you tomorrow."

"We'll be leaving at half past two."

"Okay." As Kim shifted, ready to shut the door, Riley hesitated. She wasn't ready to say goodbye. She had to try and find out what was going on one last time. "Kim, I... Have I done something wrong?"

Anguish flashed across Kim's face. "No. God, no, Riley, you haven't done anything. I know...I know I haven't been right lately, and I'm sorry. I promise I'll tell you soon, I just...not yet."

"Okay." Riley felt anything but. Kim's cryptic answers made her head swim. "I'll see you tomorrow."

"Good night, Riley."

The door closed, and Riley let out a heavy sigh, unsure which version of Kim she'd get in the morning.

⸻

As Kim, Riley, and Tyler sat in the back of an Uber on their way to the house her ex-husband shared with his new fiancée, Kim marveled at what an exceptionally bad idea this was.

It was worse than the last time Riley had accompanied Kim to a family event because at least then, when she had pretended Riley was her girlfriend, Kim hadn't wanted it to be true. Not consciously, at least.

For the last week, Kim had been trying so hard not to think of Riley at all, but for the rest of the day, they'd be side by side, acting like a couple, and Kim didn't know if she would manage to survive the day intact.

"Are you excited for today, Tyler?" Kim was relieved Riley had broken the awkward silence.

"Yeah! It's gonna be awesome. And I'm glad you're coming." Tyler gazed at Riley with open adoration. He loved her so much, and Kim had done nothing but try to keep Riley at arm's length the last few days—avoiding being alone with her, keeping their conversations brief and boring, steering well clear of any deeper topics, and insisting she was fine whenever Riley asked her what was wrong—while she tried to figure out what she was going to do.

Which she was no closer to doing.

"I told you I wouldn't miss it." Riley looked at Tyler the same way he did at her.

She didn't deserve what Kim had been putting her through. She deserved so much better—deserved honesty, no matter how terrifying that might be for Kim. She couldn't keep doing this, couldn't keep spending time with Riley, pretending that everything was normal. Pretending that she didn't want to press close to her side and kiss her senseless. Pretending that Riley wasn't everything she never knew she wanted.

Everything she needed.

Everything she'd been looking for the whole damn time.

Kim vowed then and there that after the party was over, she was going to come clean and tell Riley everything, and no matter the fallout, she'd work it out. With or without Riley.

God, please let it be with. She didn't want to imagine a life without Riley in it. The past few days had been bad enough. Awkward enough. She couldn't take much more of it.

Resolved, Kim relaxed into the seat, feeling more at ease than she had in a long time.

"And I'm excited for the zoo, too!" Riley's voice broke through Kim's distracted thoughts.

"Me too," Tyler said.

Kim's tone came out light, more casual and comfortable than in days. "I hope you're prepared to spend at least an hour watching the penguins," she warned Riley.

Riley turned to her, surprise written across her face. Kim wondered if she could sense her change in behavior.

"They're the coolest," Tyler said. "What's your favorite, Riley?"

To her credit, if she was taken aback, Riley's demeanor gave nothing away as she told Tyler, "I like lions, but they're not very interesting."

"Whenever we go, they're sleeping." Tyler said.

"Exactly—they're living the dream. I wish I could sleep all day."

"Mom's favorite is the giraffes, but I think they're boring, too. All they do is eat."

"They're living my dream," Kim chimed in. "Although I wouldn't choose to eat so many leaves."

"How much food do you think the whole zoo goes through in a week?" Riley said, a thoughtful look on her face. "It must be tons. Cari eats enough—I can't imagine what some of the bigger animals are like."

Gradually, the more they talked about their upcoming zoo trip and what Tyler was hoping to get for his birthday, they began to fall back into their usual dynamics together. By the time the car pulled to a stop outside of John and Rebecca's townhouse, Kim was feeling better.

"Hi, all." John opened the door, hugging Tyler and kissing Kim on the cheek. "Come in, come in. It's nice to meet you officially, Riley. I guess three times is the charm, huh?" He held out his hand for Riley to shake.

Kim had warned him that they'd both be in attendance—and Kim's family still thought they were a couple. John had reacted with a snicker, promising he wouldn't give the game away.

"It's nice to meet you too." Riley looked around, seeming impressed. "You have a lovely home."

"Oh, thank you. The decoration is all Rebecca. I'm hopeless."

"Nice to know some things never change," Kim said.

John grinned. "You're the first ones here." He led them to the kitchen, where Rebecca stood at the island slicing hot dog buns and bread rolls.

She smiled at them, wiping her hands on a towel before enveloping Tyler in a warm hug. "Happy birthday, Tyler."

"Thank you!"

"And it's nice to see you again, Kim," Rebecca said. "Riley, right?" Rebecca extended a manicured hand. Her red nail polish matched her blouse, and how she had the time to be a lawyer, organize a house party, and coordinate her nail polish with her outfits, Kim would never know.

"It's great to finally meet you," Riley said. "Thank you for having me."

"Oh, it's no trouble. The more the merrier."

Kim looked through the open patio doors. Plastic chairs were set around the yard, the outdoor grill smoked in the corner, and a *Happy Birthday* banner was hung around the fences.

Rare sunlight streamed into the yard, glinting off the cutlery set on the wooden table on the patio, and the sound of kids playing and dogs barking from a few doors down filtered into the kitchen.

"Can I get anyone a drink?" John offered. "I have a bottle of gin if that interests you, Kim."

"Yes please. I can help myself." Kim had been around enough times to know where the glasses were kept.

"Can I have a Coke?" Tyler said

John ruffled his hair. "Sure thing. And you, Riley?"

"What beers do you have?"

"I'll show you."

John led Riley to the garage, where Kim knew he would have put together a makeshift bar. She tried not to worry about what they were discussing.

"Do you need help with anything?" Kim asked Rebecca as Tyler disappeared outside to kick around the soccer ball John had left for him, along with a set of goalposts. Kim's one regret about living in an apartment was not having a yard for Tyler to run around in, but she couldn't afford anything bigger on her own. At least he got to experience it at John's.

"No, thank you," Rebecca replied.

"Are you sure?"

"You're a guest, Kim. Relax. Please. You've earned it. John showed me the cake you've made for Tyler—how long did that take you?"

"A few hours. The hardest part was making sure he didn't see it."

"Mom!" Tyler stuck his head around the patio door. "Come play with me."

"Is there a *please* at the end of that sentence?"

"Please come and play with me."

"Better."

Rebecca chuckled as Kim stepped into the yard. Tyler had fun skipping around her with the ball at his feet, unhindered by his broken arm. Some days, it was like he forgot about it completely.

"Nice goal, kid." Riley had joined them outside, holding a bottle of Peroni. She glanced at Kim, a smile on her lips. "Though it doesn't seem like you have much competition."

"Well, now that you're here, you can take over."

Riley left her beer on the large wooden table laden with various snacks and treats, and Kim stepped aside as Riley squared up against Tyler.

Kim had missed seeing her play—Riley went easy on Tyler, but she still tackled him, sliding the ball into the goal with much more ease than should have been possible, considering she was wearing absurdly tight skinny jeans and a pair of Doc Martens.

Riley flicked the ball into the air and kicked it upwards six times in a row, keeping it under perfect control, before passing the ball back to a wide-eyed Tyler.

"Now you're just showing off," Kim said.

Riley's grin turned to a smirk. Her confidence should have come off as arrogance, but Kim thought it was as sexy as hell.

"Can you teach me some tricks?" Tyler said.

"Sure." Riley shrugged out of her plaid shirt and tied it around her waist, leaving her in a gray tank top, her arms bare.

As Riley showed Tyler a few things, Kim couldn't help but stare, admiring the way the sunlight illuminated the ink across her skin and the lean muscle of her arms and back. What would it feel like beneath Kim's fingertips?

She could watch them all day.

Riley danced past Tyler with the ball, and he attempted to tackle her, sticking out a foot—making just enough contact to send her tumbling. Riley hissed in a sharp breath as she hit the floor, catching herself on the concrete patio.

Kim raced over to her side.

"I'm so sorry, Riley!" Tyler's voice was laden with distress, his eyes wide and his hands clamped across his mouth. "I didn't mean to."

"I'm fine, I'm fine." Riley scrambled to her feet. "I've had worse, kid, don't worry. Just don't go trying that in your first game—you might get a red card."

Kim caught a glimpse of blood on Riley's palm and suspected she was putting on a brave face for Tyler.

"Promise you're okay?" Tyler said.

"I promise, buddy." Riley held her hand behind her back. "I'm just going to go clean myself up, okay? Don't want your grandmother to see me with muddy hands and jeans—what would she say?"

"I'll show you to the bathroom," Kim said.

"You don't have to. I'm sure I can find it myself."

"I need to ask Rebecca something anyway," Kim lied, wanting to check that Riley really wasn't hurt. "Tyler, why don't you keep practicing while we're gone? Maybe you can see how your dad stacks up against Riley." Kim wrapped a gentle hand around Riley's uninjured arm. "Come on, it's this way."

"This really isn't necessary." But Riley allowed Kim to tug her inside. "I'm fine."

"You're bleeding," Kim said once they were out of Tyler's earshot. "And I know where the first aid kit is."

"It's just a graze."

"Still. My mother really will be disappointed if she sees bloodstains on your clothes, and after all the hard work we've done to get her to like you, that would be a shame, wouldn't it?"

Kim left no room for Riley to argue, dragging her to the upstairs bathroom and pointing to the edge of the bathtub. "Sit," she commanded.

After taking a long look at Kim's face, Riley obeyed, watching as Kim rooted around under the sink for the first aid kit.

"Let me see." Kim held out her hand and used her best no-nonsense voice but was still surprised when Riley offered Kim her palm.

She was right—it was just a graze—and Kim breathed a sigh of relief. "Well, I'm glad we don't have to make another trip to the ER."

"Told you it was fine."

"Considering you're a soccer player, you really are clumsy, aren't you?"

"Hey." Riley's brows creased into a frown. "Foul play was involved. Your kid tripped me."

"Still. You should be more careful."

Riley didn't protest as Kim began to gently clean the wound. Her hand was warm against Kim's.

When Kim swiped antiseptic over her palm, Riley bit her bottom lip, teeth white against pink.

"Does it hurt?" Kim's gaze flitted to meet Riley's, and, *oh*, Kim hadn't realized how close to each other they were.

Mere inches separated their faces, Riley's breath warm on her lips, her eyes dark and hypnotic. Kim could drown in them—wanted to, so very much.

"N-no. Doesn't hurt."

Kim swallowed, knowing she needed to look away from Riley's eyes, knowing she needed to break the spell, because her ex-husband's bathroom at her son's tenth birthday party was not the place to come clean and tell Riley she had feelings for her.

But Kim felt her mouth opening anyway.

"I—"

The ringing of the doorbell brought Kim crashing back down to earth, and she snapped her jaw shut.

Her mother's voice filtered through the closed door, and Kim rocked back on her heels, clearing her throat and staring resolutely at the floor.

"Here," she said, reaching for a Band-Aid. "That should fix you up. I'd better go and greet them."

Without another glance at Riley, Kim hurried from the bathroom before she could say something she wasn't yet ready for.

By the time Riley made her way back out to the yard, greetings had already been exchanged. Tyler and Kim stood with Martha and Edward beside the table and chairs.

With her palm still stinging, and aching to know what Kim had been going to say before the doorbell rang, Riley plastered on a smile and walked to Kim's side.

"This is for you, Tyler." Edward presented him with a well-wrapped box, disguising the skateboard inside.

"And this." Martha handed him a large bag of presents.

"Thank you! Can I open them now? Before everyone else gets here?"

"Go and get your dad and Rebecca," Kim said, "and then you can."

As Tyler scampered into the kitchen, Martha turned her eyes toward Kim and Riley. It was automatic for Riley to slide a comforting arm around Kim's waist when Kim tensed beside her. She wanted Kim to know she could lean on Riley for support.

"It's good to see you two again," Martha said, the words slightly stilted.

At least Martha hadn't reverted back to the version of herself that Riley had first met. She marveled at the transformation Kim's mother had made in a few short weeks.

"And you, Mrs. Jackson." Martha might have warmed to Riley, but Riley wasn't going to start being overly familiar. "Mr —Edward," Riley corrected, after a sharp glance from Kim's father.

"Come here, both of you." Edward swept them both into a tight hug. "You look so good together. So happy."

Riley swallowed. If only he knew none of it was real.

"Well, this has backfired on us, hasn't it?" Riley whispered in Kim's ear. "You wanted to piss them off, and now they think we're the perfect couple. Do you think your mom will cry when we fake break up?"

"My mother?" Kim murmured, looking straight ahead as Tyler emerged with John and Rebecca. "Show emotion? Don't be ridiculous."

Riley laughed—but it died in her throat at Kim's next words.

"They're right, you know. I am happier when I'm around you."

What the hell was Riley supposed to do with that?

What was Riley supposed to do about the way her heart pounded, about how she wanted to use the arm still looped around Kim's waist to pull her in closer? Did Kim have any idea what saying things like that did to her?

Riley shook her head. Of course she didn't.

Because she didn't think of Riley like that.

She never would.

Bea and Ash had made her download a dating app—to get her to stop moping—and maybe it was time Riley started thinking seriously about the women who messaged her on there.

The sound of wrapping paper being torn pulled Riley from her thoughts, and she had to remind herself why she was there. For Tyler.

He'd started, predictably, with the big bag of presents, revealing some new skateboarding gear—a helmet and some shin and elbow pads in red to match his new scarlet board—as well as some new clothes.

"They spoil him," Kim said as Tyler began on the box containing his board.

"What use is it having grandchildren if you can't spoil them rotten?" Edward said with a smile as Tyler tore open the box. "It's only his birthday once a year."

"Wow!" Tyler looked at the board with eyes as wide as the moon.

Riley had already seen the finished product via photographs Edward had sent her, but seeing it glinting like a ruby in the sunlight was something else, and she couldn't help but smile.

Edward had done an incredible job; Riley knew the man had spent hours and hours trying to make it as perfect as possible. She, too, had spent hours on the paintwork, making sure all of Tyler's favorite things were included, in as intricate detail as she could manage.

"You made this?" Tyler looked at his grandfather, running a reverent hand over the top of the board.

"I did. With some help. I'm sure you can guess from who. Do you like it?" Edward laughed when in lieu of an answer, Tyler launched himself into his arms for a hug.

Riley was next, and she smiled, wrapping her arms tight around him.

"Thank you." He turned to Kim with pleading eyes. "Can I test it out? Please?"

"You can have thirty seconds," Kim said, her voice stern. "And then you can put it away until your cast comes off."

Much to everyone's surprise, Tyler didn't argue, and they all watched as he did a lap around the patio.

"I should have given him his presents from me before we left. Nothing's going to live up to that," Kim told Riley as Edward talked Tyler through exactly how he'd made it.

Tyler traced his fingers over the artwork, listening with rapt attention.

"I'm just glad he likes it."

"You drew it—of course he likes it. I don't know if you've noticed, but he adores you."

"Yeah, well"—Riley glanced over at Tyler, at the excited flush in his cheeks, the bright wonder in his eyes—"the feeling's mutual."

⚬⚬⚬

Kim's leg bounced as she sat in the back seat of another Uber car with Riley—this time without Tyler as a buffer. It was John's week, so Kim had kissed him goodbye and promised to see him in the morning for their trip to the zoo.

Wracked with nerves, Kim had no idea what the hell she was going to say to Riley when they got home. Or how Riley would react.

A hand pressed against her knee, stilling it.

Riley's touch was warm against her bare skin. Kim swallowed, her heart thumping in her chest. How could such a small, simple touch set her alight?

"Sorry." Kim's eyes met Riley's in the dark.

Riley bit her lip, and once again, Kim thought about kissing her. She glanced at Riley's mouth and started to lean in before she remembered herself.

Riley's phone buzzed, interrupting the moment, and Kim recognized the notification on Riley's screen when she slid her hand off Kim's knee to check it.

It was a dating app—one Kim had used before—and her heart sank, although she knew she had no right to feel that way.

"Anything exciting?" Kim tried to keep her voice light. Tried not to let it shake.

"My sister made me join this dumb dating app last week." Riley's eye roll suggested she wasn't totally on board with the idea. "Someone has asked me if I want to grab a coffee tomorrow."

Kim's chest felt like it was wrapped in an elastic band; was her chance to be honest with Riley slipping through her fingers? "Are you going to go?"

Please say no.

Riley shrugged. "Maybe. But not tomorrow. I can't blow Tyler off for a cute woman—he'd never forgive me."

Kim forced a laugh, but it sounded hollow even to her own ears. Her, Riley, John, and Rebecca would be spending the day together. Kim's feelings for Riley wouldn't make that awkward at all.

"You okay?" Riley said as the car pulled to a stop outside their building.

"Fine." She didn't know how many times she'd said that to Riley lately, but she did know it got further and further from the truth each time.

Because Kim couldn't tell Riley now how she felt. If she was arranging a date with another woman, clearly, she wouldn't be interested in Kim. And Kim wasn't going to destroy their friendship if there was zero chance of a romantic relationship working out.

Kim wasn't that brave.

She wished she was because Tyler's party had been a perfect, beautiful glimpse of what dating Riley would be like. To finally have someone by her side again who supported her, who made her heart race and her skin tingle, someone who loved Tyler and only wanted the best for him. Someone about whom she was passionate.

But it was a façade.

And that was all it would ever be.

"Thank you for today," Kim said, when they reached their floor. She needed to get inside before she fell apart. "I'll see you in the morning—John said he'd pick us up at nine."

"Okay." Riley frowned, opening and closing her mouth a few times before heaving out a sigh. "'Night, Kim."

Before Kim stepped inside her apartment, she saw Riley unlock her phone, lips curved into a smile as she typed something.

Probably arranging a date with the woman she'd called cute. As Kim yanked her front door closed, she felt a piece of her heart breaking.

Chapter 23

WHATEVER PROGRESS RILEY THOUGHT SHE and Kim had made at Tyler's birthday party, something had clearly made it fade by the time they reached the zoo.

Kim could barely look at her and was quieter than usual—and Riley wasn't the only one who noticed. John kept shooting Kim concerned looks, and even Tyler had eyed his mom warily on more than one occasion as he dragged them from one enclosure to another.

She'd been fine the previous day—at least until Riley had gotten that dumb message in the car. But surely that was a coincidence because why would Kim be bothered about Riley having a date? Especially when she'd just been on one herself?

Dating was what had seemed to ruin things between them, and Riley wished she knew *why*.

There was one explanation she could think of, but it was inconceivable. It had crossed her mind a few times, but Riley had always been quick to squash it. Because surely there was no way that Kim could be jealous.

It was the only explanation that made both perfect and yet no sense, which meant Riley couldn't stop wondering about it.

Now wasn't the time to dwell, though. This day was Tyler's, and Riley loved seeing the look on his face as he pressed close to the penguin exhibit, his breath fogging the glass.

"Look, Riley, there's a baby!" He pointed toward a small penguin bobbing at the top of the water. "It's so cute!"

Riley had to admit they were cool to watch—if smelly—as they glided through the water, sometimes coming close to the glass and making Tyler giggle. They were much more active than the lions they'd seen earlier, whose tails had flicked lazily while soaking in the summer sun.

"Tell Riley some of your penguin facts, Tyler." John laid a hand on Tyler's shoulder. "I bet she'd like to hear them."

To Riley's surprise, she found she liked John a lot. He was a nice guy, and Riley could see what had drawn Kim to him.

"There are seventeen species of penguin," Tyler said without taking his eyes away from the exhibit. "These are Humboldt penguins. They're from South America. And they can swim up to thirty miles per hour! Isn't that cool?"

"That is cool."

"Much cooler than a boring lion."

Riley grinned. "Okay, maybe you could talk me around to penguins being the best animal."

"See? I told you! Come on, let's go to the aquarium next." He pulled Riley along by the hand.

Riley was happy to let him, leaving the other three adults trailing behind.

"Never mind his favorite animal," John said with humor in his voice as Tyler paused to watch the jellyfish, "I think you're his new favorite person, Riley."

Tyler didn't miss a beat. "You're all my favorite."

Warmth spread throughout Riley. Tyler thought of her as family.

Kim, meanwhile, stood with a faraway look in her eyes and her arms wrapped around her torso as she watched the jellyfish bobbing in the water.

Riley sighed. If only everyone else felt the same way.

"Okay, I've had enough of this." John peered at Kim from across the canteen table in the zoo's main café. "What is going on with you today?"

Kim resisted the urge to glance over her shoulder and check that Riley was out of earshot. Tyler had decided he wanted Riley and Rebecca to go with him to order their food. Looking at John's expression, Kim didn't think the decision had been Tyler's and Tyler's alone.

"Nothing. I'm fine." Kim couldn't make it sound convincing—and her behavior had been anything but. She was trying to put on a brave face for Tyler, but whenever she caught Riley's eye, her mask slipped. All she could think about was Riley with another woman.

She'd put herself into this situation, but she had no idea how to claw her way out. Not when Riley was right *there*, looking at Kim with open confusion, clearly not understanding why Kim's behavior had done a one-eighty overnight.

"Come on, Kim. I've known you for ten years—I can tell when you're lying. You were happier yesterday around your mother, so I know something must be really wrong."

Kim chewed on her bottom lip. With no idea how much longer the others were going to be, she didn't want to start this conversation.

John spread his hands out in front of him. "If you don't want to talk to me about it, fine, but I want you to know I'm here for you if you do. And I know Riley would be, too."

Kim tried not to wince at the mention of her name. Of course Riley would be there for Kim, even after everything Kim had put her through—because that was the kind of decent person Riley was.

"Unless...she's the problem?" John frowned. "Did something happen between you two?"

"No."

John looked like he was weighing his words carefully. "Do you want it to?"

She could feel her eyes narrow. "Why would you say that?"

"I don't know, Kim. I know you said you two were pretending to be together yesterday, but…you were convincing. I haven't seen you like that in a long time."

Because Kim hadn't felt like that in a long time, which was the goddamned problem.

"Look, I'm not trying to pry. Just…for what it's worth, I think she feels the same way about you. I know I don't know her well, but the way she looks at you when you're not paying attention?" John shook his head. "You can't fake that."

Kim swallowed, her chest feeling tight, because she knew John wouldn't say that if he didn't truly believe it. He wasn't that kind of guy. And for him to get involved in Kim's love life at all, he must have been convinced for a while.

"Think about it," he said, reaching over the table to pat the back of her hand.

Initially too stunned to form words, Kim didn't have the chance to respond before Tyler bounced back to their table with Riley and Rebecca in tow, each of them carrying a tray of food.

"Here you go." He passed Kim a burger and a basket of fries.

Kim eyed the giant slice of chocolate cake left on his tray. "You'd better have proper food to eat before that, young man."

Tyler heaved a dramatic sigh and pointed to a sandwich. "Riley said I had to."

Managing a smile in Riley's direction, Kim picked at her own fries. "Good. Thank you."

Trying not to dwell on John's words, Kim forced herself to engage in conversation with the others. She didn't want to ruin Tyler's day any more than she already had, at least. She could decide what she was going to do about her Riley situation after they'd all said their goodbyes.

Kim's behavior improved somewhat after lunch, but still. Riley had had enough. The constant yo-yoing was giving her whiplash, and she was going to find out what was going on with Kim, one way or another.

But she had to wait until they were alone first. John and Rebecca dropped them off outside their apartment block, Tyler chattering excitedly about all the animals they'd seen the whole way home while he clutched close to his chest the stuffed penguin Riley had bought him from the gift shop.

Riley waited for Kim to kiss her son goodbye, thanked John and Rebecca for the ride, and headed for the elevators, half expecting Kim not to follow her.

She did, but she didn't say anything, and Riley waited until they were on their floor before she rounded on Kim and let out every ounce of her frustration.

"Okay, we need to talk. What the hell is your problem?"

"What? I don't have a pro—"

"Yes, you do! I'm sick of you lying!" Riley's voice was rising, and she took a deep breath. "Ever since you went out with that guy, you've been acting different. You're distant and then you're not, and I don't think I can deal with you acting this way anymore! And today! Today it was like you could barely look at me. I just want to know why."

Instead of answering right away, Kim turned and opened her front door with shaking hands. "I'm not doing this out here," she said. "Come in."

"Will you talk to me?" Riley closed the door behind her and followed Kim into the living room, her throat tight and her heat beating so fast, blood roared through her ears. "Please?"

"I don't know how to put it into words."

"Try."

Kim looked at her helplessly, and Riley reached for her, settling gentle hands on Kim's hips. Beneath her fingertips, Kim was trembling, and Riley just wanted to know how to make things better. "Please," she said again.

Kim closed her eyes. "I'm sorry," she said, so quietly that Riley had to strain to hear her. "I know I've acted horribly toward you, and you haven't done anything to deserve it. The last thing I wanted to do was hurt you."

"Just tell me what's wrong."

Kim pulled away and began pacing in front of the couch. "I can't stop thinking about you, okay?!"

Kim's words rushed at her so fast, Riley could do nothing but blink.

"I went on that date, and he was amazing, but all I could think about was how he wasn't you. How I wanted to be back here with you. How different it would have been if it had been you sitting across from me at that restaurant. And I didn't know how to tell you. I didn't *want* to tell you because I didn't know what you'd say, and I didn't want to ruin things.

"And last night I…I was going to say something. When we were in that Uber, all I could think about was kissing you, and then you got that stupid message. And I know I have no right to be jealous, but I—I wished it was me. Today, all I thought about was you with someone else, and I couldn't stand it, and I know that's my problem to work on, but I… You're everywhere I look, Riley. How am I supposed to get over that?"

Kim stopped pacing, finally turning to gaze at Riley with wild eyes, her hair a mess from running a hand through it over and over. All Riley could do for several long moments was stare at Kim in shock.

Because her brain had surely short-circuited back there and fallen out of her skull. Kim had wanted to *kiss her* the previous night.

She'd been right—her inconceivable, unimaginable thought had been right.

Kim was jealous.

Over her.

Kim wanted her, in all the ways Riley had never believed would be possible.

"Oh God," Kim wailed, starting her pacing one more. "I knew this would happen. You hate me. You never want to see me again. You—"

Even though she still wasn't fully functioning, Riley couldn't let Kim suffer anymore and forced herself to step toward Kim and wrap a gentle hand around her wrist.

"Hey, stop it. I could never hate you."

"Really?"

Kim looked so disbelieving, tears glistening in her eyes.

Riley's throat was tight with them, too. Was she dreaming? Surely this couldn't be real.

Sliding her hand down Kim's arm, Riley tangled their fingers together and squeezed, needing to feel the warmth of Kim's skin against hers. "Yes. In fact, I'm pretty fond of you."

"You are?"

How hadn't she noticed? "Kim, I think you're the most amazing woman I've ever met. You're beautiful—I thought so the first moment I saw you. For weeks, I haven't been able to get you off my mind."

"Weeks?! Why didn't you say anything?"

"I didn't think I had a shot." A part of Riley still thought that. "I thought you were straight."

"So did I," Kim said, her voice breathy and her eyes trained on Riley's lips.

"And now?"

"Now...I don't know what to think. I just know that I like you. A lot." Kim looked at Riley with lidded eyes. "And I haven't been able to think about anything other than your lips on mine and how much I want to kiss you—if you'll let me."

"Please."

Leaning up on her toes, Kim curled the hand not entwined with Riley's around the back of her neck to pull Riley in.

Kim's lips were soft as they brushed against her own, and Riley let out a shaky breath because it was more perfect than she'd imagined. She curled a hand around Kim's hip, holding her close to her racing heart. Her thumb rested just beneath the hem of Kim's shirt, her skin blazing hot beneath Riley's fingertips.

Her mind still reeling—and half-convinced she was dreaming—Riley kept things chaste, even though she wanted to deepen the kiss.

She wanted to devour Kim, wanted to pull her into a bedroom she'd never seen, splay Kim out across the bed and never come up for air, but…she knew Kim had never done this before, and Riley wanted to do this right.

Pulling away, Riley smiled when Kim blinked at her, dazed.

"Let me take you out tomorrow night." Riley ran her thumb across Kim's bottom lip.

"Like on a date?"

"Yeah."

"I'd like that."

"Me too." Unable to resist the lure of her mouth, Riley leaned in to kiss Kim once more, then stepped away.

"Where are you going?"

Riley grinned at Kim's pout.

"If I keep kissing you…" Riley trailed off as she took in the flush on Kim's cheeks. "I don't know if I'll be able to stop."

Dark and wanting eyes settled on Riley's face. "What if I don't want you to?"

Riley groaned—Kim was going to be the death of her. "I want to do this the proper way. I'll pick you up at eight tomorrow?"

"O-okay."

"Goodnight, beautiful."

Kim's smile was sweet enough to make Riley's knees weak, and she just about made it to her front door, unable to believe the turn her day had taken.

"Shit." Kim pulled out a tray of extremely flat cupcakes from the oven.

She tossed the useless things aside and ran a hand over her face, frustrated. She was going to have to start all over again.

Hearing the commotion, Tina came to investigate.

"Did you forget to add baking soda?"

"Apparently."

"What is going on with you today?" Tina folded her arms across her chest. "You've been off all morning."

"I didn't get much sleep last night."

"You're always tired. It's never made you mess up a recipe you've baked a thousand times before. Is something bothering you? Is it Riley? I thought things would be better now that you came to your senses and told her how you feel."

At the mention of her name, Kim couldn't help but smile. Tina had been able to tell something had happened by the look on Kim's face the minute she'd walked into the bakery that morning. She must have been as relieved as Kim: the poor woman had been trying to talk Kim into confessing for days.

"Yeah, but…what if tonight is awful? Or awkward? What if she decides she doesn't like me like that after all? Or, worse, what if I do that to her?"

All of the worries at the forefront of Kim's mind—that had kept her up for most of the previous night—came rushing forth like a river.

"What if when she kisses me again, it feels wrong instead of amazing, and things fizzle out before they begin? And—not that I'm expecting it to happen tonight—what about sex? What if I'm awful? What if I hate it? What if—"

"I think that's enough of that," Tina said, cutting off Kim's rambling. Stepping close, Tina set her hands on Kim's shoulders. "I want you to listen to me carefully, okay? Because it's going to be a while before you hear me be this nice to you again."

Kim nodded.

"The only way tonight will be awkward is if you let it. I've seen you two together—you get along like a house on fire. I know it'll be hard, but don't let your nerves get in the way."

Kim nodded, taking a deep breath to try and calm her thoughts.

"I've never seen you like this before—not even over John—so I know you're not going to change your mind about her. And if she changes her mind about you, or if she can't see how great you are, she doesn't deserve you. But, for what it's worth, I don't think she will. And, darling, if the kisses are amazing already, they're only going to get better the more you do it. It's not going to fizzle out. And worry about the sex thing when you get there. Ask her what she likes. Don't put too much pressure on it. And please stop stressing. If only because we could do with a decent batch of cupcakes. We're running low."

Kim managed a laugh, and Tina tapped her cheek.

"There's that smile again. You're going to be fine. Okay?"

"Okay," Kim said, forcing herself to believe it.

"You have to say it for it to come true. Repeat after me: everything is going to be fine."

"Everything's going to be fine."

Chapter 24

DESPITE ALL OF TINA'S ATTEMPTS to reassure her, nerves somersaulted through Kim's stomach when Riley knocked on her door.

Kim pulled it open. Riley stood on the other side, one shoulder leaning against the wall. All Kim's worries fled.

"Hi." Riley leaned in to kiss her cheek, and Kim's skin burned beneath Riley's lips.

Riley visibly took in what Kim was wearing—jeans and her nicest sweater, after Riley had told her to dress warm. Her gaze trailed over Kim from head to toe, the heat of it like a touch. Kim's stomach quivered.

"You look amazing," Riley said.

"Thank you. So do you." In her ripped jeans, Vans, and leather jacket, Riley was dressed down but still effortlessly beautiful.

Kim locked her door and followed Riley to the elevator, smiling when she took Kim's hand in her own. "So, where are we going?"

Riley had been awfully cryptic about her plans.

"It's a surprise." She pressed the button for the parking garage rather than the building lobby, and Kim's interest was officially piqued.

When the doors opened, Riley led her over to a red Camry whose lights flashed as she unlocked the doors.

"You've had a car this whole time?"

She grinned. "Nah, I don't need one. I borrowed this from Ash. Thought it'd be easier than getting an Uber."

A picnic basket and two foldable chairs sat in the back seat. "And just to confirm—you can drive?"

"I am an excellent driver. Though I'm happy to hand over the keys if you'd rather be behind the wheel."

"No, thank you. I hate driving."

"How come?" Riley said once they were in the car.

"Like most of my traumas in life, it can be traced back to my mother."

"Naturally."

"Once I got my license, she insisted I drive her everywhere. I couldn't say no because she and my dad bought the car, but she was the worst back seat driver. Constantly criticized every decision I made, and over time, I lost all my confidence and refused to do it anymore. I might be better at it now, but it's been so long, I'm scared I've forgotten how."

"I'm sorry you went through that." Riley snaked a hand across the center console to squeeze Kim's hand when they stopped at the lights.

"It's fine. I don't need to drive here in the city. Although it would be nice to move to the suburbs one day."

"That was always my dream. To move out there and settle down with a family one day. Give Cari a nice big yard to play in."

"I wanted a yard for Tyler. Though I suppose by the time I can afford to move, he won't want one."

"He'll be too busy being a moody teenager, locked in his room." Riley grinned. "At least that's what I was like."

"Me too. Or I'd be out getting drunk with my friends."

"You were wild as a teenager?"

"With a mother like mine, can you blame me? I got into all sorts of trouble. And that was only the things she knew about."

"And to think—if anyone looked at the two of us, I'd be the one pegged as the troublemaker."

"Come on." Kim turned to look at Riley's profile, her cheek pressing against the passenger seat headrest. "You expect me to believe that teenaged you was an angel?"

"I was. I never snuck out—'cause I never got invited to any parties, but still. I was the quiet kid. Didn't have too many friends. I was all gangly and awkward and struggling with my sexuality. It wasn't until I got to college that I felt comfortable in my own skin."

"And then you had to drop out."

Riley shrugged. "Yeah, but it was worth it. Bea needed me, and I'd do anything for her." She pulled the car to a stop in the parking lot of Marymoor Park. The setting sun was bathing the trees in red and gold hues—it would be night soon.

"You know some people would be concerned about a first date in a park in the dark," Kim said.

"You've discovered my nefarious plan: befriend you, get you to fall for me, and lure you to a dark place so I could murder you in secret."

"I'm afraid Tina knows I'm here with you, so you might want to revise that plan."

"You told her about us?"

"Yeah, I…" Kim tried to decipher the look on Riley's face. "I needed to talk about it with someone. Is that okay?"

"Of course it's okay." Riley gave her a gentle smile. "Does she approve? She's a hard person to read."

"She likes you a lot. And she thinks you're good for me," Kim said. "Which apparently is a common opinion. I can't believe you won my mother over."

"I think I have your father to thank for that."

"Yes, because he adores you." Kim's father had loved John, but she thought Riley might have already surpassed him. "You have that effect on people in my family."

"Including you?"

"I was talking about Tyler." Kim's voice held a teasing lilt.

Riley scoffed. "Rude."

Kim kissed away her pout—because she could do that now—and smiled when she pulled away and Riley chased her lips.

"And speaking of Tyler...I'd rather not tell him about us yet."

"That's fine." Riley didn't hesitate. "Whatever you want to do, however long you want to wait—I'll follow your lead."

"Thank you." Kim glanced out the window—the sun had sunk lower, the shadows lengthening as they sat in the car. "Are we staying in here all night?"

"You mean I was supposed to plan something?"

Kim leveled Riley with a glare, and she grinned before opening her door. "Come on."

"Do you need me to carry anything?" Kim watched Riley struggle with the basket and both chairs.

"Maybe the food."

Kim took the basket and followed Riley onto a nearby path behind several other people who had arrived at the same time. Though she burned to ask what they were doing, Kim bit her tongue, suspecting all would be revealed soon.

Sure enough, when they turned a corner, a huge screen sat at the front of a wide field. People on picnic blankets and chairs were spread across the grass, and Kim put two and two together.

"An outdoor cinema?"

"Yeah." Riley looked suddenly shy as she and Kim found an empty spot toward the right side of the screen. "I hope that's okay."

"More than okay. I've always wanted to come to one of these."

Riley unfolded the chairs and handed one to Kim, who set the picnic basket in front of them.

"What are we watching?"

"*Back to the Future.*"

"I've never seen it."

"Never?" Riley shook her head in mock disappointment. "Well, you're in for a treat. And speaking of treats"—Riley opened the basket—"help yourself."

Inside were blankets, and beneath those, an array of Kim's favorite snacks—she spotted buttered popcorn, Twizzlers and Oreos amongst sandwiches and pasta salad.

"There are food trucks around if you want something from there, but I thought I'd throw a few things together."

Riley had thought of everything. Kim didn't remember anyone ever being so thoughtful—she was used to a standard dinner at a nice restaurant on a first date. The bar had already been set high. "Thank you. This is perfect."

"I'm glad you like it."

"Were you nervous?"

"Yes." Riley reached into the basket for a soda and a bag of chips and leaned back in her chair, lips curved into a smile. "Were you not?"

"Terrified." Riley deserved honesty. "I haven't been able to concentrate all day."

"And now?" There was a hint of fear in her eyes. "Are you still afraid?"

The answer was an easy one. Despite Kim's overthinking, being next to Riley felt nothing less than perfect. Like she was finally where she was supposed to be. "No. Don't get me wrong—I'm still nervous. But the second I saw you tonight, I…I knew it would be okay. This feels right."

"I feel the same way," Riley said, her voice soft. Her gaze never left Kim's face. "I know you haven't dated a woman before, so I want you to know, if you ever feel uncomfortable, you can tell me."

"I will." Based on her body's reaction to kissing Riley, Kim couldn't see that being a problem, but it was good to be prepared.

"Can I put my arm around you?"

Kim was touched that Riley had asked first. "Yes, please."

Kim leaned into the embrace, shifting closer to Riley's side so that when the movie started, she could rest her head on her shoulder.

Riley smelled like sandalwood, and in her arms, Kim felt warm and safe. When Riley drew idle patterns on Kim's arm, her heart raced, imagining what those hands might feel like elsewhere. The mere thought made her shiver as Riley's eyes met her own.

"Are you okay?" Riley's brow furrowed. "Are you cold?"

Kim felt her cheeks warm, not wanting to reveal the real reason for her shiver. "I'm okay." Drowning in dark blue eyes, Kim let out a shaky breath. "Kiss me?"

Riley smiled, cupping Kim's cheek with her free hand, tilting her head to brush her lips against Kim's—once, twice, three times. When Kim deepened the kiss, slipping her tongue past Riley's lips, she received a satisfying groan in response. Riley pressed closer, and Kim's toes curled.

They should have been doing this the whole damn time.

For their second date, Riley knocked at Kim's door at seven sharp, dressed in her best pair of jeans and a black fitted tee, a bouquet of pink, purple, and red flowers she'd picked up earlier in her hands.

"Hi," Kim said when she opened the door, wearing a smile and a floaty blue sundress with daisies on it.

"Hi, beautiful." Riley held out the bouquet. "These are for you."

"You got me flowers?"

"I couldn't show up empty-handed."

"Thank you." Kim took the bouquet in one hand and Riley's hand in the other, tugging her over the threshold and toward the kitchen.

Riley kicked the door closed behind them. Kim's cooking smelled amazing, and her mouth was already watering.

"How was your day off?"

"Good. I slept in, and I met Bea for lunch. She says hi, by the way. And she wants us to go on a double date with her and Ash, if you're up for that."

"Sure." Kim rooted around her cupboards for a vase. Once she found one, she set the flowers at the dining table's center. "I like your sister. What were you thinking about?"

"I'm not sure. There was talk of axe throwing, but I'm not confident that giving my sister any kind of weapon is a good idea. Especially if it's doing something competitive."

"Is she bad?"

"Awful. But as you've seen, so am I. We were terrible when we were younger. Were you not with your siblings?"

A timer beeped, and Kim answered as she crossed over to the oven. "Well, not in that way. We all had different interests, so had nothing to compete at."

"You mean to tell me you didn't have family board game nights?"

Kim laughed as she pulled out a roasting tray. "Nope. We played the occasional game of charades at Christmas, which I hated."

"Charades are the worst." Riley drifted toward the aromas. "This looks amazing. Do you need any help?"

"Nope. It's almost ready. Please, sit." She waved toward the table. "What do you want to drink? I have beer. Or soft drinks, obviously."

"Beer is fine."

"Help yourself."

Riley grabbed two bottles and poured them into glasses while Kim plated things up.

"Thank you," Riley said when the food was placed in-front of her. Kim had paired roast potatoes and carrots with a beef Wellington, and the outsides looked deliciously crispy. "I hope you're not expecting great things from me in the kitchen. I couldn't do this. I bet you made your own pastry, too."

"I'm a baker, Riley. Obviously, I made my own pastry."

Which was perfectly crisp and buttery, and Riley sighed happily around her first bite. "It's not fair you're good at both. I always think people should be either a good cook or a good baker—never both."

"I'm better at baking."

"I don't know. This is coming close to your brownies."

"A high honor." Kim took a sip of her beer, her eyes twinkling in the low light—she had opted for a lamp rather than overhead lighting.

"It is." Riley looked back at Kim, hardly able to believe her luck. A week ago, she'd been miserable, convinced Kim was pulling away from her, and just a few days later, they sat sharing a meal Kim had made, their calves brushing beneath the table and neither one of them able to stop smiling.

Kim's phone rang as they finished eating, and she glanced at Riley apologetically. "Sorry, it's Tyler."

Riley waved her off. "Go ahead. I'll clear up."

"You don't have to."

"It's the least I can do after you cooked."

As she filled the sink with soapy water, Riley listened to snippets of Kim and Tyler's conversation. There weren't many dishes, and Kim was still on the phone when she finished, so Riley joined her on the couch with her beer.

"Good night, sweetheart, I love you." Kim hung up and apologized to Riley. "When he doesn't want to go to bed, he keeps talking."

"You don't ever have to apologize for being a good mom." It was one of the things Riley liked most about Kim. "I know Tyler will always come first, and I'm more than okay with that. Is he enjoying Vancouver?" John and Rebecca had surprised him with a trip for his birthday.

"He's loving it. They're driving back tomorrow, but I don't think he wants to come home—I'm sure he'll tell you all about it next time he sees you."

Riley grinned, draining the last of her beer and setting her glass on Kim's coffee table. "No doubt."

Kim's leg was bouncing in the same anxious rhythm as it had in the back of the Uber the other night.

"Are you okay?"

"Hm?"

Riley pointed. "You have a nervous tic."

"Oh. Sorry." Kim's leg went still. "I guess I'm just not used to feeling like this."

"Like what?"

228

"Excited. Scared. I...I want this to work so badly, it terrifies me."

"Me too. But I also don't want to put too much pressure on us. If it doesn't work, it doesn't work. Either way, we'll be okay."

"Yeah. You're right." Kim set her own glass down and turned her body toward Riley.

The wanting look in her eyes made Riley swallow. Hard.

"Do you, um, wanna watch a movie? Or some *Grey's*? We haven't done that for a while."

"We could," Kim said, her eyes trained on Riley's lips, her earlier nerves seemingly forgotten. "Or we could do something else."

"Something else, huh? What did you have in mind?"

Kim leaned closer and kissed her. Riley sighed, parting her lips for Kim's tongue and thinking about how she could do nothing but this for hours and never get bored. She was content to let Kim set the pace, and it quickly grew more heated.

Riley melted against the couch as Kim pressed closer, her hands in Riley's hair. She felt dizzy at the soft moans Kim was making into her mouth.

When Kim shifted to climb into her lap, Riley nearly stopped breathing altogether. She dropped her hands from Kim's waist to her thighs, brushing her thumbs over the bare skin beneath the hem of Kim's dress.

Kim's kisses turned harder, more insistent, and when Kim rocked her hips, Riley groaned and yanked her mouth away. "Fuck," she said, her breathing heavy and her heart pounding. "We should...we should stop."

"Do you want to?" Kim's eyes had turned dark and sultry, and *fuck*, Riley wanted nothing more than to let Kim drag her to the bedroom.

It literally physically pained her to say it. "We're supposed to be taking it slow."

"Yeah." Looking dazed, Kim blinked. "Yeah, you're right. Sorry."

Riley brushed a strand of Kim's hair away from her flushed cheek. "I want to, believe me. But I don't want to rush this."

"Okay. Do you—would you like to stay over tonight? Just to sleep," Kim added hastily. "Although I wouldn't be opposed to more kissing."

Riley grinned. "I'd love to, but I can't leave Cari overnight. Unless…you want to come over to my place?"

"I'd like that."

"Yeah?"

"Yeah. I'm not ready for the night to end yet."

Chapter 25

THE BED CREAKED AS KIM pressed closer to Riley beneath the sheets, tangling their legs together and sliding a hand over Riley's hip as their lips brushed for the umpteenth time.

"Just to sleep, huh?" Riley said when they parted, her chest heaving and her eyes dark. Kim didn't think anyone had ever looked at her with such open desire.

It made her quiver.

"I did say I wouldn't be opposed to more kissing. And it's your fault for wearing that to bed."

When Kim had come out of the bathroom to find Riley wearing nothing but a pair of boxer shorts and a low-cut tank top, she'd all but pounced on her.

"Me? Have you seen your pajamas? If you can call them that. Those are the tiniest shorts I've ever seen."

"Are you complaining?"

"No." Riley traced her fingers along the bare expanse of Kim's thigh, eliciting a shaky breath.

All they'd done was kiss, and Kim was wrecked. She'd never been so turned on, and her shorts were soaked—hopefully, Riley hadn't noticed.

She'd had no idea things could feel so good.

She liked sex fine, but it was something she'd always been able to live without—something she *had* lived without for years, never feeling like she was missing out. But the thought of sex with Riley...

Kim might implode at the mere thought of it.

She definitely wasn't as straight as she had thought.

All she wanted was to be close to Riley, to sink into her and never come up for air. And she'd never felt like this before—it should terrify her, but instead, with Riley's lustful eyes locked on hers, Kim found it exhilarating.

"Want to go to sleep?" Riley said, and Kim loved how already, Riley was making sure she was comfortable, letting her set the pace.

"Not yet." Kim wasn't ready to let go of the euphoria coursing through her body. "Unless you want to?" While Riley might be letting Kim take charge, Kim wasn't about to push for something Riley wasn't prepared for.

Riley shook her head. "I'm good."

"Okay."

Kim pulled her in for another kiss, and Riley splayed a hand at the small of Kim's back, keeping her close. The movement pressed their chests together, and Kim could feel Riley's breasts against her own.

"Do you...do you have nipple piercings?" Kim could feel the metal—and Riley's hardened nipples—through the thin material of both their shirts.

"Um, yeah, I do." Kim could tell her cheeks were flushed even in the dark. "I got them done a few years ago."

"Can I touch them?"

"Fuck," Riley said, so quietly that Kim wasn't sure she was sup-posed to hear it. "Y-yeah. If you want to."

Oh, Kim wanted to. Kim wanted to very much.

Riley's skin was burning where Kim slid her hand beneath her shirt, and she watched Riley's face as she inched up her ribs until she reached the underside of her breast, feeling the weight of it in her palm. At the first brush of Kim's thumb against her straining nipple, Riley clamped her teeth down on her bottom lip.

The metal bar was cold to the touch, though the rest of Riley was blisteringly hot, and Kim toyed with it before circling the nipple with her thumb, feeling Riley's nails dig into her back, thoroughly enjoying watching pleasure spark across Riley's face.

"Is this okay?"

"More than okay." Riley's eyes closed. Her chest was heaving, and there was a breathiness to her voice that Kim wanted to hear over and over. "That feels so good."

Kim kissed her because if Riley kept saying things like that, Kim didn't know if she could handle it.

"You can touch me, too," Kim said when they next parted because her own nipples were aching for it.

So far, Riley's hands hadn't strayed far—never beneath the hem of Kim's shirt or shorts, but Kim wanted to feel her fingertips searing into her skin.

"Are you sure?"

"Yeah."

She sighed when Riley obliged, shifting to roll her onto her back. When Riley paused, with her hand at rest on Kim's rib cage, she added, "I promise I'll tell you if it's too much."

"Okay."

Riley kissed Kim's lips, then her jaw, then blazed a trail lower over her neck as her hand palmed at Kim's breast over her shirt and then under it, her fingers circling the nipple until it was Kim's turn to clutch at Riley's back.

She bucked her hips against Riley's thigh, which had fallen between her own. Kim was desperate for some friction to ease the building ache. *God*.

Riley drew in a sharp breath against her neck. "Fuck, Kim."

"Please don't stop." Had Kim ever sounded this desperate? This needy? She'd cry if Riley pulled away now. "Please."

Riley pressed one more kiss to Kim's neck before rising to meet her lips in a messy kiss, and Kim raised her hips once more to grind against Riley's thigh. This time, Riley moved with her. Kim's eyes rolled at the pressure on her clit, which pulsed in time with the gentle tug of Riley's fingers on her nipple.

Her hands fell to Riley's hips and over her ass, greedy to explore new skin as the two of them rocked against one another, pressure building, until—

"*Fuck*," Kim said, as her orgasm washed over her, the sensation stronger than she'd ever remembered it being, her head falling back against the pillow, her hips stuttering in their rhythm.

As soon as it was over, embarrassment flooded through her—Riley had barely touched her—and Kim threw an arm over her face, sure her cheeks were flaming.

"Oh, my God, I'm so sorry."

"What? What are you sorry for?"

"Because I—" Kim couldn't say it.

Riley gently pried Kim's arm away from her face. "You have nothing to apologize for," she said, her voice fierce.

"I don't?"

"Are you kidding? Kim, that was hot as hell."

Kim searched Riley's face for a hint she might be lying but couldn't see any.

"Please don't ever be sorry for feeling good."

Kim swallowed; she couldn't remember the last time she had been looked at with so much care. "What about being sorry for ruining the moment?"

"You didn't ruin anything." Riley pressed the gentlest of kisses to the corner of Kim's mouth. "Are you okay?"

"Yes. Are you?"

"Mm. Pretty tired, though." Riley shifted to lie back beside Kim.

"But do you not need to…" Kim trailed off.

Riley grinned. "Come? No. It doesn't have to be transactional, you know. In fact, I don't want it to be like that."

"But I want you to feel good, too."

"I do," Riley said, tangling their fingers together and bringing Kim's hand to her mouth to kiss the back of her knuckles. "I feel amazing. You're amazing."

Kim snuggled into Riley's side, the cotton sheets smooth against the bare skin of Kim's legs. Already she felt sleepy. "Thank you for letting me stay."

"I think it was your idea," Riley said, lips brushing Kim's forehead. "But I'll take the credit."

It had been so long since Kim had shared a bed, but it didn't feel wrong to have Riley beside her. In fact, it felt like Riley was exactly where she belonged.

A cold nose pressed against Riley's foot, jolting her awake.

Blinking her eyes open, Riley looked down to find Cari at the foot of the bed, tail wagging once Riley's attention was on her.

"What's up, girl? You need to go out?"

Cari whined.

"Okay, let me get dressed."

Riley glanced at Kim, splayed out beside her, still sound asleep, and sighed. She'd love nothing more than to burrow back into the sheets and wrap an arm around her waist—but duty called.

As Riley clambered out of bed and wriggled into the jeans she'd discarded on the floor, Kim stirred.

"Where are you going?" Her voice was raspy with sleep.

"I need to take Cari out for a quick walk. I won't be long—stay in bed." Riley leaned over to kiss Kim's forehead before whistling for Cari to follow her.

Outside, the sun was bright, the air warm, and Riley breathed in deeply as she let Cari pull her toward the park, feeling like she was on cloud nine.

Because when they got back home, a beautiful woman was waiting for her.

When Riley stepped back into her apartment, she was greeted by the smell of pancakes.

Kim stood at the stove, still in her pajamas, and Riley paused in the doorway, admiring the curve of Kim's ass beneath her tiny shorts.

"I thought I told you to stay in bed," Riley said, looping her arms around Kim's waist and smiling when Kim leaned back against her.

Kim flipped a pancake with practiced ease. "Are you complaining?"

"No, but you already cooked last night."

"I don't mind. I like it."

Unable to resist kissing Kim's neck, Riley brushed Kim's hair to the side.

"If you keep that up," Kim said when Riley used her teeth to graze her pulse point, "I'm going to burn these."

Chuckling, Riley stepped away. "Okay, I'll behave myself—for now. Want a coffee?"

"Please."

Riley reveled in the domesticity as she grabbed two mugs from the cupboard. She didn't remember the last time she'd had a woman spend the night at her place who had stuck around long enough to have breakfast—let alone make it.

The fact that it was Kim moving around her kitchen with practiced ease, stacking the pancakes as Cari wound around both their legs in the hope of scraps falling to the floor, made it even sweeter.

"What time do you have to be at work?" Kim said as they sat to eat.

"I have the closing shift today, so not until two. You need to leave soon, right?"

Kim wrinkled her nose. "Yeah. The curse of owning your own business—no lazy mornings. Do you…do you want to stay over at my place tonight? You can bring Cari."

Riley would love to, but—"Isn't Tyler back tomorrow?"

"He is, but John doesn't usually drop him off until the afternoon."

"Then I'd love to see you later."

It meant they would spend more time together than they had apart since their first date, but Riley didn't mind. Bea would tease her for already being head over heels, but Riley wanted to take advantage of the time they had together before Tyler came home because she knew things would have to be different once he was back.

There couldn't be nights tangled in the sheets together, romantic dinner dates, or early morning pancakes before work.

At least not until they told him they were together, and Riley had no idea when that would be.

Straddling Riley's hips, Kim admired the sight of her, face flushed and hair mussed from Kim's fingers, her eyes shining in the low light of Kim's bedroom.

Riley's hands were on her thighs, fingertips warm beneath the hem of Kim's shorts, and Kim wanted to feel those hands everywhere. She didn't want to come against Riley's thigh, still wearing her clothes—she wanted skin against skin, wanted heat and fire, wanted to sink down on Riley's fingers.

She wanted to feel Riley, breathless and shaky, trembling beneath Kim's touch.

Kim thought she'd be nervous about this. She thought it would take her weeks to be comfortable enough to do much more than kiss, but Riley—with her gentle touch, her quiet reassurances, her constant check-ins, and her way of looking at Kim like she meant the world—made Kim feel more confident than she'd ever been before.

She *wanted* more than ever before.

Riley's eyes widened when Kim curled her hands around the hem of her pajama top.

"Is it okay if I take this off?"

"Y-yeah. If you want to."

Kim yanked it over her head and tossed it over her shoulder. "I do. I want you to touch me." She bit her lip when Riley skimmed her hands over her ribs to cup Kim's breasts. "Everywhere."

"Are you sure?"

Kim nodded, her eyes fluttering closed as Riley circled her nipples, shifting her hips against Riley's stomach.

"Yes. Please. I…I don't want to wait. Unless you want to."

"No," Riley said without hesitation. "I've been dreaming about this for so long."

"I hope I live up to your expectations."

"You've already surpassed them." Riley curled one hand around the back of Kim's neck and guided her into an open-mouthed kiss.

Not content to be a bystander, Kim trailed her lips down Riley's neck and over her collarbone, paying special attention to the swirling lines of her tattoos before moving lower. Tugging the neckline of Riley's tank down to free her breasts, Kim's breath caught at the first glance of Riley's piercings.

"Fuck," Riley said as Kim pressed the barest of kisses to one of them, the metal cool against her lips.

"Okay?"

"Yes." She slid a hand into Kim's hair, her nails scratching Kim's scalp when Kim took one of Riley's nipples into her mouth.

Kim teased her tongue over the bar as her fingers tugged at the one on the other nipple. Riley's hips were restless below her, her breathing labored as little groans caught in the back of her throat. Kim loved knowing she was having such an effect on her; she could do this all day.

With Riley's reactions giving her more confidence, Kim didn't let herself falter as she shifted to slide one hand up the inside of Riley's leg.

"Tell me what you like." Kim paused inside the leg of Riley's boxers, trying not to think about how the thigh was already sticky with want, trembling beneath her hand.

"You'll be able to figure it out," Riley said. "Just go soft. And slow. I'll tell you if something doesn't feel good."

"Okay." Kim watched Riley's face as she inched higher up. Riley's lips parted in a moan at the first touch of fingers against slippery skin.

Kim swallowed and let herself explore, sliding over creases and folds—a jerk of the hips told her she'd found Riley's clit.

Kim drew wide circles, and Riley guided her into another kiss, arching her hips to chase Kim's fingers. Kim was about to ask if Riley needed more when she shuddered, her thighs trying to clench around Kim's wrist as she dug her nails into the back of Kim's neck.

"Fuck, you're amazing." Riley's head fell back against the pillow.

"No, you're amazing. I want to do that again." After feeling Riley fall apart around her, Kim never, ever wanted to do anything else. "Can you?"

"I think so," Riley said, twitching when Kim's fingers brushed again over her clit. "Though that's sensitive."

Kim slid her fingers lower, teasing at Riley's entrance. "How about here?"

"There's okay."

Pressing inside with one finger, they both shared a moan. Kim started a lazy rhythm as she added a second digit, working Riley up slowly as she kissed her deeply.

When Riley curled a hand over Kim's hip, stroking her thumb beneath the waistline of her shorts, Kim whimpered, hyperaware of the growing ache between her own thighs.

"Can I touch you, too?" Riley asked.

Kim had never wanted anything more. "Please." Her head dropped onto Riley's shoulder as a hand disappeared beneath her shorts, and Riley easily found Kim's clit, circling it until Kim was shaking.

Kim was so close, she could not keep up her own rhythm anymore. The overwhelming feelings flooding through her stilled her movements.

"I want you inside," Kim panted against Riley's neck. "I want to feel you."

Obligingly, Riley curled two fingers deep into her. Kim saw stars as she ground her hips against Riley's hand.

It felt better than she'd imagined. Kim kissed Riley hard as she resumed the movement of her own fingers between Riley's legs. Working in tandem, Kim felt Riley pulsing around her fingers mere seconds before pleasure flooded through her in waves so intense, it stole the breath from her lungs. Her whole body trembled until Riley slipped her fingers free and Kim all but collapsed into her arms.

"Are you okay?" Riley brushed the hair out of Kim's face, the fingers of her other hand sticky against Kim's hip.

"Yeah, sorry—I think I lost temporary control of my muscles."

Riley kissed Kim's forehead and wrapped her arms around her back, stroking along Kim's spine. "As long as it was in a good way."

"The best way. Am I squashing you?"

"No—stay there."

Kim was more than happy to do just that, enjoying the feeling of Riley's bare skin against her own, her arms tight around her.

It felt like home.

Chapter 26

THIS TIME, AFTER RILEY GOT back from taking Cari out to do her business, Kim was still in bed. Riley used the spare key Kim had told her to take to let herself back into the apartment. After tipping some kibble into Cari's bowl, Riley shed her clothes and climbed back beneath the sheets.

"You're cold," Kim said with a whine, wriggling away from Riley's wandering hands. "You have to warm up first."

"What do you think I'm trying to do?"

Kim grumbled, and Riley grinned but did as she was told, shifting to lie on her side and keeping her hands to herself, content to watch Kim wake.

"You can come back now," Kim said after a few moments.

Chuckling, Riley slid a hand over Kim's hip. "You're grumpy in the mornings." She kissed Kim's cheek. "How can I cheer you up?"

Kim tangled a hand in Riley's hair to bring them together. "I'm sure you can think of something," she said against Riley's mouth when their lips parted.

"I have a few ideas."

When Riley began her gentle exploration of Kim's body, picking up from where she'd left off the night before, Kim hummed.

Riley hadn't yet gotten the chance to learn all the places that made Kim tremble, and she was determined to make the most of whatever time they had before Tyler came home.

Kim liked to be kissed at the base of her neck, but her collarbones were ticklish, and as Riley descended onto Kim's chest, her nose brushing the skin there, Kim squirmed. Riley also learned that her nipples were sensitive and that the gentlest stroke of Riley's tongue along them had Kim's back arching off the bed.

Moving lower, Riley kissed the underside of Kim's breasts, rolling Kim onto her back and slotting between Kim's thighs when she parted her legs. The muscles of her stomach quivered beneath Riley's lips, and when she reached the hips, Kim whined, her hands tightening in Riley's hair.

Riley could smell the heady scent of Kim's arousal as she pressed a gentle bite to the inside of her thigh, and Kim shifted her hips, pressing upward in search of friction.

Once more, Riley couldn't believe they were here. She was in Kim's bed and had Kim breathless and writhing beneath her. Never in a million years could Riley have ever imagined on the day they'd met that it would end like this.

"Please," Kim said, the word little more than a whisper.

"Mouth or fingers?"

Kim groaned. "Mouth."

Wrapping her hands around Kim's thighs, Riley spread them further apart and dipped her head, moaning at the first touch of her tongue against slick skin. Instead of teasing—she knew she'd have endless opportunities to find all of Kim's weak spots—Riley stroked her tongue in small circles around her clit, tipping Kim over the edge with her mouth.

She didn't pull away until Kim tugged at her hair, feeling too sensitive for any more. Riley kissed her way back up the length of her body until reaching her lips.

"Okay?" Riley's nose brushed against Kim's as she waited for her eyes to open.

"Perfect." Kim was still catching her breath. "Give me a minute and—"

Kim's phone rang, and Riley rolled off her as she grabbed it, frowning when she glanced at the screen. "Sorry, it's John."

"Go ahead."

"Morning, John. Is everything okay?" Kim's frown deepened as she listened. "Sorry, no, I haven't checked my messages—you are? Already?" Panic flared in her voice. "O-okay. No, that's fine. See you in a minute."

Kim hung up, her eyes wide. "That was John. Rebecca's mom has taken a turn for the worse—they're dropping Tyler off early."

"Early? As in—"

"As in they're already in the lobby."

"Shit." Riley scrambled out of the bed, Cari bounding up in alarm as Riley scrambled to pick her clothes off the floor. "Do you think I've got enough time to get next door?"

"You're going to have to try." Kim was yanking her pajamas on.

Hopping on one foot as she tugged on her jeans, Riley shoved Cari's bed back into the bag she'd brought over last night. Once her jeans and shirt were on, she hurried into the kitchen, grabbing the dog bowls and leash before shoving on her shoes.

Glancing through the peephole, Riley couldn't see any signs of movement. "I think the coast is clear," she called back to Kim over her shoulder. "I'll see you later!"

Fleeing before Kim could answer, Riley was unlocking her own apartment door when the elevator dinged.

"Riley!"

Tyler called out her name before she could slip through the door, and Riley shoved Cari's bag of things inside her apartment before turning, forcing a smile as she lifted a hand to wave.

"Hey, buddy. How was your trip?"

"It was good." Tyler was too distracted by greeting Cari to notice Riley's disarray.

John, clearly, had no such qualms, his eyebrows raising as he took in Riley's appearance.

"We went whale watching!" Tyler's voice floated below. "And to a hockey game. And we had the best food."

Kim's front door opened, and Riley could barely look at her—her cheeks were still flushed, and her hair was a mess. "I thought I heard your voice," Kim said, her voice bright. "Welcome home, Tyler."

"Thanks, Mom." Looking away from Cari, Tyler frowned when he glanced at Kim. "Are you okay? You're in your pajamas so late."

"I overslept," Kim said without missing a beat.

Tyler nodded, accepting the explanation. "Okay. Hey, Riley, do you wanna see the photos from this weekend?"

"Maybe after I've had a shower," Riley said. "But I could come over this afternoon?"

"That's fine," Kim said without meeting Riley's gaze. "Now, say goodbye to your dad, Tyler. I'm sure he's anxious to be on his way."

Tyler hugged him—and Cari—goodbye before scampering into the apartment, and Riley heaved a sigh of relief when he was gone.

"I see you two have worked out whatever was going on between you the other day." John's words carried unmistakable amusement.

"I have no idea what you're talking about," Kim objected.

"So when Tyler and I got here, Riley wasn't running back to her apartment after spending the night at yours? Come on, Kim. You never oversleep. And you both look like you've been caught doing something you shouldn't. Plus, Riley's laces are undone, and her shirt is on backwards."

Riley looked down. "Goddammit."

"We haven't told Tyler yet," Kim said, glancing over her shoulder and keeping her voice low. "So if you could keep it to yourself for now, I'd appreciate it."

"Done," John said. "I'm happy for you guys. And welcome to the family, Riley."

Warmth flooded through Riley's chest at John's words. "Thanks."

"Right, I'd better get going. Rebecca is waiting for me in the car."

"I hope her mom gets better soon," Kim said. "Let me know if you need anything."

"I will." John disappeared with a wave.

"You couldn't have told me my shirt was inside out?" Riley said once he was gone.

"I was preoccupied with putting on pants," Kim whispered back.

Riley grinned. Kim looked good, even rumpled, and Riley could barely believe she'd gotten to wake up next to her that morning.

"I guess I'll see you later?"

Kim smiled. "Yes, for Tyler's show and tell."

Riley could think of no better way to spend her Sunday afternoon. "Can't wait."

⇢—◦◦◦—⇠

"Look at that smile on your face," Tina said when Kim walked through the bakery doors. "Tell me—how good *is* the sex?"

Kim's cheeks warmed, and she was glad no customers were inside. "Good morning to you, too. How do you know I've had any?"

"You're glowing. Come on, Kim, I'm curious! I've never been with a woman."

Kim bought herself a few moments by dumping her bag behind the counter and pulling on her apron. "It was…amazing."

"See? I told you there was nothing to worry about. I'm so happy for you!"

"Me too," Kim said, unable to stop smiling. She'd spent the previous evening with Riley while Tyler had regaled them with stories of his time in Vancouver, and Kim had seen flashes of what a life with Riley could be like.

It was everything she'd always wanted.

The worst part had been kissing Riley good night after Tyler had gone to sleep, instead of curling up beside her in bed.

"I know it's only been a week, but…I can already see a future with her."

"Damn. I've always heard the stereotypes about lesbians moving fast, but I didn't realize they were all real."

Kim elbowed Tina sharply in the side. "It doesn't feel too fast, though."

"I'm joking." Tina wrapped an arm around Kim's shoulders and squeezed. "You should move at whatever pace you feel is right. If that's saying *I love you* within two weeks—"

"I am not there yet," Kim said, laughing.

"We'll see." Tina waggled her eyebrows. "Oh, look—speak of the devil."

Kim turned to see Riley coming through the door, and her smile grew. "Good morning."

"Hi. You get Tyler to your parents' place okay?"

Kim knew spending the day in the bakery was boring for him, so when her father had offered to watch him a few times during Kim's weeks with him, she'd been eager to agree. "Yes. He's helping my dad make something, but he won't tell me what it is."

"I know what it is." Riley broke out into a mysterious smile.

"He told you?"

"Uh-huh."

"What is it?"

"Oh no, you don't—I'm not breaking his trust. You'll have to wait and see."

"You know I hate surprises." Kim tried not to pout.

"Take that up with your kid, not me."

"You two are so cute." Tina was looking between them with a sigh. "I am so glad you got your shit together, Kim."

Kim had forgotten she was there. "Yes, thank you—is there not anything in the back that needs your attention?"

"Ouch." Tina pressed a hand to her chest. "Rude. But fair—I'll give you some privacy."

When she was gone, Kim reached for Riley's collar, leaning over the counter to kiss her.

"I hope you don't treat any of your other customers like this," Riley said, her eyes sparkling.

"Just the special ones."

"Plural? Should I be worried?"

Kim kissed her again. "Singular."

"You had me worried for a minute there. I'm meeting Bea and Ash later—if they ask me about a double date again, which I'm sure they will, when works best for you next week?"

"I can do any night."

"Okay, I'll let them know."

"And I'll get your black coffee so you can head to work."

Chapter 27

THE SUMMER AIR WAS WARM, but a light wind made the hairs on Riley's arms stand on end. Kim's hair whipped around her face as she and Riley made their way through downtown Seattle hand in hand for their double date with Bea and Ash.

"I thought you said axe throwing was a terrible idea," Kim said.

"Oh, I think it is." Bea had already been talking about how she couldn't wait to whoop Riley's ass. "But I couldn't persuade them to do anything else. I'm hoping there won't be too much trash talk but apologize if there is."

"Don't worry—I can take it."

Riley didn't doubt it. "Did John say how Rebecca's mom was doing when he picked Tyler up?"

"She's out of the ICU. They're hoping she's turned a corner."

"Glad to hear it."

"Me too."

They turned onto Broadway East, and Riley waved to Bea and Ash, who were already waiting outside Blade and Timber.

"Good to see you again, Kim," Bea said. "I hope you're ready to get your ass handed to you."

"I don't need to be, because it's not going to happen."

Bea grinned. "Oh, this is going to be fun. Shall we?"

Heading inside, they were shown to their lane and given a safety demonstration, the four of them listening with rapt attention, trying to get tips on how to outdo everyone else. In theory, it seemed simple enough: throw the axe, one or two-handed, toward the target. If it embedded into the outer ring, it scored one point, with each subsequent ring toward the center increasing the score by one. The bullseye was worth six, and each person got ten throws per game.

Riley discovered upon her first throw that it wasn't so simple after all.

Her axe over-rotated, crashing off the target, and landed on the floor beneath it—much to Bea's delight.

"Let's see you do any better." Riley grabbed her axe and let Bea take aim from behind the line.

"Good enough for you?" she said when she had scored a point.

Riley huffed. "Could be better."

"Better than yours. Let's see if your girl is better than you, too."

Kim tested the weight of the axe in her hand before raising it in her right hand. It missed the bullseye—just barely—to score her four points.

"Damn." Bea blinked in surprise. "Have you done this before?"

"Nope." Kim had a saunter in her hips as she pulled her axe free. "Just naturally gifted."

"I like you. I think we're going to get along."

As the night wore on, it became clear that they would. Kim kept up effortlessly with Bea's trash talk, giving as good as she got. Riley could tell her sister was impressed.

"I'm glad you're good at this," Riley told Kim after her third dismal one-point throw in a row. Even with Kim's tips, she wasn't getting any better, but that was okay. Ash was as bad as her, so at least the teams were evenly matched.

"I'm not glad." Bea shook her head as Kim got another bullseye. "She's kicking my ass."

"Maybe you shouldn't have been so cocky at the beginning of the night," Ash said.

Bea's mouth dropped open. "You're supposed to be on my side!"

Ash kissed her cheek in apology. "I'm going to get a drink—anyone else want one?"

"I'll take a beer," Riley said. "It can't make me any worse at this."

"Can I have a Coke please, babe?" Bea said, and Ash nodded, glancing at Kim.

"I'll come with you," Kim said. "Help you carry them."

"So," Riley asked Bea once they were gone, "what do you think?"

"She's great," Bea said. "Not that it matters what I think—you're besotted by her."

Riley scrunched her nose. "I am not."

"You are. It's sweet. And don't worry—you'll get a plus-one to our wedding. Even if she does beat me tonight."

"*If?* I think you mean *when.*"

Bea smacked her on the shoulder.

In the end, Riley and Kim won both games they played, much to Bea's dismay. Riley was sure Kim would have won it even if she'd been playing against all three of them.

"That was fun," Bea said as they were leaving. "We should do this again sometime."

"I'd like that." Kim slid her hand back into Riley's once they were on the street. "See if you can find something you'll beat me at."

"How are you at mini golf?"

"So-so."

Bea grinned conspiratorially.

"Have a good night." Ash waved as they went their separate ways.

They walked back to their apartment building, taking a shortcut through the park, quiet beneath the late-setting summer sun. "That was incredible," Riley said. "Did you have fun?"

"I did—did you?"

"Yeah. And I know you were worried about making a good impression, but you didn't need to—Bea thinks you're great."

"Just Bea?"

"And Ash." Riley grinned when Kim's eyes narrowed. "And me." She pulled Kim to a stop. "I think you're amazing."

"You're not so bad yourself. Except at axe throwing."

"Rude." She wrapped her arms around Kim's back. "I have other talents."

"Yes, you do." Kim leaned up to kiss her, and Riley sighed, holding her close.

"There was something I wanted to ask you," Riley said, once they'd parted. "I know we've only been on a couple of dates and it hasn't been long, but...I want you to know I'm not interested in anyone else. I'm all in on this."

"Me too."

Kim's reply made Riley's heart skip a beat. "So...will you be my girlfriend?"

"Yes." Kim smiled against Riley's lips as she kissed her again.

Riley felt so happy, she could burst. It felt like everything was slipping into place. There was just one last piece of the puzzle missing.

"When he comes back from his dad's, I think we should tell Tyler," Kim said, and it was as if she'd read Riley's mind. "I wanted to wait until I was sure this would work, but...I think it's going well so far."

"Are you sure?"

"Yes. I'm sure about you—about us. And I want to share that with him. I don't want to have to keep sneaking you in and out while he's sleeping. I want to spend time together, the three of us—I want to have movie nights curled up with both of you on the couch, trips to the skate park, long walks with Cari."

"I want that, too." Riley rested her forehead against Kim's, content to breathe her in. "More than anything."

"Then it's settled. We'll tell him this weekend. Together. Maybe we could go out to celebrate him getting his cast off? I don't think he'll need warming to the idea of the three of us spending more time together, but it can't hurt."

"I think that sounds like a great idea."

They decided to take Tyler bowling because Kim knew it was one of his favorite things to do and they didn't go enough.

"Do I have to let the kid win?" Riley asked, a lopsided smile on her face as she laced her nonslip shoes.

"No," Kim said, getting to her feet once she had her own pair of shoes on, "but he will have the barriers up and we'll have them down, so, depending on how straight you bowl, you might be in trouble."

"I can't do anything straight." Riley's smile widened, "so it looks like I'm in for a fun evening."

"Come on." Tyler took both of their hands and pulled them toward their lane. "We only have two hours—we need to see how many games we can get through!"

Kim watched as Tyler carefully tested the weight of each of the bowling balls in the lane, eyeing his face closely for any signs of discomfort.

"Be careful," she said. His cast was fresh off, after all, though the doctor at the hospital had assured her that taking him bowling should be fine so long as he used his dominant—and not recently broken—wrist.

Tyler rolled his eyes. "I'm fine, Mom. My wrist hasn't even hurt in weeks."

"And let's keep it that way, please." Kim settled down on the bench, letting Riley key their names into the computer.

"Are you gonna go easy on me, buddy?" Riley asked when Tyler stepped up to take the first turn.

"Nope," he said with a wide smile—and promptly bowled a strike.

"What is it with Jacksons and being stupidly good at everything?" Riley stood with her hands on her hips as she gave a wry shake of her head. She ruffled Tyler's hair when he skipped past her. "Good job, Tyler."

"Your turn!"

Riley didn't put nearly as much thought into which ball she was going to use, and Kim realized why when she sent it down the lane—it tumbled straight into the gutter halfway down.

Kim found the pout on her mouth adorable.

"I think I need some tips, buddy." Riley reached for her second ball. "Can you help me out?"

Tyler bounded over to her side. "You have to roll it down the middle."

Kim bit her lip to hide a smile when Riley glared at Tyler. "I think I got that part."

"Then why didn't you do it?" He peered at Riley.

She tapped the end of his nose. "Maybe I don't need tips from you after all."

When her next bowl also didn't hit any pins, Tyler said: "Are you sure?"

Riley stuck her tongue out at him.

"Honestly, it's like having two children," Kim said, though her gaze was fond as she looked between them. She wondered if the delight of seeing Tyler and Riley getting along so well would ever wear off.

She hoped not.

"Let's see if your mom can do any better." There was a twinkle in Riley's eyes. "Though I'm sure the answer is yes."

Kim wasn't great, but she could hold her own. She managed to knock over five pins, following it with two more.

"I'm gonna have to get used to coming last at things, aren't I?" Riley said, groaning when Kim walked past her to let Tyler step up.

"Yep."

Riley took it in stride, and she did get better as the afternoon wore on—though she still came last in the three games they managed to squeeze in before their time ran out.

Tyler won. He had a spring in his step as they relocated to the café area of the bowling alley after working up an appetite. While they waited for their burgers and fries, Kim felt a flutter of nerves and steeled herself, even though she knew it was going to be fine.

"Tyler," Kim said, feeling the warm and reassuring weight of Riley's hand on her thigh beneath the table. Nevertheless, she played with the delicate bracelet around her wrist—what Tyler had been working so hard with her father to make for her. "So listen. There's something we need to tell you."

Taking a deep breath, Kim steeled herself. She'd never had to tell Tyler she was seeing someone. She should have asked John what he'd said to Tyler after getting together with Rebecca. Some days, she wished there was a parenting manual for situations like this. The last thing she wanted was to say the wrong thing.

"That you're together?" Tyler interrupted before Kim had a chance to speak. "Tell me something I don't know."

Kim's mouth opened and closed a few times as she struggled to find words. Riley covered a laugh with a well-timed cough.

"How... What do you mean you know?"

"Come on." Tyler rolled his eyes. "You went from being awkward around each other to being together loads. Plus, I caught you kissing one night when I woke up needing to pee. Which was gross, by the way." His nose wrinkled. "So, if you could at least close the hallway door next time, that would be great."

Kim wanted to tell him off for being so cheeky, but she was too shocked to berate him.

"So you're okay with it?" Riley said.

Tyler smiled. "Duh. I've been waiting for you guys to get together for ages—why do you think I told you to take Riley to Aunt Ellie's birthday?"

"You did that to get us together?" Had he really been thinking about her and Riley being a couple for so long? How had her son figured out that Riley was the best person for her before she had?

"Mostly so you could see how good you'd be together." Tyler shrugged. "Can I be the best man at your wedding like I'm going to be in Dad's?"

"Let's not get too far ahead of ourselves," Kim said, hoping her voice didn't sound too panicked. After all, she and Riley had only just made things between them official. "A wedding isn't remotely in the cards yet."

"It will be," Tyler said without a sliver of hesitation. "Can I go play on the arcade machines while we wait for food?"

"Go on," Kim said. She needed some time to gather her thoughts.

Tyler scampered away, and Kim turned to Riley in disbelief. "I was so worried about telling him, and he'd already figured it out."

"Well, at least one member of the family is perceptive enough to notice when I'm flirting with you."

Kim feigned outrage, and Riley kissed it away.

"Gross!" Tyler called out, and Kim turned to find him hovering beside one of those machines that involved throwing as many basketballs as possible into the hoops before the time ran out. "Riley, come play. This one gives loads of tickets."

"Go on." Kim kissed Riley's cheek. "Go have fun."

"You sure?"

"Yes—you've been requested."

Kim leaned back in her chair and watched them play, warmth in her chest and in her heart. She knew she'd found a keeper, found someone who loved Tyler almost as much as she did, and Kim couldn't wait to see what the future held for the three of them.

Epilogue

Three months later

KIM WAVED AS SHE SAW Bea and Ash in the distance, Cari walking between them.

Kim, John, and Rebecca had managed to snag one of the best spots to watch from the sidelines at Tyler's first soccer match. Around them, other families had gathered, and the sound of them chattering could be heard, along with the excited yells of the ten-year-olds finishing their warm-ups on the grass.

"Hey." Bea paused beside Kim and smiled at John and Rebecca. "How are the nerves?"

"Probably worse than Tyler's," John said.

Kim wholeheartedly agreed. "I don't think I have any fingernails left."

"Oh, he'll be fine," Rebecca said. "He hasn't been able to stop talking for weeks about how excited he is to finally play a real game."

In the midst of the chaotic scenes on the field—what it would be like once it kicked off, Kim had no idea—Tyler was listening with rapt attention as the unlikeliest of coaches gave their final words of wisdom.

Riley still didn't look comfortable in the role, even though it had been a few weeks. She was growing into it, and Kim knew she enjoyed it—though perhaps not on match days, based on the look on her face. Kim wondered if it was worse than when Riley herself was playing. It probably was, because at least in her own matches, Riley could affect the outcome. This time, she'd have to watch from the sidelines, hoping the kids would remember everything she'd told them.

The fall sunlight illuminated Riley's face. She wore the same kit as the kids, red instead of her usual white, but it didn't look any less good on her.

Watching Riley play was one of Kim's new favorite things—admiring the stretch of muscle, the fearless way she dove in for tackles, the skill with which she could shoot—but watching her coach might overtake it. The fact that she was doing this mostly because Tyler had asked her only made it sweeter.

"Looks like they're nearly ready to start," Ash said as the teams spread out on either side of the field. "Poor Riley looks like she's going to throw up."

Riley did look pale. But she had nothing to worry about. Even if they lost, the kids were happy just to be playing.

None more so than Tyler, who beamed as he took his position furthest forward on the field. He wanted to be just like Riley, so he was playing as a striker, and Kim didn't know whose heart that warmed more—hers or Riley's.

Riley and Tyler had grown even closer in the weeks since Riley had asked Kim to be her girlfriend. Kim had never thought it would be possible to find someone who would treat Tyler like he was their own and not like he was a burden. But Riley had embraced their family as a whole, and Kim already couldn't imagine ever being without her.

"How's the wedding planning going?" Kim asked Ash as the game kicked off. "Did you pick a venue?"

"We did." Ash's eyes lit up with excitement. "But they have limited availability. They had a spot available in December because someone canceled, but otherwise we'd have to wait nearly two years."

"December, as in two months away?"

"Yep." Bea slid her arm around Ash's shoulders. "Good thing we only want a small wedding, isn't it?"

"If you need any help finding people—caterers, flowers, officiants—then let me know," Rebecca said. "We're in the midst of planning our own wedding, so I can tell you who's good—and who to avoid."

"And I'll make your cake," Kim said. "As my wedding gift."

"You really don't have to do that," Bea said.

"It's no trouble at all." Especially considering how Bea and Ash had welcomed Kim and Tyler with open arms. While she and Riley hadn't been together all that long, Kim felt like her little family had swelled in size, and their weekly dinners with Bea, Ash and Riley were one of the highlights of Kim's week—and Tyler's, when he was with her.

Kim noticed Tyler hovering around the edge of the opposition's penalty box.

As the game wore on, Kim knew it was Tyler she should focus on, but she couldn't stop her eyes from straying to Riley.

She stood on the opposite side of the field, her arms folded across her chest and her tension held in her clenched fists and her jawline. It looked like she was following along with every pass the team made, her head bobbing and weaving, roaring encouragement whenever one of the boys ventured close to the opposing team's goal.

When Tyler slipped past the goalkeeper and slid the ball into the back of the net, it wasn't Kim or John he ran to first—it was Riley. She swept him into a hug, lifting him clean off the floor, a huge grin on her face.

God, I love her.

The thought had been lingering on the periphery of Kim's mind for weeks. She'd never felt this way before, not even with John. It was terrifying.

But so, so right.

"Look at him go." Bea clapped Kim on the back. "He'll be a pro in no time."

Tyler gave them a thumbs-up from across the field, and Riley caught Kim's attention, her smile blinding and pride shining in her eyes; Kim was flooded with warmth.

After the game, she had something she needed to tell Riley.

———◦✦◦———

"Hi, Coach." Kim's arms wound around Riley's neck the second they were back in Riley's apartment and Riley had unclipped Cari's leash, letting her bound past them and onto her favorite armchair.

Their team had won 3-2 in a tense affair, and the elation Riley had felt at the full-time whistle was matched only by tasting victory with Seattle Pride.

Tyler had scored two of the goals himself and had still been chattering excitedly about it when John and Rebecca had ushered him into their car to take him back to their house for the week.

"Hi." Riley brushed Kim's lips with her own.

"You did great today. A hundred percent success rate."

Riley chuckled. "Does it count when we've only played one game?"

"I'd say so. And it's better than a zero percent success rate, isn't it? How do you feel?"

Settling her hands on Kim's hips, Riley smiled. "Pretty damn good."

When Kim stepped closer, backing Riley up against the wall, she sighed. "Even better now."

"Yeah?"

"Yeah. How about you? Did you enjoy yourself? You know, considering your hatred of soccer and all?" Riley kept her voice teasing, knowing that, despite Kim's protestations, she was growing to enjoy the game.

"I could become a convert," Kim said. "Mostly I like watching you."

Riley swallowed. She knew that, had felt Kim's eyes on her all game. It had driven her wild.

Three months in and she still couldn't get enough of Kim, craved her like nothing else.

"And I realized something, watching you out there today." Kim's gaze darted away, teeth worrying at her bottom lip.

Concern bloomed in Riley's chest, but she didn't press, knowing Kim would elaborate once she was ready.

Kim took a deep breath and met Riley's gaze again. "I love you."

Her concern turned to elation, and Riley grinned. "You do?"

"Yeah." Kim's fingertips curled around the collar of Riley's shirt, toying with the thin material. "I really do. More than I ever thought possible."

"I love you, too." The words were easy to say back. They'd been threatening to spill forth for weeks, but Riley hadn't wanted to say it too soon. "Who'd have thought we'd be here after that first day we met in the hallway?"

"I thought we might be friends. I knew you had good taste from your record collection, at least."

"I think I have pretty excellent taste." Riley slid her hands down and into the back pockets of Kim's jeans. "And I'm very glad I moved into this apartment and not the other one I viewed three floors up."

"I think we'd have found our way to each other anyway." Kim's voice turned soft and certain.

Riley liked to think so, too. She'd never really believed in fate, but had Cari not escaped and won over Tyler in a split second, Riley didn't know what would have been.

God, she was so, so glad everything had happened as it had. Because as Kim leaned up on her toes and kissed her hard, she curled a hand around the back of Riley's neck to hold her close and Riley knew she was exactly where she was supposed to be.

Other Books from Ylva Publishing

www.ylva-publishing.com

In Too Deep
Rachael Sommers

ISBN: 978-3-96324-762-0
Length: 236 pages (74,000 words)

Lawyer Lucy's life has imploded. Escaping to the island of Tenerife results in a fun fling with a college student working at her dad's hotel.

With a backdrop of a scandal, sleuthing, and spilling emotions, just where do flings end and feelings begin?

This lesbian summer holiday romance comes with cocktails, arched eyebrows, and a side of mystery.

Honey in the Marrow
Emily Waters

ISBN: 978-3-96324-724-8
Length: 237 pages (78,000 words)

New widow Stella is facing middle age alone in LA. Without being a prosecutor and wife, who is she anymore?

When an ex-colleague, a beautiful but cold LAPD captain, helps her back on her feet, Stella can't keep pretending she's not attracted to her. And there's no way she feels the same way. Is there?

An enemies-to-friends-to-lovers lesbian romance about finding heart, hope, and second chances you never thought you'd have.

I Do

Cheyenne Blue

ISBN: 978-3-96324-829-0
Length: 212 pages (75,000 words)

Allie finds herself running a smalltown queer wedding festival and playing gay after taking her injured twin sister's identity to help her out. Now she's been given an assistant—a metalworker who loathes weddings!

A fab twin-swap lesbian romance where the toaster oven could double as a wedding gift.

Dare to Love

A.L. Brooks

ISBN: 978-3-96324-361-5
Length: 270 pages (89,000 words)

Talent-agency boss Carmen is straight, career focused, and impressed by a cool tattoo studio she visits with her best friend.

Ex-financier Ash, who runs the studio, has a broken heart and has sworn off questioning women.

When Carmen and Ash meet again, sparks fly, shocking them both to the core. The pull between them is strong but so are their fears.

A slow-burn lesbian romance about daring to love.

About Rachael Sommers

Rachael Sommers was born and raised in the North-West of England, where she began writing at the age of thirteen, and has been unable to stop since. A biology graduate, she currently works in education and constantly dreams of travelling the world. In her spare time, she enjoys horse riding, board games, escape rooms and, of, course, reading.

CONNECT WITH RACHAEL
Website: www.rachaelsommers.com
E-Mail: rachaelsommersauthor@gmail.com

Love Next Door
© 2024 by Rachael Sommers

ISBN: 978-3-96324-897-9

Available in e-book and paperback formats.

Published by Ylva Publishing, legal entity of Ylva Verlag, e.Kfr.

Ylva Verlag, e.Kfr.
Owner: Astrid Ohletz
Am Kirschgarten 2
65830 Kriftel
Germany

www.ylva-publishing.com

First edition: 2024

Credits
Edited by Lenir Costa and Michelle Aguilar
Cover Design and Print Layout by Streetlight Graphics

Made in United States
North Haven, CT
01 July 2024

54308848R00164